BEYOND BINGO

D0971464

HOROSCOPE: In some respects, the next few months will be like the ultimate free lunch for you. In other regards, it'll be like standing near a high voltage electrical line downed after a storm—which you sure as hell had better not touch. Life will be unpredictable. That doesn't mean BAD unpredictable, simply irreverent toward your plans. Under the circumstances, the best way to prepare for it might be to imagine what it would be like keeping your balance while hula-dancing on the hood of a moving car.

BEYOND BINGO

A Novel

Joan Drummond Miller
Carolyn Livingston
Julie Houy

Joan Drummond Miller

CREATIVE ARTS BOOK COMPANY

Berkeley ✦ California

For information contact:
Creative Arts Book Company
833 Bancroft Way
Berkeley, California 94710
(800) 848-7789

The characters, incidents, and situations
in this book are imaginary and have no relation
to any person or actual happening.

ISBN 088739-284-9
Library of Congress Catalog Number 99-63262

Printed in the United States of America

ACKNOWLEDGEMENTS

Our gratitude to a good friend, Cindy Dau, for all of her valuable input, including the title of our book.

Thanks go to Don Miller and Karen Kahn, and the Carmel Writers Group—McKenzie Moss, Greta Kopp, Melodie Bahou, Lisa Watson, and especially Dr. Laura Pasten and Maggie Hardy—for reading and offering editing suggestions on the original manuscript.

Appreciation goes to the anonymous members of the younger generation who helped us, in our naiveté, with background information on marijuana.

We also wish to thank Creative Arts Book Company for their encouragement.

The Low Road

[Author Unknown]

What can they do to you?
Whatever they want.
They can set you up, they can
    bust you, they can break
    your fingers, they can burn
    your brain with electricity, blur
    you with drugs till you can't walk,
    can't remember; they can
    take your child, wall up
    your lover.
They can do anything
you can't stop them from doing.
How can you stop them?
Alone, you can fight,
    you can refuse, you can
    take what revenge you can,
but they will roll over you.

But two people fighting
back-to-back can cut through
a mob, a snake-dancing file,
can break a cordon,
can meet an army.

Two people can keep each other sane,
can give support, conviction, love, hope, sex.
Three people are a delegation,
a committee, a wedge.
With four you can play bridge and start an organization.
With six you can rent a whole house, eat pie
    for dinner with no seconds,
    and hold a fund-raising party.
A dozen make a demonstration.
A hundred fill a hall.
A thousand have solidarity and your own newsletter;
ten thousand, power and your own paper;
a hundred thousand, your own media;
ten million, your own country.

It goes on one at a time,
it starts when you care to act,
it starts when you do it again
    after they say no,
it starts when you say WE
and know who you mean, and each day
you mean one more.

PROLOGUE

October 1996

HOROSCOPE: A long-running saga, more the result of collaborative friends' actions than individual, is nearing its natural conclusion. You've reached the point of no return.

"**LET ME HELP YOU WITH THAT STEP. AND WATCH YOUR HEAD.**" **OFFICER** Chris Connery puts both hands under her armpits and lifts the breathless Violet into the back of the police van.

"Thank you." She smiles her best smile. Chris is so cute, trying to look grown up in his blue uniform. Stooping low, Vi goes past Sophie and Katherine and sits on the bench right up front so she'll be near the policemen.

She sighs. What a satisfying life! I was worried about my heart when those Mafia goons were chasing me down the hill, but it's fine now. Just needed to catch my breath. I forget the name of that other policeman, the one Katherine can't stand.

The heavy armored door slams shut, and the next thing she knows the siren is wailing as they lurch along the rocky cliffs of Big Sur.

Life doesn't get much better than this, especially when you're seventy. I'm deliciously alive, without a scratch, safe in this paddy wagon, and we're flying home to dear old Butterfly Town. Thank you, Lord! *Oh, no!* Trouble is, this might give Rosie the ammunition she needs to put me away in the old people's home.

We all could have died! That snake, Peter Pellagrino. He really tried to kill us! I never liked him. Couldn't stand to watch him talk. His thick, fat, whitish tongue

I

was too big for his mouth. Imagine kissing him! That white thing flapping around, pushing insistently down your throat. He's disgusting!

"I was right about him all along," she says out loud, surprising herself.

Officer Chris Connery turns around and looks at her. She acts innocent.

"Let's get these old broads to the county jail and book 'em," the driver, Sgt. Wyatt Burley shouts to Chris over the roar of the engine.

"No. We'll book them. Take them to Monterey Courthouse tomorrow. Tonight we'll lock 'em up in Pacific Grove."

Oh, maybe *The Herald* will take my picture. Vi looks down at her dirty brown sweat-shirt, blue jeans, tennis shoes. Damn, she thinks. I'm gonna look like every other old lady in Pacific Grove. If only they could wait fifteen minutes. I'd call Nikki and have her bring over my blue azure caftan with those gold astrological signs. Perfect for my photo op!

Huddled by the heavy back door, Sophie is mute, thinking only of Jack. What does he think? How angry is he? Can he forgive her? She was shocked when he showed up at the raid, but glad he didn't see her being herded into the police van. She could still feel the policeman's large hand pushing on her back. Horrible! Her head aches, her neck feels permanently stiff, her back hurts. She drops her head to hide the tears running down her cheeks.

Poor Jack. His wife in jail! What if Mother and Daddy were alive? All they ever wanted was to be proud of me. All I ever wanted was to please them. How could I ever explain to them?

I always wanted to do good, to help people, and look where its gotten me. Why did I go along with these women? I haven't known them very long. Why did I think they knew what they were doing? I wish I'd never seen them. It's not right to break the law, even if it's a bad law. I'm sorry, so desperately sorry!

What can I say to Jack? Will he hate me?

"Guilty," she hears the judge say. Guilty! How humiliating. She imagines herself in a prisoner's uniform. They're bright orange, she remembers. I look awful in orange. Then she sees herself walking down a long corridor, walking away from Jack. His arms are outstretched toward her. She looks back over her shoulder, a long lingering look at the man she may never see again.

Dear Lord, will he wait for me?

Katherine squirms on the hard van bench, chewing on her thumbnail. What she wants most at this moment is a bathroom. Concentrate, old girl; grit your teeth, practice the Kegal exercise, think of something pleasant. Pretty damn hard, under the circumstances.

She takes a deep breath. *Don't panic.* I know I should try to see the humor in this whole thing. But all I can visualize is the evening news—the stiff reporter sing-songing off the monitor, "Three senior citizens captured in Big Sur and booked by Pacific Grove Police. Details at eleven!" Can I ever walk down Lighthouse Avenue again?

Katherine notices shredded pieces of Kleenex drifting around her feet and realizes her hands have been ripping the tissue. She fidgets with her hair, her purse, and her sunglasses. She feels her face flush as she hears the policemen talk about her.

"Ain't this a kick, Chris? Especially that gray-haired Katherine Doolittle back there. The old broad who's always storming into the station or griping on the phone about someone breaking a law!"

"Probably means well, Wyatt. Lots of nervous old ladies in our town. You know how they are."

Katherine sees that Vi's stubborn chin is jutting out. She suspects triumph in Vi's eyes. Good grief! She's enjoying this! Can you believe it?

Sophie's crying. She can feel her body shaking next to her. Her head's down.

Katherine's thoughts bounce around. She prefers thinking of the last few years. How she loves Pacific Grove and her friends. Yeah, they've changed "live and learn" into "learn to live." She'd rather not remember the past.

I should try to keep in touch with the kids more. How shocked they'll be when they hear this news. They'll think the authorities have gotten the wrong name. She shakes her head and shivers, feeling chilled. Oh, and Jerry! I'd love to see his face when he finds out I'm human after all. He'll be so embarrassed! That cheers her. That and another thought.

She straightens her shoulders, folds her hands, and says to no one in particular, "What a kick Rita would get out of this!"

(1)

EARLIER THAT YEAR

HOROSCOPE: It would be a good time to dream of taking a trip to the moon in a boat powered by firecrackers and wild swans. But, knowing your personality, it would be an even better time to fantasize about hanging out with the Zapatistas in the Mexican jungles.

LONG AGO VI HAD DREAMED AT THE SINK, WITH HER HANDS WRINKLING IN water, that someday she would take a new road. Now it was happening. Today was the day.

"Today was the day my whole life changed," Vi rehearsed the last line in her head all the way home so she wouldn't forget it.

She walked up her gravel driveway much faster than usual, rushed into the house, and didn't even lock the dead bolt behind her, her unvarying habit for the past twenty five years.

She pulled her journal from the sideboard. Out dropped all the letters she had written to her congressman, the governor, and civic officials. "Damn!" She stooped to pick them up, dropped herself into her dusty rose chair and began. "Today is the day my whole life changed." She smiled. Yes, what a dramatic opening line. Stuck for a second, she turned back a few pages to read what she had written last Monday.

The truth is I've been bored with my life for a while. But all that will change. Next Saturday, I'm going to a wonderful workshop at church called Imaging the Second Half of Your Life. I can't wait!

My boredom isn't just since Fred died. I would never tell anyone, least of

4

all you, Fred, how boring the last thirty years of our marriage were for me. Our courtship seemed pretty good, at least what I can remember of it.

The fat grey Persian cat rubbed against Violet's leg, yowling unceremoniously.

I was a wild thing. Even frightened myself. I wasn't sure who I was under all those layers of pretense. But you came along and solved that problem. I would just be a part of you. I would just be whoever you wanted me to be. You were an island of stability in an uncertain world.

I felt like a drowning woman who had spotted land. You had rules, traditions, substance. I imagined my life as your wife stretching out before me in a consistent pattern all the way to old age without a care in the world.

"Be patient, Bloomers, I'm reading something important." The cat jumped up into her lap, yowled louder, and started kneading Vi's stomach. Her wailing could no longer be ignored.

"Oh all right! I know who's in charge of this household. There'll be no peace until you've had your dinner." Vi went into the kitchen, fed the cat leftover tofu, then returned to her journal.

But when Rose was in her teens, I would sometimes have a moment when I didn't recognize her. Our daughter seemed like a stranger, and so did you, Fred. I was frightened.

I turned to you too desperately, only to find you were no longer there.

I should have left you then, but it had been over 24 years. I was 49 with nowhere to go. It was unfair for me to stay. I felt like a ghost.

She put the book down, stared into the fireplace, thinking. Why was I surprised to find Fred wasn't there any more? I hadn't been there for him in so many years. More a mother than a wife.

It was then that she spied Rose's ample frame marching up her driveway. If only she'd seen her coming she could have dashed over to Katherine's, or pulled down the shades and pretended she wasn't home.

She opened the front door and shouted "Hi, Rose, let's go out on the patio." She felt faintly guilty for not looking forward to Rose's visit. Too many of them had not been visits, actually. More like inspections, like inquisitions.

"It's windy facing the ocean. Let's stay inside." Rose marched through the door. No dissuading her. Give in graciously, Vi told herself.

"Of course, dear; I'll make some tea."

Rose followed her through the living room into the small kitchen. Vi could feel Rose's eyes on her as she made the tea. Vi loved Rose, of course—anything else would be unthinkable—but she didn't always like her.

"Mother." Her tone was strident. Rose was rummaging through Vi's refrigerator. "What are these leftovers? It looks like you've been cooking again."

"Rosie," Vi was hoping the diminutive might soften up this stern inquisitor. "I'm a grown woman. I am capable of cooking my own dinner."

Rose seated herself. Violet didn't like how erectly Rose sat in her chair, feet touching each other, hands folded. She knew she was in for it.

"Now, Mother,"—the tone became shrill. "Remember the time I came over one night at nine o'clock? You fast asleep on the couch? The oven still on? You could burn the house down with your carelessness."

Vi sighed, saying to herself: *Rose, Martha Stewart doesn't live here. Just me, a human.* She looked up at her beloved cuckoo clock and waited until she could trust her voice to speak. She was able to best Rose if she had to, but she didn't like manipulating her own daughter. Rose always brought up the one time Vi forgot to turn off the oven. "Come on, Rose, didn't you ever forget to do something?"

If Rose had ever done so, Vi thought, she didn't choose to remember or didn't feel like admitting it. She wouldn't answer, just got up and transferred her inspection to the cupboards.

"Did you eat all the tofu I brought over day before yesterday?"

"No, to tell the truth, Honey, I didn't really like it. But Bloomers did, so I gave it to her."

"You fed my tofu to the cat?" The tone warned Vi to backtrack fast. Rose had gotten to be really funny about food. Always checking up to see if you were finishing your spirulina. Bringing over cold bowls of leftover fava beans. Whatever possessed the child? Vi remembered when Rose was little she'd scarf up Vi's homemade pies and doughnuts just like all the other neighborhood kids. Now when Vi offered her some pie, she acted like she was trying to poison her or something. Vi got the feeling she was talking to her own mother instead of her daughter.

Only one solution here. "I ate almost all of it," she lied, turning her back on Rose to look for the tea strainer so Rose couldn't read the fib in her eyes. Finally, when Vi could stall no longer, they sat down, eyeball-to-eyeball, over the delicate Limoge tea cups and the silver tea ball.

"What I really wanted to discuss with you, Mother—"

Oh, oh, the build-up. Here it comes. Vi knew that voice. She was in big trouble. Rose had come to lecture.

"Mrs. Callahan called me this morning. She saw you drive through a stop sign without looking right or left, then try to parallel park, give up, just shut off the engine in the middle of the street and go into the Grove Pharmacy. Mother, I've warned you before . . ."

"Oh, Rose, please, no lectures today." That snitch Hannah Callahan squealed on her again. "Look—the sun is shining. Why don't we go outside and watch the seagulls. Listen to the surf!"

"Don't change the subject. You've got to stop driving. Do you understand? You're too old to drive."

Vi chose silence as a response. Rose was a Republican and a member of the Christian Coalition. To Vi's way of thinking that was just in name only. They didn't behave much like Christians, she thought. So judgmental! She didn't like the way Rose said "family values" as if it was a term that just applied to some families. Mainly hers.

"Answer me, Mother!" Rose punctuated her command with her finger. Vi really didn't like to have fingers pointed at her. Especially not Rose's. She decided to keep silent.

"Very well, Mother. If you're not going to talk to me, I'll just say what I came to say and go. I feel it's time for you to move to The Grove Rest Home. I've made an appointment with the director for the first of the month. He'll show you around. Answer any questions you have. Give you a tour of the place. You know, it's really very nice. They have all sorts of classes, even have a painting studio."

Be careful, Vi cautioned herself. You've gone too far already. Don't make Rose mad again. Maybe she can get you committed. Act grateful. Don't say much.

Vi reached over and touched Rose's hand.

"That's really thoughtful of you, Dear. I'm sure you're looking out for me and maybe it's a nice place, but . . ."

"Now, Mother—"

"Life there is too predictable. No surprises. You know you will have red jello on Wednesday and fish on Friday. They make you feel like a child. Don't mean to, of course, but I've heard . . ."

Rose broke in. "Oh, you don't know that, Mother. You've never been there. You don't know anything about it." She spoke through clenched teeth.

"I'm fine here," Vi stated as strongly as she could, pulling her five foot, one inch frame to its most commanding height. Rose's stare didn't change.

"Mother, my mind is made up. You can't afford to fix the roof. You can't manage the yard. You don't eat right. Someone has to be responsible for you."

Vi looked away. Her eyes lit on the dust caught in the refrigerator's grill. Rose thought Vi was a terrible housekeeper. Said she couldn't see well any more. Vi wanted to tell her the truth. She could see fine. She just couldn't see the point of housework anymore. She didn't want to waste any more of her days. Regretted the hours and days she had wasted. She wanted to describe her great longing, her passion to see more of life before it was all over. Rose would never understand.

The room was silent. They avoided each other's eyes. Neither moved.

"I don't want you to live alone, here," Rose finally spoke. "What if something happened? Who would know? Carmel Valley's a long way off. I can't be over here every minute checking on you."

"Katherine lives right next door, Rosie. She's my best friend. She'd know right away if anything happened."

Rose's turn not to speak. She picked up her black over-the-shoulder purse and headed toward the door. Once there, she turned around and delivered her final ultimatum.

"Remember, Mother. The Grove. First of the month." Then softening, "Be careful." And she was off, marching down the driveway.

Vi stood at the window watching her disappear. They won't take me to The Grove without a fight, she thought. This did not comfort her, though. Rose was capable of almost anything. Who knew if she could get a court order saying Vi was incompetent?

She had not told her about the weekend seminar, and how excited she was to be starting a new life. Forming her own club. Good thing she'd kept her mouth shut. If Rose heard about it she was certain she would have forbidden it. Vi didn't want to be disobeying Rose. She would if she had to, of course, but it was easier to keep secrets.

Forgetting she'd already fed the cat, she shuffled back into the kitchen for a can of tuna. She turned to Bloomers and put her finger to her mouth, "Mum's the word, Bloomers. We won't tell Rose."

She went back and picked up her journal. Read her first line: *Today is the day my whole life changed.* Crossed it out and wrote: *Today is the day I changed my life.* She smiled. "I'm in charge now," she said aloud. Then she stoked the fire in the fireplace, tore those last few pages out of the book, threw them in and watched while they burned.

I'm starting my new life, she thought to herself. No more letters to Fred. This book is about me from now on. Anyway, what if I had a heart attack? No sense leaving something like that around for Rose to find. She had always preferred her father. They were so much alike. Even looked alike. What she doesn't know about her father and me is just as well.

Bloomers, now stuffed with her second dinner, jumped up on Vi's lap and settled into a ball for napping.

"Don't get too comfortable, Bloomers," she said as much to herself as the cat. "There are going to be quite a few surprises around here. You're going to be second fiddle. I'll be first." She hesitated. "And I'm changing your name. From now on we'll both be 'Late Bloomers'."

(2)

———

Horoscope: You have a strange talent for being alone in the midst of a crowd. You're lost in your own world even as you interact with others. Your peninsula has turned into an island. Surprises whirlpooling your way in the next twelve months will change that!

KATHERINE WAS IN A SOUR MOOD AFTER CALLING THE POLICE STATION TO complain about illegally parked vehicles on her street. Unfortunately, Sgt. Wyatt Burley answered the phone and gave her the "meddlesome old broad" routine. He was a hard-line cop, with a perpetual cigarette hanging from his lips. He had a beer belly and cold eyes. He didn't like Katherine ever since she reported his cousin for having a "drunken brawl" and playing his stereo too loud. I'll ask for Officer Chris Connery from now on, she thought. He's nice to me, probably because I'm a friend of his mother's. He's grateful that I take her grocery shopping and to the poker games. At least *he* treats me like a lady.

"I've got to get out and take a walk," she said to the telephone, as if in apology for slamming down the receiver. She was nervous, couldn't get Rita's call an hour earlier off her mind.

She hoped a stroll along the shore would melt her tenseness. After six years in Pacific Grove, she had finally succeeded in erasing most of her self-pity. She loved the magic carpet of purple flowers along the cliffs, the quaint Victorian downtown. She loved the solitude of living alone in this perfect place.

But the surf and rocks could not distract her today. As she walked along the beach, thoughts of Rita returned. Rita was her opposite in every way—gregarious, boisterous, risk-taking, classic in style and social grace; a blend possible only for the very rich.

Katherine wanted to do something, anything, to change her mood. She thought about taking the pins out of her hair to let it fall and blow in the breeze. No; it would look messy. She tried to put joy in her step as she walked home, but felt silly as a young jogger passed her and laughed. *Is he laughing at me?* she wondered.

On the phone, Rita had said: "It's been a long time since we talked, but I'd really like to see you. I'm up at Community Hospital . . . Oh, I'm okay, just need to talk to someone. Can you come to see me? Visiting hours start at ten." She had heard a crack in Rita's raspy voice.

What on earth could she want to see me for, and why the heck is she in the hospital?

Katherine drove to the hospital, clutching the steering wheel in the precise ten–two o'clock hand position and keeping a nervous eye on the speedometer. Old memories of Rita swirled like the fog drifting in. After nearly missing the turn-off to the hospital nestled in the forest, she parked and walked briskly toward the entrance.

Slowing her pace as she walked to the information desk, Katherine glanced at her reflection in the window. She tried to straighten her slouchy shoulders, smooth her salt-and-pepper hair into its tidy bun. Hoped no one would notice her skirt was wrinkled. Was it too short? Did the flowered blouse go okay? Should she have worn a contrasting color? She was never sure what would look best and be proper.

"May I have the room number of Rita Rich?" She suppressed the smile that automatically twitched whenever she said Rita's full name.

Katherine, straightening her rounded shoulders, opened the door. Reclining in the bed was the same old Rita—meticulously coiffed and made up as if posing for a Vogue cover. Even her bed jacket screamed I. Magnin.

"Hi, Katherine—I'm so glad you came! I'm going nuts. Did you know they don't allow you to smoke in this place? Not even outside? I've got to get out of here, at least long enough for a hefty drink and a cigarette, and maybe dinner with Mr. Tall, Dark and Handsome."

Rita was babbling, but Katherine broke in with "How are you? What are you doing here? You look . . ."

"Like hell," Rita finished the sentence. "Oh, Katherine . . . I know we haven't seen each other for months, but I had to call you. Since Ray died I've felt so alone with no one to talk to."

Katherine looked out the window. Ha! she thought to herself. Yeah, right; she's been lapping up Pebble Beach society and dating rich golfers in her open husband-hunting quest. Turning to Rita, she said, "Seems to me you have friends at the club." Katherine saw Rita bristle, recalling some of the recent debates they'd had about men.

"Just because you shit-canned all men as despicable monsters with their brains between their legs since Jerry dumped you for a younger, less prim and proper babe, doesn't mean I can't recapture the joy of having a man take care of me."

Silence permeated the room as Katherine slouched down in the visitor's chair, wondering why she had bothered coming, even questioning their friendship. Things and people change. Yes, she and Rita had a history together, but now their lifestyles were different. She resented Rita and the way she lived. Wasn't sure she still liked her.

Rita had an air about her even before she married into money. Her concept of life meant upper class material wealth. They corresponded for years after Rita was widowed and moved to Pebble Beach and Katherine was still suffering the boredom of the valley. She lived vicariously through Rita's adventures, wondering what it would be like to have her outrageously gregarious lifestyle. They got together frequently, at first, when Katherine moved to Pacific Grove after being jilted. But Katherine knew her own reverse snobbery and her inability to cope with their differences inhibited their friendship.

"I'm sorry, Katherine. I didn't mean to be nasty. It's just . . . it's just that I can't think of anyone I can really dump on." Rita squirmed and reached for the night table drawer. "Oh, damn! I can't smoke. Here, take these and get rid of them for me before the witch nurse finds them."

Katherine felt victorious as she stuffed the nasty coffin nails and matches in her purse. She hated the habit. Seeing Rita's vulnerability softened her.

"Okay, so what's the problem?"

Rita blurted out, "They found The Big C—cancer—the death warrant. Oh, they tell me they probably got it all; total remission is possible. But, just in case, they've got me started on chemotherapy . . . Oh, Katherine!"

The tears were making black streams of mascara trickle down Rita's hollow cheeks. Katherine sat dumbfounded, her blue eyes unblinking as she watched a stranger emerge from behind Rita's face. She studied the gauntness about her, the worry lines looking like corduroy disguised with powder.

Rita sputtered on. "You can't imagine how repulsive and degrading it is to be overcome with nausea—to lean over the toilet and heave and heave until nothing's left but dry retching. Pain like I've never known shoots through my body. And dear God, I may even lose my hair!" With this, her tears turned to sobs.

"Is there anything I can do?" Katherine handed Rita a Kleenex. What an inadequate comment—*like what?*

Rita dabbed her eyes and composed herself. "Well, actually . . . I realize you certainly aren't the person to help me directly, but like I say, you're the only one I know I can pour my guts out to, figuratively speaking. There's Guido, of course, but I save him for bigger and better things," she giggled. A hint of the old Rita. Guido was obviously the new stud.

"I think I'm getting immune to the pain-killing drugs." Rita paused. "I need some research—a little snooping to find out about—availability . . . "

What is she getting at? Katherine thought. Her impatience with the old Rita was returning. "What can I . . ."

Rita chose her words carefully. "Remember in high school, our senior year, with Dick and Phil? After the dance? Behind the gym? Dick had those joints they lit up? You panicked and wanted to leave, but I had one and really enjoyed it."

Katherine felt the chilling in her veins as she remembered that night. Her only thoughts were of getting caught, of her parents finding out, of getting suspended or even put in jail.

"Yes, I remember, but what's the connection? That was fifty years ago." She didn't want to remember the only time she'd been close to illegal activity.

"Well, even then there was talk about the good things marijuana does." Skepticism crossed Katherine's expression as Rita rushed on. "No, seriously, therapeutic qualities have been known for thousands of years. I could show you research if you doubt it."

"Think of all the druggies! There's a reason for the laws against it."

"Hey, all I'm interested in is that it helps the pain and the nausea. I could enjoy food again and not dread the damn chemo because I'd know I could take it without tossing my cookies, I could ——"

"Visiting hours are over," said Nurse Witch from the door. Katherine was glad to have the conversation interrupted.

"Well, I'd better go. I'll come back tomorrow." *Why did I say that,* she thought. "Promise? I mean really—you will, won't you?"

Vulnerability again overshadowed the Perfect Rita mask. "Of course I will."

(3)

HOROSCOPE: The more adventurous and outrageous you feel this week, the better. The eccentric influence of Uranus on your ruler Mercury is urging you to push back boundaries. Much can be achieved and enjoyed through a fling. Whatever happens, you won't be bored.

VI STOOD IN THE CENTER OF HER KITCHEN. THE CLOUD OF ROSE AND A headache hung over her. She picked up the phone to call Katherine. Thank God for Katherine living next door. I'll ask her to pop over. She'll know how to cheer me up. I need to giggle with her.

I'll imitate Rose glaring over her tea cup and she'll pop off a wise-acre remark. Then we'll screech till Rose shrinks down to human size and I won't feel so scared.

No answer. She slammed down the phone. Better take some Tylenol. Maybe a hot shower will wipe out this queasy stomach.

Suddenly Katherine flung open the kitchen door.

"Oh Vi, get me some tea. I need your help." She rushed to the dusty rose chair and freefell into it. "I just got back from seeing Rita. She's in the hospital. You remember hearing about her, don't you?"

"Yeah, Mrs. Got-Rocks of Pebble Beach. I can't imagine you two as friends from what you've told me."

"I know. When we were young and living in San Joaquin—well, we weren't so different. Rita's a changed person since she came into money when her husband died."

"I thought you disapproved of her sleeping around." Vi was trying to size up the situation. Katherine looked like she would cry at any moment.

"Oh, her gigolo adventures are just her way not to grow old."

"You're defending her? I thought she really got on your nerves."

"But you should see her now, Vi. She's dying. Cancer." Now the tears surfaced and her voice was almost inaudible. "She looks so sad. I think I'm her only friend. I just can't desert her."

Today was not the day for Vi to tell all about Rose and The Grove. Right now Katherine needed Vi to be strong. The role felt good.

"Of course not." Vi left the tea kettle to put her arms around Katherine. Not many people got away with embracing Katherine. She tended to back away if someone stood too close. But Vi was an exception. They looked like Mutt and Jeff as Vi reached up to pat Katherine on the back. After the hugging and crying and tea, the story came out. Vi was amazed.

"She wants you to buy her some marijuana?"

"Yes. I didn't agree. But I did tell her I'd go back tomorrow so I have to say something. I don't know what to do."

"That's easy," Vi said. "Just go get her some."

"What?" Katherine grasped the arms of the chair. "Even for *you*, Violet, that is a preposterous idea! I'd be breaking the law! And I don't have any idea where to get it. What if I'm arrested?"

"Don't worry. I'll help you. I think I know where to get some."

"You? How would you know?" Katherine's face betrayed her shock.

"Adrian told me her mother smokes marijuana all the time. I'll ask her."

Vi enjoyed seeing Katherine's eyes grow wide. "Mrs. *Pellagrino*? Why she's eighty if she's a day!"

Vi called Adrian who said she would talk to her mom. "Meet us for the early bird dinner tonight at the Monarch Cafe," she said, and Adrian agreed. Vi figured Katherine would be cheered up enough by then. She was anxious to broach the subject of their new adventurous lives.

"Did you check the paper today, Vi?" Katherine asked while they were waiting for dinner.

"It's inconsistent with your general skepticism, Katherine. Why, of all things, do you choose to have faith in your horoscope?"

"I guess I'll look to just about anyone for direction, even the stars," Katherine laughed.

"Well, I have to admit I read mine today and it's perfect. It tells me to have a great fling."

Vi decided not to mention that Rose was planning to ship her off to the old people's home. Don't start with a downer when you're launching a sales campaign for a wild new adventure, she reminded herself. The situation with Rita could be an opening.

"How would you like to change your life?" she asked between bites of chicken stew. They were comfortable at their favorite table by the plate glass window with lace curtains.

"More money and travel." Katherine's tone was vague, as usual.

"But where would you go?" Keep it light, Vi thought. Don't want to sound like a prosecuting attorney.

"I don't know . . ."

"Some traveler. You won't even drive over the hill three miles to Carmel!"

"I'm afraid the brakes might not hold on such a steep grade coming back."

Katherine was turning out to be a scared dud. Her imagination was shot with Novocaine. How could Vi explain all about "Imaging the Second Half of Life" to her?

Today Vi could taste it out there—life. It was waiting for her to grab it. She wanted to wake up tingling with excitement every morning. Jump out of bed with no idea what the day could hold. No more predictable. Her prayer to the universe was for surprise. What was wrong with Katherine? Why didn't she want to grab at life while she still could?

Luckily, somewhere between the chicken stew and berry pie, Adrian turned out to be a great ally. Funny, Vi had never really felt close to her. Thought she was secretive and withdrawn. The three women worked together at the church thrift shop. Adrian was at least fifteen years younger. She was beautiful, with olive complexion and dark hair, but hard to know. That evening, Adrian seemed electrified by the idea of something, anything, new. Her dark eyes were alive and her usual scowl was replaced by a look of excitement. She jumped in with Vi and they ganged up on Katherine.

"I don't need to change anything," Katherine said. "I'm happy."

"We could get a tattoo."

"Join a motorcycle gang."

"Rob a mini-mart."

Vi saw they shouldn't be kidding her. Katherine looked nervous.

After Vi asked Adrian if her mother might give them some marijuana, Adrian suggested they should smoke some themselves. Katherine wet-blanketed.

"But what if . . . what if we get caught? What if we get sick?"

"But what if . . .", Vi mimicked. "That's your life's slogan. You should put it on your license plate."

"And I had my heart set on 'Back Off'," Katherine replied, sarcastically.

"Take a chance for a change," Vi said. "There's more to life than thrift shops and weekly bingo games—we're going beyond bingo."

Katherine glowered. "I don't do bingo." There was no budging her.

Finally Vi was forced to manipulate. Didn't want to, but there was no other way. "You owe it to Rita. You need to try it so you can advise her. If it's harmful or dangerous, you should know about it. Then you can talk Rita out of it. If you think it's okay, you'll feel better about getting her some."

After dinner Vi felt smug. Her nervousness almost gone. She had done a good job of convincing Katherine. What was really funny was how easy it all was, once they decided.

"Do you think your mother would mind? I would like to help Rita," Katherine said, remembering her manners.

"Yeh, she's smoked it ever since I can remember, and she's eighty. Can't be too bad for you," Adrian replied. "I'll ask her if we can smoke some at her house. I assume you think the neighbors might catch you if you do it at home."

(4)

———

HOROSCOPE: Display pioneer spirit and courage to let go of routine, status quo, security. Have an adventure of discovery: Suddenly you're free!

AND THAT'S HOW EASY IT ALL WAS. THE NEXT EVENING THEY WERE SITTING in Mrs. Pellagrino's living room by the wrought iron balcony filled with geraniums, smelling the faint remains of basil and garlic from homemade gnocci.

Adrian went to get her mother while Vi, filled with self-satisfaction, cuddled down in the big, lumpy chair. Let the adventure begin, she told herself.

"It's so lovely of you to invite us over, Mrs. Pellagrino. You can't know how much we appreciate this opportunity. We're open to new experiences because, well, you know how you can get old just doing the same things." Vi saw Adrian wince and realized she was babbling. She stopped talking as Adrian sat down on the floor by the fireplace, smoothing her stylish long challis skirt over her legs.

"Make yourselves comfortable," Adrian's mother said. "We're just here to have a pleasant evening."

"Welllll, yes," said Katherine. "But the main reason I'm here is because of my friend Rita." She was pacing the room, peeking out the windows. "She's really miserable from chemotherapy and needs some help. Violet said I would feel better about it if I tried some myself. I don't know. Maybe I shouldn't get involved with this."

Mrs. Pellagrino smiled. "I'm not expecting the police at the door."

Katherine fussed with the curtains and then sat down, clutching a small pillow to keep her hands still.

"Do you girls want a drink before we start?" asked Mrs. Pellagrino.

"Is it all right to mix liquor and drugs?" asked Vi. Adrian closed her eyes and sighed.

"I'd like a glass of Chablis," said Katherine. Things were suddenly looking up for her.

"You'll drink any old time!" Vi grabbed her arm. "You can tell what generation we're from."

Adrian got the wine and handed everyone a glass.

"Okay, let's get to it," Mrs. Pellagrino said. She pulled a little packet out of her apron, laid it on the table. There was some weedy-looking stuff and some cigarette papers in a snack-size, zip-lock bag.

"Oh my, what if we get caught?" asked Katherine, gulping wine.

Vi swatted her on the leg. "How do we do this, Mrs. Pellagrino? she asked.

"Call me Mercedes," Mrs. Pellagrino said as she dumped a little pile of the dried greeny-brown substance on the tiny paper. She picked it up, carefully licked the edge of the paper and, with her well-worn hands, expertly rolled it into a miniature cigarette. "Here are the ground rules. We'll smoke just this one joint, just this one time. That's it. Take the rest to Rita. After this you're on your own."

Mercedes slowly brought the cigarette to her lips and inhaled deeply. She closed her eyes and held it in for what seemed forever. The room was silent; nobody moved. She let it out and opened her eyes. "That's what we do. Hold it like this." She demonstrated. "Inhale, hold it in, and let it out." She handed it to Adrian, who did as she was told and handed it to Katherine.

"But I've never inhaled anything!" Katherine protested, but she went ahead with it.

"Don't worry if you cough a little," Mercedes said as Katherine coughed. "It's natural."

"I didn't know we all were going to smoke the same one," said Katherine between hacks. "Is that sanitary?" She handed it to Vi.

"It's a social thing. A bonding experience." Mercedes smiled at Katherine. "It's okay. You'll be fine."

Vi put her glasses on and was peering down her nose, checking the joint. "Aren't we supposed to stick a pin in it? I saw in a movie once where they stuck a pin in it."

"Inhale, Vi. We can't let the thing go to waste. It's too expensive," said Adrian.

"You're thinking of a roach clip, Violet," said Mercedes. "That's what we'll use to hold it when it burns down to the end so we don't lose any of it."

Vi took a deep hit and held it a long time. Exhaling, she said, "Oh, I love it! I feel altered already! Is it supposed to happen this fast?" She handed it back to smiling Mercedes.

Mercedes took a long drag, passed it to Adrian, and pushed herself up off the couch. "Well, that's it for me, girls. You all have fun now." She gave each of them a wave and headed toward the stairs.

"So how do you feel?"

"How do *you* feel?"

The joint was smoked, Katherine stopped coughing, and the three of them snuggled into the furniture, smiles on their faces.

"I thought I'd feel light-headed, but I don't. It's not like wine. I feel . . well, kind of . . . relaxed," Katherine said as she flipped off her shoes. She gazed at her toes and wiggled them.

"I feel nice, too," said Vi. "Do you know that I woke up this morning really stiff— my hands, elbows, knees—the usual arthritis flare-up. Seems to be gone now. Look, my fingers work better." She demonstrated, making little animal-shaped shadows on the wall.

"Well," said Katherine, "I'll have to admit I was having all kinds of butterflies in my stomach. This works better than Tums . . . even better than Valium!" She looked proud.

"I think you're feeling good, Katherine," said Adrian.

"Call me Kathy. Katherine is so stuffy," she said as she twiddled her toes. Kathy . . . It sounded right.

They were walking toward the shore in the moonlight. Vi hadn't felt this close to anyone since she and Fred were courting. Or maybe this was better. She wasn't sure. She told the others about Rose and the home. She wasn't frightened any more.

They marched down the hill in the middle of Butterfly Lane, trying not to giggle and trying not to fall down. It was like a pajama party. Vi said something about Judgment Day as they arrived at the bottom of the hill.

"You're assuming that I'm going to heaven and be presented with this Master Voice saying, 'What are you doing here?'" Kathy asked.

Vi was confused by the question but didn't want to ruin it all by asking what she was talking about. She said, "I guess so. What I'm thinking is it'd be something like a job review. God is your boss. He tells you there are some things you do good and a few things you could improve on. That's the way my husband's evaluation interviews were. The boss asked him if there's anything the company could do to make his job better. If I go for that Last Judgment and God asks me if there's anything He can do to improve the world, I'll have a couple of suggestions."

Kathy started to laugh. "Come on now, Violet. What do you know about improving the world? You haven't been outside a ten-mile radius of the Monterey Peninsula your entire life."

Kathy had her there. Old friends were like that. Vi had to giggle. Linking arms with the taller woman she said, "Well, you're right; I don't know too much about the world. But from what I see on CNN it's not going too well. Maybe I should just give God a few hints about what to do in Pacific Grove."

"There you go," said Kathy. "This is fun. I could think of a few serious improvements, if God were so inclined. "Why did He make me a woman at all? And if He was really bent on it, why didn't He make me Rita Hayworth—or Kate Hepburn?"

"Well, I wanted to be Humphrey Bogart, or at the very least Claire Trevor," Vi said.

Kathy and Vi leaned against each other and roared with the fun of being their movie idols. Then Vi noticed Adrian wasn't laughing. "So, Adrian, if you could tell God a thing or two, what would it be?"

"Well, maybe nothing." What was she sounding so angry about? "We can't expect God to fix everything. People have to fix things. We could stir up some action."

"Have you ever tried to present anything to the City Council? They are what you might call 'polarized'. Everything is about growth or no growth," said Kathy.

"Forget the City Council," Adrian said. "Lord, that could take forever. We don't need government to get things done. Let's do it ourselves." Adrian paused. "Wait till you meet Sophie, my college roommate who just moved here. She's a real go-getter."

Somebody said something Vi didn't understand. The moon was brighter than she had ever seen. She started to sing, "Oh show me a home where the buffalo roam . . . and I'll show you a dirty house." Then she laughed.

They arrived at Lovers' Point. The moon outlined the cypress trees and the jagged promontory. It felt magical. They sat side by side, like three birds on a branch. Vi felt deeply content, in love with her friends. Was it the marijuana? No, she was sure it had no effect on her.

Adrian was getting enthusiastic, waving her hands around. "What we get down to is Rita. We can't stop the suffering in the world, but we can help Rita."

Kathy concurred. "There's a lot of stuff we have no control over, but this business of helping Rita . . ."

Adrian said, "I'll ask my brother Peter where to get the pot."

It was settled. They looked at each other and smiled. Vi saw them as three happy old birds, just sitting quietly on their bench, intoxicated with pot and the moon and each other. At least that's what she felt. What a glorious night!

The next morning, Vi was surprised to feel good. She was afraid she might have a hangover like she always did with too much booze. Sitting on the edge of the bed, stuffing her feet into her ancient slippers, she thought the pot smoking evening a success: a good time, they didn't get busted. Later in the shower, she recalled the walk to the beach in the moonlight, the conversation about God and the Last Judgment. What stood out was the decision to help Rita, but she liked that part about Kate Hepburn and Claire Trevor.

"Better get on the phone and plan the new pot caper with Adrian right now," she said to Bloomers, also completing her morning bath and disdainfully disinterested.

Right after Vi finished dressing, before she could get to the phone, she spotted Rose puffing up the walk. "Damn that woman," she said. "I'm too busy for her nonsense today."

"Hi, Rosie," she called out, hoping to disarm her.

"I'm a grown woman, Mother; no diminutives. Please call me Rose." The grim-faced figure marched through the front door.

Vi sighed. It was going to be a long day.

On her walk the next morning, Kathy stopped to rest on the bench overlooking Kissing Rock. She gazed reflectively at the waves rolling in, pounding over and through the two large rocks that were joined together in a kiss. She agreed with Vi that things needed improvement in both their small world and the big one out there, but to her, this place on earth was the best place to be.

Was she the same person as the Katherine of last week? "I don't think so," she muttered. She liked being called Kathy. She was thinking of cutting her hair to get rid of the librarianish bun. But smoking marijuana? That was a real detour out of her comfort zone.

What a contradiction! Jerry always wanted her to be a perfect lady, not to say or do anything that would bring dishonor to his name. Ridiculous! He dishonored his *own* name! When he dumped her for that vamp who didn't know the meaning of inhibition, he told Katherine she should break out of her inhibitions. Stupid hypocrite!

She remembered the previous night when Vi and Adrian had said the same thing. She remembered how the crystal hanging in Mercedes' window sparkled, reflecting glorious colors on the opposite wall. How absolutely sensuous the music sounded.

Rita used to tell her to break loose, too. Once she said, "Honestly, Katherine, I just don't understand you! When you were active in community theater in Modesto, some of the roles you played were like a resurrection of your hidden inner self. Why can't you do that in real life?"

Last night had really been wonderful. She felt close to Vi and Adrian. "No, I don't think I want to get in the habit of this. Addictive personalities need to be careful. Been there, done that," she mused.

Katherine had always needed to rationalize her actions; Kathy, too, felt it necessary. "If it really does help pain . . ." She hated to feel pain, to see signs of it. Even as a small child watching her father put baby kittens in a gunnysack and dunk them in a tub of water, she felt the pain. She remembered when her mother was taken to the over-crowded, under-staffed emergency room after her accident. She was screaming with the pain of twisted, shattered bones, writhing in her own excrement as they waited for a doctor, and all Katherine could do was watch helplessly.

Kathy recalled her own pain the night Jerry hit her—beat her—that night he saw her kissing Tom at the community theater. Some things you just don't tell. And she never had.

She shook herself back into the here and now. Straighted her shoulders and got up from the bench with a strong determination. *I will not have Rita in pain if there's something I can do about it.*

(5)

———

"JACK," SOPHIE CALLED AS SHE WALKED IN THE FRONT DOOR, "GUESS WHAT? I met the most fabulous women at the 'Shop and Pray' and I'm going to give a lunch for them as soon as I get the good china unpacked."

"Hey," Jack said, "first things first," as he rose and grabbed her to him in a happy hug.

"I've missed you and there's nothing to eat in this house. Do you realize this is the first time you've gone anywhere without me in a couple of months and left me home to starve?"

"I thought of you once," she said. She still wasn't quite used to having an almost brand new husband, but was ever so glad she did.

"I was having so much fun at the 'Pray and Save'."

"I thought it was 'Shop and Pray'."

"Oh, you know what I mean. It's a darling thrift shop on 18th street, so very Pacific Grove. Painted blue and white, Victorian like a little old lady, with red geraniums in blue pots on the porch. There are several rooms and a kitchen and they are full of stuff. Adrian introduced me to Violet and Katherine. They're so different but fun and I'm happy to make some new friends. I love you," all in the same breath, then she gave him a big kiss.

24

"Tell me more about these women. I want to know anyone who's in your life."

"How sweet." She began to cut up vegetables for a stir-fry and Jack joined her at the kitchen table with his drink and peanuts.

She thought, *I enjoy having a man to cook for after all these manless years, but it is somewhat inconvenient. I need to plan my party.* But she said, "Aren't you glad we retired and moved here? If Adrian and I hadn't written and talked on the phone so often, it wouldn't have occurred to us. Pacific Grove is such a homey place."

"Yeah, I love America's Last Hometown." He came up behind her and squeezed her around the waist.

"When I visited here the first year I was teaching, I thought it quaint, but in twenty five years it's changed a lot. Has retained its charm, though."

"Just like you," Jack added. "Describe these new gals."

"Violet's the short one, dark and gypsy-like, kind of bossy. Katherine, tall, white-haired, dignified-looking, seems to do what Vi tells her to, but I don't know. They're funny and fun together. Kid around a lot. Witty. They seem fond of Adrian, and were nice to me. The shop has neat stuff. I hope I'll find dolls to add to my collection.

"When I walked in that shop today I felt I found another piece in the puzzle. You know what I'm talking about. I've mentioned it before. How life is a puzzle and you keep finding different pieces that fit together although you don't know exactly why they do, but they do all through your life. Finally you find the last piece, and voila, that's your whole life, although you don't know it at the time—when you've found the last piece, I mean."

Jack looked at her, bemused. "What a theory. I don't know how logical it is—that's not your thing. But sweetie, I think we have just gotten started on a whole new puzzle, and I don't want you finding any last piece for years and years. I don't even want to think about it."

"Well don't," she said. "I know I'm so excited about living right now I feel reborn—until I look in the mirror. It's amazing to be finished with teaching school forever, when school was my life, the students my children. To have this whole wonderful new world out here and a darling husband for the first time in my life. A fifty five year old 'Old Maid' finding a sexy man like you. Lovemaking is heaven on earth and I never knew what I was missing." She paused.

"Let's skip dinner and go to bed!"

The next morning, after they cleaned up the tiny kitchen and walked their two miles on the beach, Sophie began to unpack the blue and white china she'd found at a garage sale. Staffordshire, and what a bargain! She loved it. The small dining room had a perfect corner cupboard for display and the old drop-leaf table looked great. When she knew her new friends a little better, she would feel comfortable inviting them for lunch.

What would she make? The safe hot chicken casserole she had been doing for years for her bridge club (that barely got through two rubbers), or something from the new *Silver Palate* cookbook they gave her for a wedding present?

She smiled to herself as she thought of her old Moundsville, West Virginia friends. She missed them somewhat, and the teacher gossip that centered mostly on which high school students were doing it, and which faculty were involved in hanky-panky. Now that she was finally doing it herself she understood their wild urges better, although she deplored the promiscuity. After all, sex without love would be like dinner without dessert. Not at all complete. She loved Jack so much.

She hummed a few bars from their song, "It Had to be You," and as she put the last plate on the hutch, the phone rang. It must be Adrian, she thought. I wonder what's happening. It was good to be living close to her old college chum.

"Good morning. Oh, Adrian honey, isn't it a glorious day? Guess what I'm doing. Getting ready to have a party! Yes. For you, and those darling women you introduced me to, Katherine and Violet. I'm so glad you took me to the thrift shop. It's going to be fun. I can hardly wait to work there!"

(6)

———

VI, STILL RUMPLED IN HER RATTY GREEN CHENILLE ROBE, STOOD INDECISIVELY in front of her closet. What in the hell do you wear to meet a woman in the hospital who is dying? She already regretted her promise to Kathy that she would go along to deliver the marijuana. Kathy had told Adrian that cigarettes weren't allowed in the hospital, so Adrian mixed up a syrup using the recipe she got from her mother—a mixture of marijuana and rum.

Let's see. Kathy always talks about how wealthy Rita is. Maybe the new Harve Benard suit she picked up at Shop and Pray yesterday would do. And just to show she wasn't stuffy, she could wear her Greta Garbo-style straw hat.

No, too formal. Kathy wants to keep it light. Like a party. Dressing up like that might be too funereal. Need something outrageous. From all she'd heard about her, Rita *was* outrageous. She would like recognizing one of her own. Don't think like you're going to a PTA meeting with all the Pacific Grove mothers, she reminded herself. You're in a whole new life.

She pulled out her sweatshirt drawer. Maybe something with a smart aleck slogan. "The last time I used a broom, I flew somewhere."

She really liked her red one with the little yellow birdhouse that said, "So . . . it's not home sweet home . . . Adjust!" and she was about to put it on when she

27

remembered she had a hole in her matching red tennis shoes, so she settled for the blue "Don't let reality ruin your life."

She wore her white ducks and blue tennis shoes, white sailor hat. Checked it all out in the mirror. She thought it made a pretty good statement. Saucy, casual, almost boyish. Yeah, she liked it. Just right for Rita. She grabbed her wallet and rushed over to Kathy's.

"I don't know if this is such a great idea," she said to Kathy as they walked down the hall of Monterey Community Hospital.

"Please, Vi. I can't face her alone. I need you to keep things light. She looks so terrible, I can't be cheerful. I don't know what to say to her sometimes. And I'm scared carrying this marijuana."

"Don't be silly. It just looks like cough syrup!"

They were at the door of Rita's room. "I've always said I would do anything for you, Kathy, and this certainly is a test of that. What do you expect me to say? I never even met the woman."

"Oh, just be your funny self. Just carry on. You know—bubble a bit."

As she entered the room, Vi thought how lovely for a hospital. Not that terrible sterile white. A soft green. The Del Monte forest on display outside the double window. A bouquet of peach tea roses on the night stand.

As Kathy was discreetly putting the bottle of cough syrup into Rita's outstretched hand, Vi tuned out, looked Rita over. She was sitting up in bed, propped by pillows. Vi was relieved to find her looking less terrible than she'd imagined. Pale, of course, a little shrunken at the cheekbones, neck crepey; but all in all, vibrant, pretty, even a little stylish in her maroon bed jacket. She's had plenty of top-notch plastic surgery. Must get a stylist to come in to keep her hair that honey color.

Rita smiled as she put the medicine under her pillow. Kathy sat by the bed. Vi stood at the foot. A young nurse brought in an extra chair, but Vi still stood, indecisive. Must act silly, she said to herself, trying to implement Kathy's wishes.

Kathy looked worse than Vi felt. She heard the tremor in her voice as she introduced her. "Rita, this is my friend I wanted you to meet because you're so alike. She reminds me of you in high school."

That's some intro, Vi thought. What does she mean? That I'm immature? Better do something funny. But what? A joke. *My mind's a blank.*

"I'm Violet Farnsworth," she said, doing her best cross jig and curtsy. Never mind how stupid you look, she told herself. *Just cut the tension. Get them moving.*

"What a hoot you are, Violet." Rita's voice was strong, loud. She was beaming. "But what an awful name! Is that really your name?"

"I'm afraid so. My friends call me Vi. I discovered my *real* name when I was nine and saw Hedy Lamar in *White Cargo*. I should have been Tandelejo, but mom just didn't know. She called me Violet and my sister, Daisy. Some dumb floral fixation."

Rita laughed. "My name was originally Victoria VanHolt. I picked Rita after seeng Hayworth in *Gilda*, and I married Raymond Archibald Rich because I liked the last name."

Ahhh. Like taking off your pantyhose, the relief of tension in the room was blessed. *Give her more of this,* Vi thought. *Quick.* She was really beginning to enjoy herself. Kathy was right. The woman lived for smart remarks. Life in the hospital was too serious. She just wanted to volley with someone. Throw around her wit. Get a little admiration for her smart mouth.

Rita leaned forward, throwing out her arms in a big sweeping gesture. "It's not too late for you to change your name. Tandelejo just might suit you fine. Why not change it?"

"I hate paper work. Just too much trouble. Confuse the social security department, get a new driver's license, and worst of all, I'd have to explain it to my daughter. She'd never get it, not in a million years!"

"Why?"

"Well, she's the daughter my mother wanted instead of me, and her name, Rose, says it all."

Silence. Oh, oh, Vi thought. Keep it moving. *No silences.* Kathy wasn't helping just sitting there with a dumb expression. What's her problem? Don't let the pace lag. This is a tough gig; three old ladies in a hospital room, a party with no alcohol and no men.

"I liked hearing you say 'hoot', Rita. Haven't heard that good old word for years!"

"Yeah, I like to say it to someone who doesn't say, 'What do you mean?' The best thing about young people is their beautiful bodies . . ."

"But the best thing about old people is they know what you're talking about, and they've seen all your favorite movies, and they can sing all your songs," Vi interrupted, still wondering why Kathy was sitting like a zombie in her chair.

"You're the bee's knees, Vi. I can hear you're hep to the jive. You're in the groove."

"Yeah, I'm reet to the beat!" They both laughed.

"So what's your story, morning glory?"

"Whadya wanna know?" Vi asked with a gleam in her eye.

"Brag! Be a bratty kid. Tell me what you do well."

"Oh, that's an easy one. I was a Meglan Kitty."

Now Vi was really excited. *Damn! Why do I have on these tennis shoes. If I only had my taps.* Doing her best under the circumstances, she gave Rita her best tap, kick, kick.

"That's where Shirley Temple was discovered, but I was good, too. She was just lucky."

Rita picked up an empty plastic ice bucket from the night stand and started to beat on it with a pencil.

"You're in luck today, Shirley! It just so happens I can do a double paradiddle. Legacy of a beautiful drummer I used to date." She started to drum. She was transported, and Vi could see, behind the sickness and the wrinkles, the girl Kathy had loved in high school. *I've taken her back to her good old days.* Vi got the beat and did a buck and wing and a double shuffle.

Kathy was sitting there frozen and, starting a little side tap step, Vi made her way toward her chair with Rita still drumming and humming her accompaniment. She grabbed Kathy's hands to get her up on her feet.

"Come on," she encouraged. "Take a step. Just like this, Kathy. You can do it. Just one step."

Kathy was on her feet now, but didn't move. Pulled her hand away and sat back down.

"Yeah, yeah," Rita chanted it to the beat, "what are you waiting for? Inspiration?"

"Or a signal from heaven?" Vi was doing great with her patter and dance. She and Rita could put this show on the road.

"Your youth to return?" Rita was half-chanting, half-singing.

"A fool-proof deodorant?" Vi sang now as she danced. She was staring right at Rita's bright eyes. This was turning into a glorious contest.

"The return of your figure?"

"Your ship to dock in Monterey Bay?"

"Next year?"

Rita and Vi were allies in pushing, playing, wanting to see Kathy break loose.

"Permission from Mama?"

"From God?"

"Jerry? Or the bimbo?" Rita giggled, looked proud of herself for this smart zinger.

Boy, are we a perfect pair, Vi thought, returning the gibe. "Are you waiting for the neighbor's permission? The lady next door? Hell, I'm the lady next door. You've got my permission!"

"I'm the friend who knew you when." Rita was changing her drum rhythm to a faster beat now. "Hell, you've got my permission, too!"

Vi was wheezing with the effort to speed up her tap dance. She knew she was out of shape, but what fun! She delighted in the brain-storming moment, proud for cheering Rita up. She thought she was going to pop out of that bed any minute and start tapping her heart out.

Then she saw Rita's face go dead. Her arms reached out. "Oh Katie, I'm so sorry. Come here." And Kathy was on the bed, sobbing into Rita's embrace.

"I was just wishing I didn't feel so out of place while you're having fun," Kathy said.

Vi felt foolish. She had missed the signs of Kathy's distress.

"We were just playing." Rita's voice was soothing now. "Vi and I were just having too much fun teasing. We're born to tease. You're my best friend. You know I wouldn't hurt you for the world."

Vi was relieved to hear Kathy's old strong voice. "Never mind, Rita; it's silly for me to be hurt. You're both right. I know that I don't loosen up easily. It just hurts to feel left out."

"How could I do that? You've been a part of my life too long." Rita was patting her on the back. Kathy's head jerked up.

"This is something, Rita. You're the one with all the problems and . . ."

"Go ahead, say it, Kathy. I'm the one who's dying."

"And here you are, comforting me."

"I like it. It feels good," Rita said.

Now Vi felt left out. She stood motionless at the foot of the bed, separate from their intimacy. "Vi's sorry, too," Rita shouted. "Come over here and give old Katie a hug."

Relieved Rita provided an opening, Vi rushed over to the side of the bed. Gave Kathy an awkward hug. "I am sorry, Kathy. Rita and I are just a bad combination. You said we'd get along and have fun, but we got a little carried away."

As they finished their goodbyes and were starting to leave, Rita grimaced with pain. She took a heavy swig from the syrup bottle. "Thanks gals." Smiling weakly, she said, "Come over here Violet Farnsworth."

Vi approached her bed. Rita grabbed her fiercely for a hug, then pulled her down to eye level and said in a mock serious voice, "You and I, Tandelejo Farnsworth, could get into some serious trouble!"

⟨7⟩

HOROSCOPE: Your sensitivities will be on full alert over the next few weeks. Beware. An invitation to join exclusive group offers startling opportunities. Find balance. Altruistic urges should be subject to common sense.

FINALLY THE DAY OF THE PARTY CAME. SOPHIE POLISHED AND SCOURED everything. The table was set with her blue and white china and her grandmother's silver on the white and blue woven coverlet from Appalachia, one of their wedding presents. She was pleased how well it all looked together, informal yet elegant. Just the right note to entertain Adrian, Violet and Katherine. In Moundsville she'd had many good friends, and she missed them. Having worked with these women for awhile, she really liked them, and wanted to know them better. Sometimes she noticed the three of them exchanged glances and stopped talking when she came around. She tried not to feel hurt.

After today and her special hot chicken salad and onion tart, they would definitely accept her. Her chocolate silk pie should settle it. They would know she was an excellent cook.

She glanced out the window and saw them. Adrian wore a long red skirt, Katherine was in a blue tailored shirtwaist dress. Violet must have bought that green outfit Sophie had liked yesterday at the thrift shop. They were chattering as they came up the walk.

As she dashed to the door she brushed back her messy curls. "Welcome to Mountain Manor," she said. "That's what Jack calls our house in memory of our

32

romantic encounter, no matter how inappropriate for the seaside. I'm so glad to see you." She enveloped them in a group hug, genuinely pleased to have them there. "Katherine, you look nice in blue."

"Thank you; but please call me Kathy."

"Where's Jack?" Adrian asked.

"I persuaded him to join the local golf club so he'd have an interest in something besides me, since I work at the shop. I still have to push to get him out on the course."

"Really? You might be sorry," Kathy said. "I couldn't get my ex *off* the course."

Vi scoffed, "I don't think she has to worry. Look at that figure."

They all looked at Sophie in the pale blue twin sweater set and the pleated skirt. Sophie blushed. "I'm not worried yet." She steered them into the dining room.

They oohed and aahed at her primrose-in-a-basket centerpiece, then sat down and sipped the crisp rosé she poured.

Sophie gulped a good bit of her wine and got up her courage to ask, "Tell me something, will you? You girls have a secret. Something that happens at Shop and Pray?"

They looked at each other in surprise.

"Uh, oh," Adrian looked at the others. "I told you she was sharp, didn't I? We don't need to keep any secrets. Trust her."

There was silence all around the table. Then they all began to talk at once.

"My Mom has smoked pot for years."

"My friend Rita has terminal cancer and she asked me to try and get her some marijuana for her pain. I've heard it has many medicinal qualities."

"We just tried it for a kick—a new experience . . . ."

"We won't do it again," Kathy added.

"We got a little of it for Rita."

"We're going to have to find more. We want to help Rita," said Vi.

"We'd like you to join us," said Adrian.

Sophie was stunned as they continued. She wanted to be friends with these women; she wanted them to feel she was trustworthy and one of them. She liked the idea of doing good. But can you do good by doing bad? She felt confused. What was she, a girl from Moundsville, doing with friends like this? Friends who casually broke the law, who thought it was okay to buy marijuana.

"I don't know what to think," she said. "I'd love to help Kathy's friend, but what would Jack think?"

"Come on, Sophie. He doesn't have to know everything, does he?" Adrian said. "Can't you have a secret of your own?"

Sophie chose her words carefully. "I don't know what to say. Jack and I are so close I think he might sense I had a secret. And I'd feel guilty being involved in something he'd disapprove of."

"But how do you know? Has the subject ever come up?" Vi asked.

Kathy added, "You're an individual. In a marriage you don't have to share every little thing. Don't you want some independence?"

"You don't know how Jack feels about it. You haven't known him long enough to know his opinions," Adrian said.

"Think it over," Vi chimed in. "We don't want to spoil the party. Do you share your recipe for hot chicken salad? I'd love to have it."

Sophie felt relieved when the conversation changed topics. She didn't have to share her doubts. They laughed, sipped a little wine, and enjoyed each other's company. Adrian told Kathy she was more fun when she drank wine, and added she'd like to see more pizzaz in her wardrobe.

"What do you have in mind?" Kathy asked.

Vi started giggling. "Remember that book by Marabel Morgan? She suggested wrapping yourself up in cellophane and all that sort of stuff to be more sexy. I think it was called *The Total Woman*."

"Oh, yeah, I remember that. I trashed it." Adrian waved her empty glass at Sophie.

"Sounds interesting to me," said Sophie as she stood up to fill everyone's wine glass.

"We thought it was so emancipated. Like a bunch of hookers trying to appeal to our husbands. I fibbed, telling my husband I didn't have any underwear on at a P.T.A. meeting," Vi confessed. "I thought it would be a turn-on. He made me go home."

"But did he go with you?" Adrian asked, laughing.

Kathy interrupted. "I would never package myself like that! And I sure wouldn't dress in cellophane for my husband."

"I'm sorry I even read the book. I never did anything except lie about it," said Vi.

Kathy took a sip of wine and smiled. "Well, I suppose if I had followed that broad's advice maybe Jerry wouldn't have taken off with little ol' Blinky-eyed Susan."

"Or he might have taken off sooner after he saw you in the plastic," Vi laughed.

They cleared the table and moved into the living room. "It sounds to me like this town has lots of real home town activities. What's this 'Feast of Lanterns' they mentioned down at the thrift shop?" Sophie asked as she poured the coffee.

"Believe it or not, it's a festival based on the Blue Willow Legend, the story of a plate," Vi said.

"Oh come on, Vi, it's more than that!" Adrian exclaimed.

"It's marvelous," said Kathy. "Especially the pageant where they enact the Pacific Grove version, which really doesn't have anything to do with plates, by the way. About a Chinese Mandarin's daughter escaping a planned marriage to run away with a poor scholar. They somehow change into butterflies in bursts of light and come to Pacific Grove every year."

"There are huge crowds around Lover's Point and when it starts getting dark they light candles inside paper lanterns. It's a beautiful sight," said Adrian.

Sophie looked confused.

"And then they shoot off fireworks and play patriotic march music over the loudspeakers," Vi added.

"And if that isn't exciting enough for you, wait until you see the Butterfly Bonanza in October when small children dress up like butterflies to welcome the monarchs to their winter home," Kathy said.

"Well . . . it all sounds fascinating," Sophie said.

After the party was over, Sophie cleared the table, still skeptical about what the women were doing with marijuana. "God, I had no idea. They want to do good, but does that make it right?" A Staffordshire plate shattered on the floor. "Damn!"

After dinner that night, Sophie curled up beside Jack on the couch.

"Honey, I want to ask you something. I told you how much the women at my luncheon enjoyed the party, but I didn't tell you what they are trying to do." She glanced up at him.

"So tell me now, silly. What are these nice ladies doing?" He gave her a squeeze.

"Well, Kathy has a friend seriously ill with cancer. She asked Kathy to find out about getting some marijuana."

"What!?"

"Listen until I finish." She mustn't stop now. "Kathy doesn't want to smoke it herself, but she studied about it at the library and in the articles being written supporting the ballot proposition—I think it's Prop 215—about medical use. It sounds like it really could pass," she said hopefully. She hesitated, but as Jack opened his mouth to speak, she rushed on.

"Anyhow, I found out when I asked them what they were up to. It seemed to me they had a secret. I noticed they stopped talking when I came into the room at the shop. I don't know yet where they plan to get it." Sophie stopped and let out a big sigh, realizing she was talking too fast.

"But it's illegal," Jack said. "I don't want you getting involved in something illegal."

"I won't do anything against the law," Sophie answered, cuddling up tighter in Jack's arms. "But if I know they do, am I guilty by association? I want them to like me, and we're just beginning to know each other."

"I realize you knew many people before I came along, and I know, even as much as we love each other, I can't be everything to you." Jack spoke softly, smoothing her hair with caressing hands. "I know you've been reading the publicity supporting passage of Prop 215, but I don't agree with it." There was silence as they both stared into the dying embers in the fireplace.

"Tell you what," Jack said. "I trust you to know the difference between right and wrong. You do what you think is right."

(8)

HOROSCOPE: Today marks the point of no return. You will find professional strengths and talents you didn't know you had. Dress appropriately for business venture.

VI WAS NERVOUS. HER OLD '73 PLYMOUTH VALIANT SOUNDED LIKE IT WAS missing. Traffic was backed up from the Pebble Beach on-ramp. Stalled in a line of cars that weren't moving at all, she checked out her makeup again in the rear-view mirror and decided that she looked professional.

She thought about Mr. Peasou. Such a lovely name. He must be French. Even if she didn't like Peter, she had to admit it was nice of Adrian's brother to get his name for her.

Vi checked over her clothes, moving her hand inside her suit jacket to adjust an off-kilter shoulder pad. She would have felt much more secure if she could have talked to Nikki. She was a great friend and always knew what to do, but only Bertie Wattle was on duty at the library when she went in. She didn't know anything. Vi found "How to Dress for a Successful Job Interview" by Ms. Mary Lexison in *Managerial Woman*. It's true, she wasn't applying for a job, but Bertie assured her the outfit would be just the same for a modern business meeting.

Vi liked the sound of "modern business meeting." According to Ms. Lexison, clothes were not as severe as in the 80s. Lighter colors were the word for the 90s. That was good because Vi liked her powder-blue bouclé suit. She wore a white silk blouse (without the jabot—too fussy for business). Her high heels were Selbys, but she noticed that one of the heels was worn down. Oh well, it would have to do. She debated about the pearls but, remembering Barbara Bush, decided they would be all right.

No earrings. ("Too much jewelry," Ms. Lexison had said, "indicates you are not to be taken seriously.") Vi definitely wanted to be taken seriously. Her proudest possession was the Louie Vuitton attaché case that she'd purchased yesterday at the thrift shop. It was a little worn, but that gave her an air of experience. Made it look like she had been through many business deals. No need to announce she was an amateur.

The car in front of her inched forward. Violet took her foot off the brake and let hers roll almost to its bumper.

Her dilemma was the clutch purse. How did you carry an attaché case and a purse? The two together? Or one in each hand? She had considered her Jackie Kennedy pillbox hat for a jaunty touch, but took it off in the car as the article made no mention of hats.

She had made a mistake on the cologne. Ms. Lexison forgot to cover that. She was tired of violet cologne. Everyone always gave it to her because of her name, but she definitely didn't feel like a violet. In a bold move she had sprayed on "Obsession" but now, with time to reflect, she felt it was too bold for a business meeting. Fine time to think of it! It's too late to get it off now.

She looked at her watch. Late! Now she was nervous again. ("Lack of punctuality makes a bad impression at a business meeting.") She wished she had a business card. Would it be going too far to carry a cellular phone? Probably, and she didn't have one. At last the traffic began to move.

Violet rushed into Starbucks at the Crossroads Shopping Center and quickly scanned the room for Mr. Peasou. There was a distinguished older gentlman at a corner table. "Mr. Peasou?" she inquired in her best business tone. He shook his head. Relieved not to be late, she sank into a small wire-mesh chair with a tie-on cushion and prepared to wait.

Ten minutes passed; twenty, thirty. No one. Just some homeless-looking person wearing a shirt with the sleeves cut off, torn at one shoulder. She didn't like him sitting so close. He smelled.

"God Almighty, Pea Soup! I told you not to sit down in here. Think I want to have these damned cushions cleaned again? Take that coffee outside."

The homeless-looking person glanced sideways with a touch of resentment at the big blonde behind the counter, but slowly moved out into the fog.

Vi had a sinking feeling. Was Pea Soup Mr. Peasou? She was afraid he must be. She followed the retreating figure outside.

He sat on a metal bench. His jeans were loose on his lean frame. He bent over the cardboard coffee cup for warmth, clutching it with both hands while he endured a convulsive coughing fit. Violet noticed his hands. Strong-looking hands covered with freckles. His freckled face was worn out. It had seen too many miles.

"Mr. Pea Soup?" Vi's voice no longer sounded business-like in her ears. Just timid, frightened.

He scowled at her. Then starting with her shoes, looked slowly up to her outfit and then her face. At this moment she was glad she had abandoned the pillbox hat.

"Who wants to know?" He narrowed his eyes, started scratching his scalp.

Vi hoped nothing would jump off him and onto her.

"Mr. Pellagrino sent me on a business matter." She got a little more reassurance in her voice this time.

"Shit he did," he laughed. At least she thought he meant it as a laugh. She had never heard a noise quite like it before.

"Yes he did. Mr. Pellagrino, Adrian's brother. He sent me here to purchase some marijuana."

His eyes opened wider. "I dunno what you're talking about." He made a move to get up.

"No, no, don't leave, Mr. Pea Soup. I probably made some mistake, but I'm really sincere. Look, see, I have money!" She opened the clutch purse and took out a handful of bills. "Poor Rita really needs it. She has cancer, you know, and she's in terrible pain. Please, you're the only one who can help!"

He stared at her a while. "You're not a Fed are ya?"

"What's a fed?"

This time she was sure he was attempting a laugh. His hand gestured for her to sit down. He leaned forward, looked a little less menacing. Vi felt relieved. She seemed to have passed some kind of test.

"How much do ya want?" His voice sounded almost like he was teasing.

Now she was rattled. That was a question she hadn't thought about. She had his confidence. Better not show insecurity now.

She tried for a casual tone. "A pound."

"A pound?"

"Maybe two." She could see he was startled. Good, she impressed him at last.

"I only got a half ounce," he said.

"Can you get more?"

"No. You want it or not?"

"I guess so. What's the cost?"

Now he squinted at her again. "Five hundred dollars." He was bluffing. She could tell by the way he was trying too hard to look matter-of-fact. She had no idea what it should cost.

"I'll give you two hundred."

"No, three hundred."

"Sold." Why quibble, she thought. Rita needed it right away. She counted out the money and handed Pea Soup the cash. He gave her a little bag. She quickly opened her attaché case and dropped it in.

Mr. Pea Soup folded each bill carefully, into halves, then quarters, and placed only one in each of his many pants and shirt pockets. Now it was Vi's turn to stare.

"It's good stuff," he said. "Big Sur's best. Second only to Acapulco Gold. No shit in it. Pure and good." He looked in her eyes for the first time.

For a second Vi thought if you cleaned him up he would look something like her Uncle Jeffrey. She'd always been fond of Jeffrey.

"Thank you, Mr. Pea Soup." Vi extended her hand. He formed a half smile and shook her hand. Her first business deal was sealed.

(9)

———

HOROSCOPE: The New Moon on the 7th sheds light on your relationships. Time to confide in new friends. Delay important decisions. Things are not as clear as they could be. The views of loved ones are worth seeking, but they are not infallible.

SOPHIE WAS GLAD THEY HADN'T PUSHED HER ON THEIR PROJECT. SHE COULD stall by talking about something else. She didn't know Kathy and Vi very well, but since they were flirting with drugs they must be broad-minded.

"I never thought I'd do this, but today I feel like telling you how Jack and I met." Sophie nervously smiled at the three women seated around the tea room's fake marble-top table as they sipped their jasmine tea.

"Glad you brought him into the shop today so we could meet him," Vi said.

"I love his gorgeous curly white hair," said Kathy.

"You certainly haven't told me much," Adrian added. "You might as well know we've all been talking about you behind your back. After fifty five years of being a virgin, what made you take the plunge?"

"He did. He found me at Blackwater Falls Park at an environmental seminar. He gave a speech against dumping waste products in the Kanawha River. He remembered the damage that was done in the 50s before people's consciousness was raised. It was last fall, October 13 to be exact, and we were married over Thanksgiving."

"Fast work. You've left out a few details," said Vi.

"I was sitting on a log in the woods. My friend Mary Ann went home early.

There was no one else I wanted to see again so I was at loose ends. It was gorgeous there—red, yellow and orange covered the ground and a great elm tree and some maples almost met overhead. It smelled good in the woods and it was unseasonably warm for October. I could hear the falls in the distance, otherwise total silence."

"Doesn't she describe it beautifully?" Kathy leaned forward.

"Get to the good part. Cut to the sex," said Vi.

"Violet!" Kathy looked shocked.

"I had the whole weekend ahead of me before I needed to return to school. I longed for something, but didn't know what. Adventure, change. A different life, maybe. I was tired of being a schoolteacher. I always loved teaching and most of my students, but too many rules, too many rule-breakers. I was beginning to get tired. I would never admit my life was a tad boring, but I guess maybe it was."

"Sounds like it," said Adrian.

"I took off my shoes and socks, let my hair out of its bun, took off my cardigan. The sun felt fantastic on my feet and arms. I stretched out . . . and this man walked out of the trees straight toward me.

"'I've been watching you,' he said. 'You are a wood nymph. I suppose you'll disappear, but your hair has a halo of gold in the sunlight. . .'"

"Oh, nobody talks like that!" said Vi.

"Weren't you frightened?" Adrian asked. "I would have been scared out of my underwear!"

"Sounds like a psycho," said Kathy.

"I was startled and a bit afraid there in the woods, but I didn't say anything.

"'Hope you aren't going to stop with just your shoes and socks.' He added, 'I should have stayed hidden to see. I didn't want to be a voyeuer. I wanted to hear your voice. Find out if you were real.'

"I was dumbstruck. I wasn't used to meeting a man who was so direct, and he left me breathless."

Adrian and Kathy smiled at each other. "He's gorgeous," Adrian said, "but that's not enough. Why were you in such a hurry?"

"Why do you think? I'd waited my whole life."

"What happened next?" Vi asked.

"We walked to the main falls. The water felt wonderful on my feet. Suddenly I was deliciously happy. I couldn't say why. It was the combination—this perfect day and this man who already felt like a friend. He invited me for dinner at his cabin. I was anxious to go. I didn't have anything exciting to wear; just a pair of khakis and a green sweater. I hadn't been on a 'date' in years. I hadn't even looked at a man. Jack was different, but I didn't know much about him yet. He told me he was lonely. His wife had died a couple of years ago."

"Is he retired?" Vi asked. "He seems kind of young for that."

"We're both fifty five and we have so much catching up to do, we can't keep working. It was lucky our retirements kicked in. We sold our houses. We're okay. More than okay. Comfortable."

"You sold your house? What's wrong with you? You didn't give him all the money, did you?" Adrian sounded accusatory.

"We pooled our money. We share it. But that's not what I was going to tell you."

"Yeah, what happened that got you from there to here?" Kathy asked.

"He seduced me," she said primly.

They all laughed uncertainly. "Really?"

"We never did eat that evening. The moon was full and there in the moonlight he enchanted me. I haven't wakened from his spell yet. I had never felt beautiful, till then. I never really wanted anyone that way before. He was magic. *I* was magic. The moonlight made us mythic creatures and the leaves were a mattress under us." She stopped, embarrassed by her frankness. "I think we were made for each other."

"Lucky you," Kathy whispered.

They all sighed. Not jealous exactly, but . . . reflective.

Sophie took a deep breath. *I wonder if I should have shared all that*, she thought.

Vi said, "I remember being able to create love stories like that when I was in college, but not after I married Fred. So many wasted years."

Kathy shook her head. "I find it hard to believe any man can be like that."

Adrian did not speak. The silence hung over all of them.

(10)

HOROSCOPE: Suddenly you are in charge of your own fate. You can rewrite the script of your life. Focus on power, authority, ability to win friends among the high and mighty. A new acquaintance figures prominently.

VI WAS SELF-SATISFIED. SHE'D FINALLY PRIED KATHY OUT OF HER PACIFIC Grove cocoon and launched on some real adventures. Adrian couldn't go because she had to work, but Kathy, grumbling a little, agreed to ride over the hill and around the bay with her all the way to Santa Cruz. Vi could tell that Kathy's mood was different when she came out the door. She was wearing the red muu-muu Rita had given her.

Kathy relaxed in Santa Cruz, far enough from home to cut loose a little. They had an espresso in a sidewalk cafe and talked to some street people right out of a 60s movie. They bought a few second-hand books at Logos Bookshop across the street. Not quite the adventure Vi had dreamed of, but the important thing was Kathy had a good time. She was funny, less tense, and promised to go again next Sunday.

Pea Soup had proved a reliable provider for Rita's needs. Life was peaceful for a week, but Rita couldn't keep her mouth shut. She was feeling so good she just had to tell everyone in the cancer unit, and word got to the Hospice Center. The demand grew.

"Can you get a little more for Abigal? I told her how great I feel—she wants to try it." Same scene for every delivery, and every time Kathy said, "Honestly, Rita, I wish you wouldn't tell everyone. We could get caught."

44

Pretty soon Vi was sent for pickups every day and her life became more exciting. She and Pea Soup got along better. He knew she wasn't a Fed, and she remembered not to wear her blue bouclé suit. They chewed the fat now and again as they sat over coffee outside Starbucks.

He told Vi that he dropped out of high school in Chicago to run numbers. He'd always wanted to come to California where the sun was shining. He had to change his specialty when he got here, as there wasn't much number running on the peninsula.

"Pea Soup, I think I need more stuff," Vi said. "Is there any way I could get several ounces at a time?"

"Jesus, I've got other customers, ya know. Why don't ya go up to the Wolf at Yankee Point for what ya need?"

"Don't you want my business?" She tried not to sound hurt, but she was. Surprised, too. Didn't businessmen like to expand?

"Naw," he said, "you're taking up too much of my time and eating up my supply. I'm just small potatoes. I don't want to get bigger."

And so it was settled. She needed to see Wolf—Mr. Big.

The next day Vi drove down the coast on Highway One toward Yankee Point. What a day! Not a cloud in the sky and the ocean a sheet of blue.

The adventure was expanding. Already she was referred by Pea Soup to the Wolf. She liked the sound of the name. Just like an old Edward G. Robinson movie. The Wolf must be Mr. Big. The real boss. The tough guy. Now she was going to the top.

She wasn't sure how to approach this cold-hearted crook. Remembering how she had taken the attaché case for her first meeting with Pea Soup, she'd left it at home, feeling more confident now. No more suits. Her red and white striped T-shirt, jeans and tennis shoes were just right for the big event.

Take a page from Bogie, she told herself. Be cool. Don't gush. Stare him down, and make him speak first. Don't look at his eyes. Sit down slowly. Fold your arms across your chest, feet flat on the floor. The Wolf had to respect her. Know she was cool enough to handle a bigger stash. Give her a couple of lids a week with confidence. Maybe she should flash the cash early on. Rita gave her five thousand dollars just in case they could make a big buy. Maybe the sight of the money would tame the Wolf.

She was a little scared, but mainly just excited as she pulled off Highway One and headed down the long driveway toward the ocean.

What a house! She loved the aging Spanish mansion hanging on the cliff's edge, red bougainvillea spilling over the eaves and windows. It was on a sheltered cove.

She imagined sea otters and seals crawling up on the rocks below to sun themselves and sleep.

Her hand felt clammy as she reached for the doorbell by the big glass wall. Mr.
Big was nowhere in sight.

She rang. No one came. She rang again.

She opened the door half-way and called out, "Mr. Wolf?" Was his name Mr.
Wolf or just Wolf, or maybe Wolf was his first name. She should have asked Pea
Soup for more information.

Down at the end of the tiled hallway she saw a tall white-haired woman. Beautiful! Wearing an elegant azure blue caftan that billowed out at the sides as she
walked, like Beatrice in a Renaissance painting. Tiny gold astrological symbols
were embroidered on the filmy fabric.

At that moment Vi thought she felt her whole life move in some strange unpredictable direction. This woman, this exotic beautiful older woman stood before
her like Fate, embodying everything Vi wanted to become.

It was like looking in the mirror and suddenly knowing your future. Now she
knew her life was going to change; at seventy she was in school. She was being
initiated. A whole new person was being born. She could feel it—gratitude to God—
or someone—consumed her. Someday, she told herself, someday Violet Farnsworth will become this vision.

She was too moved to speak.

The woman approached.

"Won't you come in?" The deep voice was just as she knew it would sound.

"I'm Violet Farnsworth. I'm looking for Mr. Wolf." She was suddenly shy.

"I'm Running Wolf." The woman smiled. "Come in. I was expecting you. I've
chilled some wine."

Vi was speechless. *This was Mr. Big?*

"What's your connection with Pea Soup?" the mystic woman asked.

"He was our supplier, but Rita has involved the whole cancer unit and hospice
now."

"I do have some access."

"What would the cost be?"

"Well, for now let's not discuss that. Tell me something about yourself, Violet."
She was steering Vi into a high-ceilinged living room. Everything was cream-
colored and the ocean view dominated the room. She was settling Vi into an
enormous overstuffed couch and pouring chardonnay into a crystal glass. "Give
me your whole life from the beginning."

✷ ✷ ✷

Three glasses of wine later, the sorceress saluted her with her wine glass. "Good for you, Vi. It's never too late to reinvent yourself."

"I hope you're right. I want to be just like you." Vi knew she sounded like some mooney star-struck teenager, but she couldn't keep the admiration out of her voice.

"Thanks." Running Wolf smiled. "I invented the whole thing, you know. I was born Rebecca Bernstein from Chicago, your usual bright Jewish girl. Met Bernie in college, studying to be a lawyer. Mother liked him. Three children later I knew I was sick of it."

"Just like me," Vi said.

Running Wolf walked over to refill her glass. "Funny, I never told my mother. There wasn't really anything to bitch about. Bernie never drank, didn't sock me, wasn't even cruel or stingy. Just dull. What could my parents do about that? I tried to pretend nothing was wrong. I tried to do what was expected of a nice, bright Jewish girl according to Bagel Belt standards. Succeeded by marrying the nice Jewish boy with good salary, raising orthodox kids. To be chosen—that was what it was all about. An old maid was a disaster. I pretty much did what was expected of me." She paused, looking out at the crashing surf.

"Then one day I saw the first wrinkle in the mirror and knew what was coming. I should now act my age. Go sit in a corner somewhere like Whistler's mother, some grandchild's bubby, knitting. Fold my hands, spew wisdom, wait patiently for death. I panicked. Felt myself vanishing. I knew I couldn't act my age. How do you act sixty? I knew I had to run for my life. You see, I'm not finished yet."

"Oh, I know just what you mean." Vi was nodding.

"I left Bernie a note. I know that was a coward's way. I came to California and found my world navel was Big Sur and my real name was Running Wolf. I do psychic counseling, aura adjustments, and I'm into harmonic convergence." Looking at Vi's confused expression, she continued. "Vi, the best way to predict the future is to invent it. I've never been sorry."

Vi was transported by the courage, the boldness of it all.

Running Wolf disappeared down the hall. Returned moments later with a grocery sack.

"I love your caftan. It's who I want to become someday," Vi said as Running Wolf flowed across the room toward her.

Running Wolf laughed. "Oh, this isn't exactly who I am either, Vi. Rebecca Bernstein isn't altogether gone from this body. She still comes back from time to time and stirs up a kettle of matzo ball soup and a little trouble. I really wear the caftans because people like a psychic consultant and astrological guide to look different from the woman on the street. I used to be a marketing director in Chicago.

People like to see what they expect. Can't disappoint the customers, can we? When I meet with the wealthy pot growers from the old Big Sur families you could just as well see me in a St. John's knit. There's plenty of me in here for everyone."

Yeah, Vi thought. You could get good costumes for all your parts. She made a mental note to go shopping, and not at Shop and Pray this time, either. The mall, or maybe Carmel. Couldn't wait.

"Got to run, Wolfie." She decided to shorten the name as a sign of affection. As Running Wolf handed her the Safeway bag filled with stuff, she asked, "What do I owe you?"

"When you come back next week, we'll go into financial arrangements. The price list is in the bag. Clarify what you want and how often. I'll donate this bag, one half kilo, to make sure the sick ones who have no money get some, too."

"How kind." Vi grabbed Wolfie's hand. Her face must have showed her surprise because Running Wolf stuck her tongue out.

"Even dealers have hearts, you know."

Vi was floating along the mountain road from Yankee Point, singing. She was going to enjoy this. Running Wolf was Vi's new model. Just what she wanted to be when she grew up. They would become fast friends. Vi would get a blue caftan, too. Maybe she would change her name to Tandelejo after all. They would have bold adventures together. Vi might take up harmonic convergence with her. She liked the idea of telling her friends, "I'm into harmonica convergence." I bet Adrian would know what it was. Kathy would be shocked. Rita would clap her hands together in delight and pronounce it just right. Sophie would withhold judgment.

What the hell is harmonic conversion? Vi wondered. *Who cares. I'm not going to miss anything, especially not now. At seventy, I've already missed too much. I want to be included. Never again left on a shelf. This may be my last big production—only a starring role will do. Full speed ahead!*

An old song came on the car radio. She sang along as loud as she could as her foot bore down on the accelerator.

Oh, it's only a paper moon
Hanging over a cardboard sea
But it wouldn't be make believe
If you believed in me!

Naturally, Kathy had to call a meeting to discuss plans for distribution of the medical supplies. Even if she didn't share Vi's wild enthusiasm, she knew things had to be organized and handled efficiently. Vi scoffed and said "hell's bells, we pick it up and take it to those who need it. What's the big deal?" but she went along with discussing Kathy's Plan A and Plan B proposals.

Adrian arrived with Sophie in tow. "Jack hates the idea, but I'm an adult. I believe we should help Rita." She paused, looked hesitant. Kathy could hear the tremor in her voice, but eagerness, too. "I don't want anybody to know about it, especially Jack. I hope I can do things that will keep me in the background!"

Vi gave her a hug. "Don't worry, you can work behind the scenes. You're great at Shop and Pray, and a wonderful cook. You'll be in charge of recipes and covert activities."

Adrian smiled. "Who would've thunk it back in college?"

"Okay," Kathy said, scratching her head with her pencil, notebook poised. "Let's figure out what day Vi gets the goods. How frequent do the pickups need to be?"

"Listen to her! Talk about 'who would've thunk it'!" Vi laughed. "I want all of you around for moral support, at least the first time. We'll need to do it weekly. What day would be best?"

"Tuesday's out," said Sophie. "I have my book group that day."

"Wednesday won't work," said Kathy. "That's the day I get together with the poker group. They would get suspicious if I quit after I started it."

"Thursdays we help at Shop and Pray. Can't very well combine those two things," Vi said.

"Well, Fridays are impossible. That's the day I work on the books down at the office, and I don't dare miss a day. I'm nervous about what Peter's up to." Adrian looked worried. She was very involved in the bookkeeping for the Pellagrino family's fishing fleet business.

"Saturday is the day Rose comes by to check up on me. All I'd need would be to have her catch me hauling in my bag of pot and I'd be in The Grove in a minute!" Vi exclaimed.

Sundays wouldn't work. Sophie had church, Adrian spent Sunday with her mother, Kathy took her meditation walks, and even Vi didn't think it would be right.

"So what about Monday?" Kathy looked at each one. Amazement. They checked their calendars and nodded. "Okay, for this week anyway."

And so the initiation of the Monday Club.

(11)

———

HOROSCOPE: This is not the moment to expect too much of other people, especially when they have their own agendas. Shoulder your own responsibility to understand old friends. New acquaintance casts shadows.

"I STILL DON'T UNDERSTAND, RITA." KATHY TRIED TO KEEP THE FEAR OUT of her voice. "The doctors said the chemo and radiation might work if you stayed and behaved yourself."

Rita inhaled on her cigarette, closed her eyes and then blew a huge cloud of smoke out the open window as they drove into Pebble Beach. "You need a new car . . . "

"You're evading the issue," Kathy interrupted. She was surprised when Rita had called her that morning and asked—no, demanded—that she pick her up at the hospital and take her home. Kathy answered the summons immediately. She had walked in on a discussion Rita was having with the three doctors who were arguing adamantly against her leaving.

Rita snuffed out the cigarette, immediately lit another. "God, I'd rather have a joint! You did get some more stash, didn't you?"

Kathy could feel her face flush. She was still having difficulty realizing she was involved in the lawless demand and supply of marijuana. "Yes," she said, "I hid it in the trunk under the spare tire. Vi found a real ally in this strange woman from Yankee Point. And can you imagine? Even sweet Sophie is getting in on the act with some recipes Vi got from Running Wolf."

"Recipes? You've got to be kidding; you just roll it up and smoke it," Rita chuckled. "Seriously, you gals have been great." She patted Kathy's arm and took a deep draw on the cigarette. "The visits from you and Vi were fun, listening to Glen Miller and Stan Kenton tapes, reminiscing about the 1940s and 50s, and how naive we were then. Remember the time you dressed up in a full skirt with crinoline underneath?"

Kathy smiled. "I really worked to get that outfit together, especially the saddle shoes."

"Vi was a corker in her pedal pushers and penny loafers," Rita said.

Kathy rolled her car window down. The cigarette smoke was bothering her. "I'm glad you got acquainted with Adrian and Sophie, too. At least they cooled down the hypothetical terrorist plots you and Vi were making up to disrupt the dull hospital routine."

"You all have jazzed up my hospital life. Sophie is sweet but lively. What's with Adrian? She's the mysterious one. You're all different, yet strangely compatible." Rita paused. "I'm lucky to have such good friends."

"We come as a package," Kathy said. Suddenly a thought struck her. "I do hope our new medicine isn't what convinced you to stop treatment."

"Hardly!" Rita laughed. "No, I weighed all the info and decided I was educated enough to have a choice—and screwed up enough to make one. Anywhere I hang my hair is home. I don't want more chemo or radiation, and I want to smoke the pot instead of disguising it. Having the Monday Club at home is much more my bag. Besides, I'd rather spend the time I have at my own little Shangri-la with my boy-toy Guido on beck and call."

"I'm afraid to ask, but what's he like?" Kathy had visions of Rita lying on a chaise lounge with her Adonis dropping peeled grapes in her mouth between sips of gin and puffs of smoke.

"You'll be meeting him in a few minutes. He's at the house. That's why I asked you to pick me up. I didn't give him much notice and he had to get things straightened up."

"He's living there?" Kathy couldn't keep the shock out of her voice.

"Don't be such a prude. Of course he is. Look—there he is now." Rita waved wildly at a tall dark figure as Kathy pulled into the circular driveway.

A face appeared at the passenger door—a little like Tony Curtis, but with a sexy outlaw look. A hand led Rita out of the car into a passionate embrace.

Rita came up for air, laughing. "Guido honey, this is my best friend in the whole world, Katherine Doolittle, but call her Kathy or . . ."

"Or Katie old girl?" Guido finished. "Yeah, the little woman here talks a lot about you." He eyed her up and down as if she were a side of beef on a hook. With a smirk he said, "Not bad, as the stories would lead ya to believe."

Guido puffed out his chest, thrust his hips forward, and clasped Rita's thinning body to his in undulating gestures that didn't leave much to the imagination. Kathy averted her eyes. She began to perspire (Vi often told her she was too repressed to sweat). He was watching her as she carried Rita's hospital bag up the walk to the grandiose mahogany door. "Macho cum laude," Kathy whispered under her breath.

Guido put his hands on Rita's rump and said with a short laugh. "Run play with your frigid friend while I finish some business in town. We'll play our games later." Kathy saw Rita wince as Guido gave her a harder than necessary pat on her rear. Kathy's and Guido's eyes met briefly. She was relieved to see him leave.

"Guess I'll go now and let you rest," Kathy said after getting Rita settled in her bedroom. She found it hard to make conversation; she felt unsettled about Guido. After all, it wasn't any of her business. She didn't dare say he was no good, but it was her gut reaction.

"Don't go yet. You don't like Guido, do you?" Rita was, as usual, perceptive and blunt. She laughed. "It's okay, Kathy. You can be honest. We never did have the same taste in men."

Kathy hesitated, looking at all the gold-framed mirrors in the bedroom and realizing that "men" wasn't their only difference in taste. "Well, he appears anatomically correct." Rita's pencilled eyebrows arched up. "I don't know what to say, Rita. He makes me nervous."

"Why? Are you comparing him to Phil or Danny or Paul? You disapproved of everybody before I married Ray."

"I don't hold you accountable for past mistakes, Rita. I'm afraid for you. He's using you. I don't trust him. Those eyes." She shuddered. "Can I get you some coffee?"

"No. A martini sounds better. You can bring it after you get the package of medicine out of the trunk," Rita barked.

Chores accomplished, Kathy again tried to leave, but Rita's quieter tone of voice pulled her back. "Please. I need you to understand, Katherine." The use of her formal name indicated Rita was serious. Kathy sighed deeply, determined not to speak her mind any more than she already had. The silence was deafening. Rita guzzled her martini and her trembling hand illustrated the tension in the room.

"I need Guido. I need to feel someone's hand in mine. I need someone to say I'm a joy instead of a pain before I die—that I'm beautiful and important." Rita looked down at her wrinkled hands and then up through her mascaraed eyes at Kathy. "Can you understand that?"

"I think I do. But do you ever question his sincerity?"

"I'm not stupid, Kathy." Rita glared. Silence.

"Doesn't it bother you that he's using you? After your money?"

"He's not exactly poor. He just paid cash for some land in Carmel Valley."

"Where does he get that kind of money if he doesn't have a job?" Kathy asked.

"None of my business—or yours. It just proves he's not after my money. Besides, who else would sleep with a dying woman?" Kathy couldn't look at her, afraid it was too true. "Life's a witch and then you fly," Rita added softly.

The phone rang. Kathy was glad for the interruption. "Hello.... Hello...? Shit! No one there." Rita slammed down the receiver, reached for her drink and a cigarette.

Probably some bimbo for Guido, Kathy thought to herself.

"Oh, I almost forgot!" Rita seemed to perk up as she stood and went into the den, dragging Kathy by the hand. "I have a surprise for you. I had Guido pick them up last week."

She picked up a large bag and beamed as she handed it to Kathy before getting back in bed. "They're cellular phones. All programmed and set to go. For you and the Hash Hens so you can keep in touch with each other better—and with me too."

Kathy stammered, "But I, . . . but we . . .Gee, you shouldn't have . . . Why?"

"You're babbling, Katie old girl. Don't fret about it. Consider it a small token of gratitude for making things better for me and my buddies. It's just a start. I've got my heart set on getting that old clunker you drive replaced."

Kathy knew Rita well enough to soft-pedal the protesting.

Guido returned, strutting in on their conversation. "Hey, there KD, you still here? Did you bring us some Acapulco Gold?" Kathy pulled away from the arm encircling her waist, his hand suspiciously high enough to touch her breast. She transmitted her disgust with her eyes, but a tingle she hadn't felt for a long time intruded her body. "It's certainly not for you," she said.

"Maybe you'd like to share some?" He again put his arm around her, this time his hand slowly descending to her butt, where it rested briefly. Kathy heard herself whisper "No" as Guido turned and plopped on the bed next to Rita. "After all," Guido continued, "Rita shares everything she has, don't you Sweetie? But maybe we should get her some heroin, eh? Would that be better? I have connections, too, you know."

Kathy saw Rita gritting her teeth. She knew the look well from back in high school. "I sometimes close my teeth so what I'm thinking doesn't come out through my mouth," she'd told her. Kathy couldn't stand to see Rita dying, needing Guido, gritting her teeth. Even though she felt afraid to leave Rita alone with Guido, she took her leave without saying anything. What could she say?

Driving back to Pacific Grove, Kathy didn't even look at the blue water or hear the sound of the surf. Only the sound of Rita's and Guido's voices as she was leaving echoed in Kathy's ears. The words weren't clear . . . "That prissy broad . . . " from Guido; Rita's voice shouting accusations about what he'd been doing when she was in the hospital. Kathy wondered too. Her mind bounced between thoughts of mortality, morality and macho men; to friendship and Vi's ideas of adventure.

On an impulse, tired of thinking, she pulled into the parking lot of Pebble Beach Lodge. She took a phone out of the bag, played around with some buttons, gave up and read the directions, then dialed a number. By the time a voice answered, Kathy was out of her car, leaning on the fender of the Mercedes next to it.

"Hello. Mizzz Viiiooolet Faawrnswaarth?" she started in a dignified English accent before her voice betrayed her by sounding like a kid as she continued, "Vi! You'll never guess where I'm calling from!"

The beat of the Monday Club went on even stronger after Rita got home from the hospital. Instead of asking her friends to deliver to her hand-picked customers, Rita opened her Pebble Beach home as a gathering place for picking up the medicine. But then it began turning into a party. The patients would kick back and smoke joints in her living room. People started bringing in food and drink, with plenty of alternatives for those who didn't want to smoke their pot.

The living room got too small for the music, dancing and mingling so they moved up to the ballroom on the third floor. There was an elevator for those too weak to negotiate the circular staircase. Designated drivers were required, although their sobriety was questionable due to the level of second-hand fumes in the room. Word got around; maybe not all of them were sick. It didn't seem to matter. Rita told Kathy all about it, and they argued frequently. Kathy preferred not to hear most of it.

Rita said that the friendships were genuine. There was enormous assistance and love in the dying, and lasting group support for those who grieved afterwards. People who'd had trouble sleeping slept more soundly with their pain diminished. Those who lost weight during chemo found themselves enjoying food again. There were hands to hold against the coming of the night.

(12)

HOROSCOPE: What you want to do and what you think you should be doing are different sides of the same coin. The trick is to flip it so that each is face up. Rumors stir the pot. Don't let logic interfere with your instincts.

THE FOLLOWING WEEK, AS VI GOT HOME FROM AN AFTERNOON BINGO SESSION, she saw Hannah Callahan waving at her. She knew Hannah was excited when she saw Vi drive up next door because she forgot to pretend that she was watering. She just bolted over the hedge with a spryness Vi wouldn't have believed possible.

"Violet, oh Violet, you'll never believe what happened today." Her voice sounded different.

Vi got out of the car and had a chance to look at her. Hannah even looked different. Her face was animated. Hannah looked younger, wearing her enthusiasm well. Her beady old eyes had a softness. Her quick, bird-like gestures were a change from the slow, whiney deliberateness that had so often greeted Vi in the driveway. For a brief second, Vi actually could imagine liking this square little German woman. Then she remembered that Hannah was Rose's spy.

She had to admit she was intrigued, so intrigued she let the witch in the house. Hannah was probably too excited to evaluate the house cleaning anyway, and Vi could keep the shades drawn so the dust wasn't terribly visible.

"Come on over, Hannah. I'll make you a cuppa tea."

Vi heard the words coming out of her mouth and couldn't believe them herself.

Tea and biscuits with Attila the Hun? Oh well, something was very different about her today.

Hannah clapped her hands together like a child. "How nice of you to ask me, Violet."

As soon as Vi opened the front door, regret set in. She had forgotten that the Sunday paper was still spread all over the couch where she had demolished it yesterday, and Late Bloomers had pulled some more of the stuffing out of her old cat pillow after Vi left. Little balls of Kapok were all over the living room rug.

"Don't mind the mess, Hannah," Vi tried to dismiss it. "I've been on a really tight schedule today. I'll just pop into the kitchen and put on the kettle."

But this news had to be big. Hannah didn't even look around the living room, just followed Vi right into the kitchen, eyes glittering with her story and started to spill it out.

"You know, I went to Pebble Beach today for the Suppers for Seniors golf benefit at Poppy Hills . . ."

"Oh, yeah. I think Rosie mentioned it." Vi had the kettle filled and was rummaging through the drawer for the tea strainer. Hannah grabbed her arm. Vi froze at the unexpectedness of a touch from the cold one. She looked up to see the grim face transfixed, almost attractive.

"I was making a crucial putt when Margaret Ackerman came running across the green with one shoe missing, her hair falling down in her eyes. 'There's a mad goat chasing me,' she said. The first thing I thought was, poor Margaret's lost her mind!"

Vi gave up the search for the strainer and sat down at the kitchen table. Some of Hannah's excitement was beginning to rub off on her. She leaned forward, speaking slowly.

"You think Maggie Ackerman's lost her mind?" She pronounced each word slowly. This was a delicious thought. The staid, sanctimonious mayor of P.G., stark, staring mad? What could happen next?

"No, no; that's what I thought!" Vi could see Hannah was enjoying the attention she was giving her. *She's going to string it out now that she knows she's got me hooked.*

The kettle was sputtering and screaming its brains out, but Vi ignored it. *Just tell it, Hannah.* She felt like reaching over and grabbing Hannah by the throat and yelling, spit it out! but she knew she had to remain polite.

"Well, Violet, you remember reading in *The Beacon* last week the Pebble Beach Company was trying a new system of putting goats out in the wooded section of Poppy Hills to eat the poison oak? It was a way to avoid using pesticides."

"No." Vi couldn't see where all this was going.

"It was one of those goats that attacked Margaret. Another tried to eat Jennifer's golf ball. Some of them were just standing there like statues. They were out on the green, falling down and running around, and then this one just took out after poor Margaret. She had on a red golf shirt. I bet that's what set him off."

"You're thinking of bulls, Hannah. Bulls don't like red."

"Well, you could be right. Anyway it was some commotion. Rose called security. A big crowd gathered. The police came. But you'll never guess what caused this commotion."

Here we go again, Vi thought. She's going to withhold the story to get more attention. Vi turned to the screaming kettle and finally locating the strainer, poured the water into the little brown teapot. She wanted to convey complete indifference to the story. That ought to drive the old biddy into spitting it out. She was arranging some lemon bars on a paper doily when Hannah jumped up from the table and followed her to the stove again.

"The goats were all strange because they ate a patch of marijuana! The police found it. Growing in a thicket right down close to the green. The goats ate the marijuana instead of the poison oak and wandered out onto the golf course. Isn't that something? They're very unfussy eaters, you know. The police rounded up the goats and questioned all of us. The photographer from *The Herald* took my picture. He said Margaret and I might be on the front page." Hannah smiled. Maybe, Vi thought, for the first time in her life.

"There's going to be a big story about a possible drug ring. Someone growing marijuana on the Poppy Hills golf course and selling it in Pebble Beach. Angela Willis said that some wealthy woman who lives there has drug addicts and dealers living in her house. The reporter told me he can't wait to get to the bottom of this. He's always wanted to do investigative reporting. Woodward and Bernstein are his heroes, but he was afraid nothing really big would ever break on the Monterey Peninsula."

Vi couldn't answer. Could feel the back of her throat tighten. Knew she should respond. Try to breathe normally, she told herself. Don't let Hannah suspect; she's Rosie's spy. Don't look at her. She might see it in your eyes. Get up and go to the sink. She felt a flutter around her heart as she fought to rise to her feet. *Slow. Calm*, she thought to herself. *Slow. Calm.* Hannah should see no reaction at all. Supporting her weight at the counter, Vi put the lemon bars in a plastic bag and sealed the top.

"I'm a little tired, Hannah. Think I should lie down. Here, take the lemon bars with you for after supper." A long silence. Then she could hear the chair being pushed back from the table.

"Well of course." A pause. Hannah was standing behind her now. She could feel her suffocating closeness. "Sorry to wear you out, Violet."

Another pause, but Vi was afraid to turn around and meet those eyes, afraid they would see too much. She held the bag of lemon bars out to the side, but kept her back to Hannah. She felt the bag lifted from her hand.

"All right. I'll see you later then." She heard the words, but no steps on the floor. Why didn't she leave so she could go tell Kathy? She was just standing there. Vi could feel her eyes staring at her back.

"See you later." Vi heard her own voice from a faraway distance and at last the sound of footsteps retreating to the door. She heard the latch opening, the door being closed. It was over.

(13)

HOROSCOPE: It appears that you are being pushed to the limit by someone close, and in typical fashion you've suppressed your anger. A show of temperament could pave the path to better understanding. Sometimes you have nothing to lose.

DRIVING OVER TO SEE RITA, KATHY REVIEWED THE WHOLE SITUATION. IT ALL began when Rita passed the word around the hospital and hospice. The volunteers turned a blind eye and deaf ear when they saw how much better patients were doing. Those receiving home care got in on the network, and the Maryjane tea, Sophie's bongo brownies, the magic formula in brown bottles (since smoking wasn't allowed in the hospital) were so popular that Vi had to increase the orders. It was getting out of hand. Luckily, that was when Rita left the hospital; the Monday Club moved to Pebble Beach.

Kathy, Vi, Adrian and Sophie were at the first "meeting" of the Monday Club at Rita's, but felt out of place and decided this was Rita's gig. "I'm still alive, Kate," Rita had told her. "And until I'm dead I'm going to stay alive—keep on living. That means having Guido. Having people, parties and fun. I need that. It's what we all need. We need that as much as the marijuana—to forget what's hanging over us."

Kathy was impressed at that first party in the ballroom. She enjoyed the interesting people who talked about real issues. Some laughed. Some cried. They danced, even sang. Kathy talked with Sharon, a petite lady in her mid-forties, dressed in a pink and blue plaid jogging outfit with matching turban. She was undergoing radiation treatment for her cancer, as well as dealing with a drug addict son. With a smile, she assured Kathy that things were better. Her son had successfully undergone a drug treatment program, and the marijuana helped the pain from her radiation-induced osteoporosis. She hadn't told her son about the Monday Club. "I'd rather be a hypocrite than in pain."

"How can you cope with all this? Isn't it hard to face reality?" Kathy asked, reaching for one of Sophie's brownies without remembering the secret ingredient.

"Whenever anyone says 'face it,' something really unpleasant comes after it. I like the T-shirt your friend Vi is wearing." Kathy glanced over at Vi and Rita line dancing, with Vi's "Don't let reality ruin your life" shirt swinging in rhythm.

"I don't need reality," Sharon continued, looking down for a moment. "I need hope. I ignore statistics. The odds tell all of us we're going to die. But doesn't everyone, some day? I cope with hope, even if it may be unreasonable hope."

Not knowing what to say, Kathy put her arms around her and gave her a light hug.

But now Rita had gone too far. Was she really growing pot at Poppy Hills? Kathy slammed the car door, marched up the steps of Rita's front porch, and with face flushed, fire in her eyes, shoved the door open screaming, "Rita! What the hell is going on? Where are you, Rita?"

Rita peered over the stairway railing. "I'm up here. Been straightening up the ballroom after the Monday Club meeting. Got a little raucous yesterday. Come on up—I could use some help. Guido took off somewhere."

"Thank God for small favors," Kathy muttered under her breath as she mounted the stairs. It seemed quicker to run up the circular staircase than wait for the elevator. This stark, formal house with its blinding white, marble and crystal might be high Pebble Beach fashion. She found it cold.

"Now what are you ranting about? I've never known you to burst in without ringing the bell." Rita led Kathy by the arm to the veranda overlooking the rose garden and poured her a glass of iced tea from the white wrought iron serving table. Kathy knew Rita was ignoring her anger. "Did you know Angela Willis is spreading rumors after what happened at Poppy Hills?"

"You mean the stoned goats?" Rita laughed.

"The guy at the Pebble Beach gate even said something weird . . . " Kathy was flinging her arms around as she sputtered, "Josie down at the drug store heard rumors . . . I've noticed a police car parked across the street from my house sometimes. I think they have Vi and me under surveillance. The Monday Club has turned into wild pot parties! It wasn't supposed to be recreational." Rita tried to interrupt but Kathy was on a roll. "Even the barbers are gossiping to all their customers about Pebble Beach pot parties."

Rita chuckled.

"Not funny! Medical purposes, remember? It's supposed to be just for the terminally ill, and now it's a social club for druggies. Damn it, Rita! I mean, really! What's going on?"

Going over to the built-in bar behind the glass mirror panels, Rita reached for two wine glasses. She filled hers with Jack Daniels, and Kathy's with an unpronounceable French wine, exchanging it for the empty ice tea glass. "Sit. Clean-up will wait for Guido. Breathe. Drink. Life is too short for tirades."

Kathy took a deep breath, a sip of the exquisite wine, and sat down on the blue velvet settee. Another deep breath. "Rita, I'm frightened. Stories going around town make us sound like dope peddlers— and the parties are for anyone who wants to get high and not just sick people and how do we justify that and . . ." She talked in unpunctuated phrases falling over each other until Rita interrupted.

"Wait! First, how do you define 'sick'?" She stood, turned her back hiding her face from Kathy. "You don't know what it's like!" Silence. "No, you don't. Fine line between physical and psychological pain. Marijuana helps one thing that's not often diagnosed. Depression. We need companionship. We need pot."

"But it's illegal!"

Rita turned around and shouted, "So what? When you're dying, who cares?" Setting her glass down and lighting a cigarette, she continued. "Look, Kathy. I know you're concerned, but think about this hypocritical society. Prescription drugs like Prozac and morphine have worse side effects."

"But the morality of it. Kids. Getting doped up doesn't teach them to face life's problems."

"What are you talking about? There are no kids in the Monday Club!"

"Marijuana is dangerous; it destroys your initiative and drive. It screws up your mind."

"So why do you drink?" Kathy didn't answer. "If you're against one addiction, why not all? Pot, alcohol, tobacco, Prozac, Excedrin? You know damn well we're in a drug culture. The legality argument here is the big guys versus little guys. Tobacco and alcohol companies don't want competition. Big pharmaceutical supply companies like Sandoz don't want competition."

Kathy watched as Rita paced back and forth in a cloud of exhaled smoke. "But . . . "

"Bristol Myers can't patent marijuana; any shmuck can grow it," Rita continued. "There's no government revenue coming in. No profits on Wall Street. No TV advertising."

Kathy jumped up as she saw Rita falter and grasp the back of the white damask Queen Anne chair. "Are you okay?"

"I'm fine. I just need to lie down and rest. Help me into my room—I'm not finished yet." Kathy held Rita's elbow as she guided her down the hall, noticing how thin and brittle her arm was. She was shrivelling. *Why do I forget she's dying?* she thought.

Rita continued. "The Feds think it's un-American to grow your own marijuana with no middle man. After all, the drug of choice has to have a brand name like Jim Beam or Tylenol." Her voice was softer now, still raspy, but tired.

I'm getting her upset, Kathy thought. "I should go," she said, as Rita removed her wig and lay her fuzzy head on the mountain of satin bed pillows.

"No, wait. I didn't mean to lecture. Sit with me for awhile. I want you to understand."

"I try, I really do. But I worry."

Rita laughed, her husky sarcastic laugh. "There's a lot more you could worry about. Why all this emphasis on marijuana when pollution is killing more people than drugs? There are people in the Monday Club who have horror stories to tell about the hushed-up polluters and skeletons in the closets of Ft. Ord and Monterey Bay."

"I try not to think about it," Kathy said softly. She couldn't admit the real reason she was worried was fear. Afraid of getting caught.

"Your drug of choice, Kate old girl. Detachment. You're addicted to detachment. From life. From emotion. From men. Even from your kids for God's sake!"

Kathy stiffened. Rita could be cruel. "I suppose you're right. But it's how I cope."

"So allow me and my friends to cope in our way. It's more than smoking pot. It's our form of denial, our detachment from the thought of dying. We need each other for support. Some can't afford it. I can—for me and for them. I need purpose, since I don't have much to look back on—or forward to. Let me do what I do best. Give parties and have fun."

Kathy stayed until Rita fell asleep. She felt drained. Why did she feel empty? So alone?

When she got home, Kathy noticed something under the door. It was words from a newspaper cut and pasted on plain white paper. "GET RID OF MONDAY CLUB. YOU ARE BEING WATCHED." She whirled around but could see no one. Where was that spying police car when she needed it?

She slammed and locked the door and set the burglar alarm. After making sure the automatic sensor light was turned on, she grabbed the phone to call the police. Asked for Officer Chris Connery, then hung up. She felt so close to Chris, almost as if he were her own son. She couldn't let him know about the Monday Club. What could she tell him?

⟨14⟩

HOROSCOPE: Transform dull routine. You're an old dog being exposed to new tricks. Learn, then play your own tune and let others dance to it.

VI PACKED A TUNA SANDWICH, SOME CARROT STICKS AND THREE OREO COOKIES in a sack, carefully closed the front door and drove down her street to the library. Today was Tuesday. Tuesdays she always had lunch with Nikki at the Pacific Grove Public Library.

"Hi, Vi," Bertie waved and smiled. "Nikki said she'll be a few minutes late. Go on in the back."

Vi opened the door to Nikki's office, made the coffee, stared in the fridge, finally decided on a Hansen's orange soda, and settled into the couch.

"Sorry to be late, Vi." Nikki came in like a summer wind. Vi had the same guilty thought again. Nikki seemed like the daughter she should have had instead of Rose. Or better yet, Nikki was everything Vi should have been at thirty four if she hadn't stupidly married Fred.

"What's new with the Monterey Mafia? Isn't that what Rita calls you?"

"Don't tease an old lady, Nikki. Rita's going to get us all in trouble. I'm worried."

"What's Pebble Beach's wild one gotten herself into now?" Nikki was heating a can of Campbell's cream of chicken soup on the hot plate. Vi put place settings on the end of the desk and pulled up an extra chair.

Vi felt such a rush of love and pride. She was proud Nikki called her a friend. She was ashamed when she remembered that she hadn't always acted like a friend to Nikki.

The first time Vi had seen her was a morning last February when she was shopping at the Granary downtown. She looked like one of those new movie starlets: chic haircut, flawless face, perfect breasts and rear end. She could have been a Penthouse advertisement for "Clueless." She had on tight white shorts, a gold-buttoned naval jacket and a white captain's hat with gold braid. Vi thought any minute she might salute or start tap dancing like someone out of an old Busby Berkeley musical.

"Who's the new one?" She motioned toward the door after the stranger left. The clerk laughed out loud. You'll never believe it, Vi. That one's the new librarian!"

"My friend Kathy used to be a librarian, but I bet she never looked like that!" They exchanged knowing looks. "This one's probably an airhead," Vi said.

Now she shifted her weight uncomfortably in the metal folding chair. She had never confessed all this to Nikki. She should come clean and apologize. She was too quick with a judgment. She was wrong so often you'd think she would learn to wait with her early conclusions.

In her own defense, (Vi was not about to beat up on herself indefinitely—that was Kathy's department), Nikki was easy to misread. Her soft vulnerability and sultry laugh probably led certain men to think they were more charming than they were; that she might be an easy lay or at least a good flirt. But the wrapping was not the package and any man who got close enough would discover too late that Nikki was not exactly as she appeared at first rapture. Her great good looks and flair for colorful clothes gave the jealous biddies of Pacific Grove endless material for gossip. She had confessed to Vi she was sometimes lonely in Butterfly Town.

"Want a brownie?" Nikki interrupted. "I made them last night with big chunks of white chocolate." That was another great thing about Nikki. She ate like a horse.

"Of course." Vi folded up her baggy and put it in her brown lunch bag, then folded the bag and put it in her purse. "I love how you eat, Nikki. If you go to a restaurant with my daughter, Rose, she spends ten minutes pouring over the menu and another ten grilling the waiter about fat content, canola oil, and the contents of the salad dressing."

"I know, that's most of the women in this town." Nikki put the paper plate with the brownie in front of Vi and sat down. "You'd think chocolate was a variety of poison or that sugar was another name for Satan. Want more coffee?"

"No, I'm through." Vi sighed and pushed the paper plate away.

"Good! I have a big afternoon planned. You're into learning new things and having new adventures, Vi. I have a great one. I'm introducing you to the Internet."

"I don't think so." Vi tried to sound firm. "I'm not good with machines and I think it's too late to teach this old dog new tricks. Besides, I hear you have to be profound and smart and . . ." She could hear her own voice trailing off indecisively and knew she would lose this argument.

"Don't be silly. You got used to your cellular phone, didn't you? Besides, your new life is full of challenges. Quit your whining and come on."

No one could resist Nikki. Vi followed obediently behind.

"I've already picked out your e-mail names. You'll be Top Chick, Kathy could be Hep Kate and Sophie, Henny Penny. Adrian's got her own."

Later that afternoon on the way home, Vi used her cellular phone to call Kathy. "Come to the library with me tomorrow. You won't believe it."

"What now, Vi? We certainly don't need another project."

"It's not a project."

"Your finger is in one too many pies for your own sanity, Jack Horner."

"That's a good one, Kathy, but I can't imagine too much pie in my life. Anyway, this isn't work. It's just a great lot of fun. More adventures. I've logged on the Internet. Wait until you see. I know you're going to love it."

"You always say that. I'm not up to learning something new, and I'm not comfortable with computers."

"Grumble another minute or two and then agree to meet Nikki and me for lunch tomorrow. I promise, it's a ball!"

"Oh, all right, Vi. Anything to shut you up. Just don't ever talk me into jumping off a cliff."

"Eleven thirty tomorrow." Vi deftly closed her cellular phone and, running the stop sign at the corner, careened into her own driveway magnificently self-satisfied.

HOROSCOPE: An old friend figures prominently; expect to be chosen for assignment of transforming fantasy into reality. A chance to step back and recall what is truly important to you. You will be in a much better position to satisfy those who need your help.

SMILING AT THE GUARD AT THE PEBBLE BEACH GATE, WHO NOW KNEW HER by sight, Kathy glanced in the rear view mirror and ran her fingers through her slightly mussed hair. She still hadn't gotten used to it being short and casual, but it felt good!

As she pulled into the circular driveway, she saw Guido getting ready to leave in Rita's Jaguar. Well, thank God he won't be around, Kathy thought to herself. She accepted Rita's need for men and various diversions to keep her mind off the cancer, but honestly! Guido was half her age—admittedly with a fantastic body. It was difficult for Kathy to keep from voicing her mental nickname of Greedo whenever she spoke to him. She wondered what he was up to when he wasn't with Rita. She didn't trust him.

"Hi, Kathy—your timing is great! Come have a glass of wine while I finish getting dressed," Rita shouted from the bedroom. Good old Rita—some things never change. Brazen and open about everything she does, Kathy mused. She went into the bedroom and was surprised that Rita was climbing back into bed, properly dressed in a stunning red jumpsuit. It wasn't like Rita to loll in bed during the day—at least not without Guido. She pulled up a chair so that they were facing each other, but Kathy had trouble looking her friend in the eye. *She looks like hell in that wig, and her face is drawn even with the globs of make-up,* Kathy thought to herself, but aloud she said, "You're looking great, Rita! Are you getting used to the wig after having it a couple of months?"

"Hell, no—it itches. I only take it off when Guido's out and I have my eyes closed. One thing about being bald is that it cuts the time wasted on hairdressers. Kind of a 'bad news—good news' thing. You're told you're going to lose your hair— but you can have the ease of wearing a wig."

"That's a weird way of looking at it."

"Hey, you have to have a sense of humor to get through the last phase of your life." The smile on Rita's face started to fade. A chill went through Kathy. She filled her wine glass. As Rita lit up another cigarette, Kathy could not restrain her thoughts and blurted out, "I can't believe you are still smoking!"

"Why? Do you think it's going to kill me any sooner?" Rita's glare was somewhat obliterated by the exhaled smoke. She had a way of always looking you straight in the eye. Kathy thought to herself, *I bet if she were a Catholic and went to confession, she'd rip the curtain open and say 'look at me when you talk to me, damn it!'* She could easily picture the scene. Kathy had to escape the penetrating gaze. She had enough trouble talking in words; she feared what her eyes might say.

Feeling uneasy, Kathy squirmed in her chair, got up and walked around, giving unusual attention to the view of the sea through the cypress out the immense bay window, then petting the sleeping cat until he stretched, mewed nastily and moved away from the window-seat to settle under the bed. She wondered if she could say the right things. As Kathy adjusted her long necklace to cover the small spot on her knit shirt, Rita spoke. "It's okay, Kate old girl; I don't mind talking about it. Go ahead—ask those questions I see swirling in your head."

Kathy hesitated and then asked, "What's the prognosis, Rita? There's been all this fun-and-games stuff going on. You've been leading the Monday Club to raucous heights. I thought you were feeling better with the marijuana, but today you seem different."

"Believe me, the pot helped by making eating a joy again after chemo, and it sure beats that slow morphine drip for pain.... But it doesn't cure."

The silence was deafening before Rita continued. "The chemo and radiation didn't help. They finally admitted it. I let it go too long before checking with a doctor and it simply spread too much. No one to blame but myself. It won't be long now."

Kathy took a gulp of wine to stifle the sob she felt in her throat; tried to control the tears by blinking her eyes rapidly. Her mind was racing but she dared not use her voice. *I can't stand to watch Rita like this,* she thought to herself.

"I feel like junk food," Rita said. "Go raid the fridge and see what goodies Guido has provided."

Amazed at Rita's talent for shifting emotional gears so suddenly, Kathy felt obliged to follow her lead, even though she was acting a part. She had to prove her loyalty by not showing she saw through Rita's bravura act. As she got back from the kitchen with a loaded tray, they started to banter like in the old days. Rita was escaping back to high school, retreating into safety, as they talked silly 1940s talk, interspersed with cold pizza, oreo cookies and cherry flavored coke.

"Yuk, this tastes icky!" Kathy said.

"Ah, but remember you can acquire a taste for anything," Rita replied, with the old gleam in her eye.

"You certainly acquired more tastes than I did. A tiger can't change his spots."

"That's leopard, Kathy."

"Whatever."

"Hey—try it, you might like it. Still waters may run deep, but rapids are more fun. Let it all hang out and get rid of that complacency. It's no fun being perfect. Do you understand me?"

"So you want me to take the bull by the tail?"

"Will you ever get one of those things right? No. What I want you to do is take the bull by the balls and run with it! But I'll have to admit I've noticed a change in you. You even look different. There may be hope for you yet! And certainly we've both gotten past where our mothers were at our age. Remember their Stitch and Bitch Club?"

Kathy chuckled. "Sewing Club. Those ladies were too dull to bitch. If we'd followed our mothers' mind set we'd be in rocking chairs watching soap operas to get our kicks in between sewing and cooking. God, how I hate the thought of getting old!"

"It beats the alternative . . . I'd much rather live my soap opera," Rita replied. "My life's been a rough draft of one, you know. Guess I've run out of script."

As soon as the words were out, both women fell out of their frivolous mood. "At least my mother doesn't have to watch me die."

Kathy got up, adjusted the window to let more breeze in, looked at her friend who, in spite of all her bold talk, seemed vulnerable. She fluffed up the pillows and removed the bed tray as Rita stretched out.

"What's it like, Rita?" Kathy surprised herself by asking the question she never dreamed she would dare ask.

"I cuss a lot. I have frustrating dreams about the things I can't do—and never will."

Kathy poured herself a glass of wine, leaned back, and met Rita's eyes.

"Sometimes I panic—I don't want to die. But other times I feel bored with waiting. It feels like my body's asleep but my mind is wide awake. And when the pain hits, it can be intolerable. That's why I'm so grateful to you old passive terrorists for the pot. Like I said, it does help."

Kathy nodded. "I still have real mixed emotions about the whole thing."

"That old legal-beagle thing still there, eh?" Rita said.

"Well, like I told you before, since Vi made the connection wih Running Wolf for getting it in bulk, and then the goat episode and all the rumors, I'm even more afraid. The Monday Club has gotten out of hand."

"As far as you're concerned, it's strictly for medical use. You guys haven't been branching out into the recreational world, have you?" Rita was smiling. "You haven't gone to the Monday Club since the first meeting, and I told you I'd take the rap for any problems." Rita lit another cigarette, exchanged the cherry coke for some Jack Daniels.

Kathy knew Rita was teasing, but she blushed anyway. "It's just with all the publicity about drug use among teenagers. It's possible it could lead them into some decadent life-style, and . . ."

"Oh, come on, Kathy," Rita interrupted, "since the beginning of time I'm sure parents have faced similar challenges of keeping their kids away from some danger or other of the adult world. It's like alcohol, sex, and other good things—it's a matter of being adult or mature enough to handle decisions, to be aware and informed of all the consequences and understand moderation."

"I'll feel better if and when the medical use gets approved," Kathy said.

Rita reached for the paper. "Did you read this article about 50,000 people gathering in Boston Common Park in favor of legalizing marijuana? It was a hoot, considering there were only 5,000 at the anti-drug demonstration across town in the same city!" Rita smiled at Kathy's shocked expression, and then continued.

"Tell you what. In my will where I, Rita Rich, being of sound mind even though deteriorating body, designate Katherine Doolittle—to do much—" she snickered, "to act as executor of my last will and testament. . ."

"Oh, Rita, no. You can't be serious?"

"Why not? You are the closest friend I have, other than Guido, but somehow, even though he is *much* better at some things, I think I trust you a little more."

Kathy wasn't sure which emotion was strongest. Reluctance, panic, fear of what Guido's reaction would be. But rising above all was the sinking in her heart that Rita was going to die soon.

Rita continued before Kathy could say anything. "I want you to administer the disposal of all this 'stuff' I've accumulated, and handle the cash disbursements to the hospice and the cancer therapy and recovery groups. As for the Monday Club, I've arranged for Sharon and Martha to take charge. They'll alternate houses for the meetings. All your Monterey Mafia has to do is be the liaison between Running Wolf and the Club with under-the-table help on the cannabis.

"Now about my memorial party." Kathy was shaking her head as Rita handed her a small red leather datebook. "The names and addresses of the chosen are here—all the great ones of the Monday Club. And Running Wolf, of course. A few have lines drawn through their names. I crossed out Leo Nast because I got mad at him. The other three have died."

"No pot party!"

"Please, Kate. I'm counting on it. We've been planning it for the last month. I invented it for them so they could have some way to deal with my death."

Ignoring Kathy's protesting "But . . .", Rita rushed on. "We decided to copy Truman Capote's famous party based on a scene in My Fair Lady. Everybody has to wear black and white and wear masks. Here are the funeral invitations." She handed a box to Kathy. "I had them printed myself with just the date left blank for you to fill in. Don't you like the bold black and white graphics? And the 'Rita Rich requests the pleasure of your company at her memorial and last pot party at 7:00 p.m. in the ballroom of her Pebble Beach home. Dress: Gentlemen—black tie, black mask; Ladies—white dress, white mask.'"

"You've got to be kidding!"

"No, Kate, I'm not." Kathy noticed the 'Kate' and realized it was always Rita's way of telling her to loosen up. "Let me throw this last fling. It's the only thing I did well in my life. I always gave great parties. Great parties and great sex. Put it on my tombstone. You four can come about 6:30 and oversee the food. Maybe say a few words about how much you love me and then go home. It's not a party you'd like, but let them do it. I promised."

Kathy knew she was holding her mouth the way Rita made fun of, but she couldn't help it. She did not like the idea at all.

"In my will I'm leaving $200,000 to the D.A.R.E. program."

Still shocked, Kathy managed to find her voice. "That's some drug program isn't it?"

Rita referred to some papers on her nightstand and read off: "Drug Abuse Resistance Education. I knew you'd worry." Kathy was amazed. Couldn't answer.

"Well, anyway, my attorney is coming out tomorrow to update all this legal mumbo-jumbo. By the way, I've given Guido permission to stay here in the house until the estate is settled." Kathy tried not to show her disfavor but grimaced as

Rita continued. "Oh, I know you think he's a golddigging gigolo, but give him credit where credit is due. He's letting me die like I lived."

Rita took off her wig, put it on the nightstand. She closed her eyes for a moment and then said, "Before I die, I want you to know if I had to go through it all again—the years back in school until now—I'd choose to do it with you. You have been the reason my life was worth living these last few months." She opened her eyes and continued. "Now get out of here and let me get some rest."

Kathy swallowed hard as she blinked back tears. Maybe some from guilt for not being a better friend. "I'll phone you tomorrow," she said, bending down to kiss Rita on the cheek—something she had never, ever done before. Rita blinked her eyes in acknowledgement of the gesture, then waved her dismissal from the room.

(16)

HOROSCOPE: A change occurs over which you have no control. You have reached the point of no return. Decide whether to take up challenge or cool your heels. A promise must be fulfilled.

THE PHONE WOKE KATHY OUT OF A SOUND SLEEP. LOOKING AT THE ILLUMINATED dial of the clock and seeing it was five thirty A.M., she moaned and stretched over to lift the receiver, mumbling a grunt of "hullo."

"Katherine Doolittle? This is Guido. On my note of instructions from Rita, number one is to phone you. She's gone. I guess you need to make arrangements or something. She said she'd mailed you a letter. I'll be at the house."

That was it. No explanations, no emotion, no opportunity to respond, even if she knew how, before the line went dead. He just hung up. Good. Kathy could concentrate on being angry at the no-good son-of-a-bitch jerk-faced bum instead of thinking about Rita dying. How did it happen? Why didn't Rita call so she could go out and be with her? Damn Guido!

Even with all these thoughts popcorning in her head, she could not let the tears flow as she went through the motions of starting her day—showering, washing her hair, fixing her cereal and fruit, glancing through the paper but not knowing what she was reading. It was a form of numbness that protected her. Rita had asked her not to come out—had quit partying, got Guido to pick up whatever she needed. But every day they talked on the phone, Rita's voice huskier, less cheery each time.

At 10 A.M. the mail came, and Kathy's fingers trembled as she opened Rita's letter.

72

✻ ✻ ✻

Katherine—Kathy—Katie; good friend of so many years, through thick and thin, and even when you didn't approve of me or like me—I need to let you know some things to put that nervous mind of yours at ease.

The time has come when life isn't fun any more. It's okay to leave now. I've sent Guido down to get a bottle of Jack Daniels to wash down every pill I've stored up, and then I'll send him off to the golf course, write a note to him, and take control. I want to be in control of how I die as well as how I lived. Don't feel sorry, or guilty, or sad—just be happy that I lived a great life and I valued having you in it.

Call my attorney—I gave you his card—he has the will and more specific instructions on what to do. You may balk at my "service" ideas, but remember that garbage of granting last wishes. I've arranged for a caterer to handle the mundane parts of my memorial party—you just set the time. Make it a rip-snorter for you, Vi, Adrian and Sophie—and the Monday Club. Ignore what you don't want to be involved in. Running Wolf has agreed to co-host, so you could leave early and let them celebrate in their own way, as they know I would.

So the purpose of this note is to let you know everything is okay with me and to once more plead with you to leap before you look. I'll be watching you from above (or below) for the results!

Raise your glass of chablis to *carpe diem*, Katie. Thanks for everything. Cheers! Rita

Now the tears flowed down her face and dripped onto the letter held loosely in her hands. "Damn you, Rita! Why did you have to die just when I was beginning to understand you?"

Getting up from the couch, the crackle of the plastic cover jolted her memory of Vi and Rita both teasing her. "What are you protecting things from? Why are you so tidy? For whom?" Wiping her tears off with her sweater sleeve, she ripped the plastic off the couch, disarranged the magazines on the table, and stalked out to the kitchen to get that glass of chablis.

"Here's to ya, Rita!"

Mr. McGrath, the attorney, was prompt in arranging for the reading of the will, since instructions for the final arrangements were included. His office in Carmel was luxurious—the rich kind of stuffy. The mahogany desk was so immense it seemed to dwarf the bespeckled man who had greeted them. "Cold fish hand-shake," Vi had whispered in Kathy's ear. Kathy glared at her.

Guido's eyes seemed to be staring holes into Kathy's face. She couldn't read what he was thinking—probably just as well. "He's mentally undressing you, Kathy!" Leave it to Sophie to be sexually positive.

"No, that's not anything close to a friendly look," Adrian whispered in the other ear.

Kathy again had mixed emotions. Every time she saw Guido she shuddered, not knowing why. *He frightens me*, she thought. At the same time, she had to admit that feeling was back, the one she felt the first time she'd seen him, starting in her thighs, up through her pelvis and upper body and into her arms, coming to rest in her flushed face.

Mr. McGrath cleared his throat. "If you don't mind, I have a busy schedule today so I will dispense with the portions of the document that deal with whereases and therefores, and as Rita . . . I mean Ms. Rich would say, 'cut to the chase'." He looked down at the papers before him. "Ms. Doolittle, of course will have a copy for reference. I understand she is aware of Rita's . . . Ms. Rich's intentions."

Guido was pacing the floor, having refused to take one of the plush leather chairs as the others had. He stopped abruptly at hearing the last sentence. Kathy squirmed, crossed her legs, put her head down, thinking she never really knew Rita's intentions about most things.

"To continue. 'To Guido, my eternal gratitude for all the nights you held an old shriveled body in your arms and pretended you liked it.'" Kathy blushed. Guido leered. Mr. McGrath didn't look up. "For services rendered, dear Guido, keep all the toys I bought for you plus $50,000 cash. You also get the Jaguar. But when you get some bimbo in the back seat, just remember I'll be watching. This car is haunted by me. You can have the old Morgan (I know it was your favorite). All this only if you pack up and get out of the house in 48 hours. I'm leaving the house and everything in it to Katherine, and you know she doesn't like you. I don't want you aggravating her. You can now be dismissed—the rest of this document is a secret."

Guido stormed out of the room, not looking at any of them. The pictures on the wall bounced as he slammed the door. The women exchanged surprised looks—Kathy was in shock, not only from the will but that Rita had finally kicked Guido out.

"I have wrapped packages for you from Rita. I understand there's a note in each one. I assume you'll want to open them privately." He handed the gaily wrapped presents to them. "Here's something else." He reached into a large shopping bag and pulled out four over-sized red sweatshirts monogrammed with big bold **MM** in bright gold and Monterey Mafia underneath. Dignifed attorneys sometimes smile, and Mr. McGrath couldn't hide his as the women accepted the shirts, apparently with no question about the label's meaning.

He gave Kathy a sealed envelope of instructions for the Memorial Service. The reading of the will continued, with each revelation more surprising than the last. Kathy was reminded of her promise to keep the Monday Club going now that she had the money. "If you don't want to join the club, Katie, at least see that they have the resources." Kathy took a deep breath at that one.

There was a listing of all the cash, money in banks, the house, the jewelry, the bonds—the works. A special provision was made for a $200,000 grant, to be administered by Kathy, to the Pacific Grove Schools for an effective drug education program. Besides the wrapped gifts and sweatshirts, Rita's "going away" presents to the four women were new cars. A red Alfa Romeo for Kathy (Rita's idea of a joke, no doubt) with personalized license plate reading "Carpe Diem". Vi got a yellow Subaru with an even more elaborate cellular phone and a note—"try not to kill yourself in this, Vi." Adrian got a purple mini-van. Since Sophie didn't drive, Jack got a Cadillac to drive her around in.

"You may pick the cars up at the Rich estate. She made arrangements for them to be delivered there while you were hearing the will. Goodbye and good luck to you all. Let me know if I can clarify things for you, Katherine." Kathy nodded like a robot, rose mechanically from her chair and shuffled out the door in a daze.

On the way out to Rita's, Kathy and Vi alternated between shocked silence and nervous chatter. Adrian and Sophie were picking up Jack and would meet them. As Kathy drove through the gate into Pebble Beach, she saw Guido heading out in Rita's familiar sports car.

"Oh, God! There's Guido. Who is that with him in the Jag? Hope he didn't see us." Kathy nearly ran off the road stretching her neck to look behind her.

"Good Heavens above, that's Adrian's brother, Peter Pellagrino!" Vi shouted.

"What? Impossible! Why on earth would they be together?"

Both were puzzled, but they had bigger things on their minds—picking up their new cars!

(17)

———

HOROSCOPE: Reach beyond the immediate by letting others know you intend to fulfill your mission with a flourish. What seemed impossible will be available. Chance to hit financial jackpot.

VI WOKE UP WITH A START. HER NECK HURT. THEN SHE REMEMBERED. SHE had been sleeping in the back of Adrian's purple van. She looked in the rear-view mirror, ran a quick comb through her hair, picked up her purse and hurried back to the house. It was after four. Only a couple of hours left of Rita's estate sale. How could she have slept so long?

"Hi, Roy. How many do you think are left?"

The security guard at the front door looked at his list. "Well, I passed out two hundred numbers by three and only a hundred have come out so far. If a hundred are still in there, it means we have that many more waiting around somewhere for their numbers to be called."

"Damn, I doubt we can push them all through by six. Can your staff work overtime?"

"I dunno," he said, but his face told her a definite no. "Fifteen, twenty minutes maybe."

What to do. She wasn't sure. Where was Kathy? Probably gone to the bank to get rid of the cash. She must have made five trips today. She got nervous with all that money. Where was Sophie? Vi ran through the living room, past the cashier's station to the kitchen.

"Martha, have you seen Sophie?"

"Not lately. She was serving refreshments to some of the people waiting in line out front the last time I saw her."

This added annoyance of the refreshments was Rita's idea. Put it in her will. "Give them champagne and little cookies. I want everyone to be happy and a little drunk when they paw through my things at my last garage sale." So Rita! But it was a nuisance. Some people probably came just for the booze and to gawk at the house. Too many people had already heard about the notorious Monday Club and wanted to get a first-hand view. They were in the way. Too many of them. They'd started lining up before eight this morning and there hadn't been a moment of let-up since. Finally had to start giving them numbers and assigning them a certain hour of the day. Now that wasn't working either.

She'd better find Nikki. She looked on the sun porch. Most of the furniture was gone. Just a potted plant or two left. No Nikki.

Thank goodness for all the help. She saw Ida putting "sold" stickers on the stereo equipment in the study. "Nice sale, Ida. Keep up the good work."

"Thanks." Ida looked as tired as Vi felt. "It's been quite a day! I guess we'll all be glad to go back to our Suppers for Seniors posts and leave the retail business behind. I don't know how you girls at the Shop and Pray do it."

"Have you seen Nikki, Ida?"

"No."

"Or Sophie? Or Kathy? Or Adrian?"

"No, sorry."

Vi tore up the stairs. The top floor was clotted with people grabbing things in a frenzy. She finally spotted Nikki over by the linens and started pushing in her direction.

"Hi, Vi!" Nikki sounded like she was having fun.

"There's still a hundred waiting in the wings and this crowd shows no sign of leaving. We only have a couple hours left. I don't know what to do."

"Did you ask Kathy?" Nikki shouted past a few people.

"No, I can't find her anywhere. Or Sophie and Adrian either. I'm worried."

"Oh, come on, Vi. Get with it. You were having great fun this morning. You're just tired." Nikki handed a young man his box of monogrammed white towels.

"I just don't want to be the one to go out there and tell a hundred people they can't come in. There could be a riot!"

"You'll think of something."

"Nikki, come out on the balcony. I can't even hear you in here."

Nikki and Vi pushed their way out on the balcony and it was suddenly quiet. Nothing left for sale on the balcony.

"Nikki, my daughter Rose was here earlier with my neighbor Hannah, and I think they had a photographer from *The Herald* with them. I don't want anything ugly to happen that could show up as a headline in tomorrow's paper."

"Yeah, I see what you mean. The Monday Club doesn't need any more publicity. Do you really think there will be trouble if these people don't get in?"

"I don't know. I just don't want to take any chances." I'm beginning to sound like Kathy, Vi thought.

"All right. Let's let them in. So what if the security guards go home. There really isn't all that much of value left anyway."

"But how can they all fit in the house?"

"This mansion can hold hundreds. They just won't be able to see much. Some will probably get disgusted with the crowds and go home."

"I guess you're right."

"Sure. It'll be OK. I'll keep all the library staff on after six. Lots of these people are just curiosity seekers. They'll look around the house, then they'll go home."

Still outside, Sophie watched the last of the customers or sightseers file into the house at Vi's invitation. Vi then put up a sign that said "Closed." Sophie sighed with relief and glanced ruefully at the trampled and littered lawn. She might as well be useful. The more work she did the quicker she could get home.

She started cleaning up the discarded paper cups and napkins that dotted the grass like a fresh fall of hailstones. She felt depleted, exhausted really. No hope of getting out of here until it was all in good order, even if they were going to come back tomorrow for final clean-up. Still so much to do she felt like crying.

The estate sale had been hugely successful, but even though she hadn't known Rita long, she felt sad for her. People pawing over her things, dropping some of them on the floor. "I would hate that," she said to herself, and felt a tear drip down her cheek.

Rita had been a vibrant personality. Even though terribly sick, she smiled and joked with everyone around her. Sophie was sorry that she had taken her own life. To give up all hope—she must have felt an awful moment of despair. Such a generous and caring person too, under the flippant façade. It wasn't fair, Sophie thought. So many things to live for, so much money, and no one there to hold her hand.

Just then she looked up and saw Kathy striding up the walk after her quick run to the bank. She looked tired, but neat in her sage green pant suit; not at all bedraggled like Sophie felt as she tried to smooth her hair.

"We've closed the sale. The last people are inside, but there's almost nothing to buy. They're probably just nosing about the house," Sophie said.

Kathy threw her arms around her. "Thank goodness. You've been great, Sophie. I feel like I've known you a really long time. You're such a take-charge person. Everyone has been super. We've made tons of money." She helped pick up the trash on the lawn as she talked.

"Rita would be glad all her things are going to help a lot of people. Who would have thought she would have turned into the kind, benevolent person she became. There was a lot to my old friend—much more than I realized." Kathy grabbed Sophie by the hand and led her toward the house. "Let's go inside, find the others and drink to Rita. We can finish this tomorrow."

They all gathered in the cheery kitchen where Rita never cooked a meal that they knew of. Nikki, Ida, Vi, Kathy, Martha, Sharon, and Sophie. Sophie missed Adrian, who left early for an appointment. They fell into various positions on the floor. No chairs left. Kathy went to the sink where they had dumped all the ice and buried two bottles of Pieper-Heidseick champagne.

"It will taste just as good in a paper cup," Kathy said. "Rita would understand, since there isn't a single piece of crystal left in this house, or anything else of value."

"A toast," Sophie raised her cup, "to Rita, Pacific Grove's secret benefactor."

Vi held up her cup. "To Rita, God bless her. I bet she was laughing at us wherever she is when she saw us working our tails off today. We did a great job, didn't we girls?"

They all nodded in agreement and sipped their champagne. "I'm proud of us. It's what Rita wanted," Kathy chimed in. They began to clean up the kitchen and pack up their things. No one paid any attention to Sophie who was pouring over Rita's recipe box, forgetting to finish her champagne. "The first thing I'll make will be from this new one for brownies."

"What have you got?" Vi stood over the seated Sophie.

"Recipes. Dumplings, just like my mother used to make with stewed chicken. And I swear this is the same pumpkin pie recipe my Aunt Ella used for all our special occasions from Halloween to Christmas."

"I know what you mean," Vi said. "I remember Sunday pot roast with sweet onions and collard greens."

"These recipes bring back some pretty sweet old memories," said Sophie.

"You can chart the changes in our lives by our recipe boxes." Kathy joined the conversation. "My childhood was mostly recipes for macaroni, tamale pie, tomato soup casseroles. Now it's about tofu and raddiccio."

"These faded recipe cards are like old friends. Somebody's life is in this box," Sophie said. "I can't just toss it out like it meant nothing. Someone should care."

The next day was clean-up. What a mess! Plastic cups, paper napkins all over the window ledges, shelves, and still scattered across the lawn. It looked like a flock of doves had landed. Spots of white speckling the green.

"Reminds me of the old days. Before a game we'd go out and toilet paper somebody's yard and house," Vi said.

"You would." Kathy's voice was filled with disapproval. "I can't understand how people can be such pigs."

Sophie was unavailable for griping. She was already out on the lawn with three volunteers, picking up the trash. "The truck from Shop and Pray will be here at noon to pick up anything worthwhile that's still left," she shouted to anyone interested.

"What would that be?" Vi said to Kathy. "The vultures have pretty well picked this carcass clean."

"Let's have a look." Kathy was tying a scarf around her head to protect her hair. She had on her worst looking grey sweats. Working clothes, Vi concluded. Boy, did she look like hell. This evidently wasn't one of her perfect grooming days when we cared what the neighbors thought. Something about her face looked bad, too. Kathy wasn't herself today. *Be careful*, Vi thought. *Be humble; be gentle with your friend. She's so fragile right now. Think before you speak for a change.*

A commercial van pulled up and unloaded five Hispanic ladies who didn't speak a word of English. The side of the van said "Maids on the Move. We Are Specialists in Cleaning up Dirt." Funny how everyone has to be a specialist today. Vi herded the pretty young women into the house and they really did seem to know what they were doing. In just a few minutes there were buckets and mops, swishing vacuum cleaners and trash compactors, and all evidence of the estate sale vampire bats began to be washed away.

Vi wandered through the rooms surveying what was left. Luckily, they had removed all the really valuable things of Rita's in the first few days after her death. Nikki and Running Wolf really came to the rescue. Amazingly, they found that Rita had kept excellent records of her husband's and her own many extravagant purchases. Most of the art, antiques and antiquarian book dealers they contacted were only too happy to buy back the things the Riches had purchased from them, often at two to five times what had been paid for them.

There were a few surprises, though. She had an early Bishoff painting of Point Lobos that went for $350,000, and a Dorsey was on consignment at Rocky Point Restaurant. Who knew what it would bring? Also, between The Post Ranch Inn and Rocky Point Restaurant they had pretty much disposed of Rita's wine cellar for a cool $400,000. Vi had insisted Kathy take some of the chardonnay so she'd learn to appreciate wine in bottles instead of jugs.

Nikki took over on many of the first editions and autographed books. She was still researching their value. Not that Rita ever read them. "I just use them for decorator books, sweethearts. They make a library look so British—all that Morroco binding and the faint smell of old leather mixed with good cigars. It reeks of money."

Vi sat down on the built-in window seat in the empty library. She kept remembering things Rita said. Remembering the going away gifts and notes she left for them with her lawyer. Vi's gift was ruby-red slippers. Of course they weren't the real ones Judy Garland wore in *The Wizard of Oz*, but they were perfect facsimiles and in just Vi's size, complete with taps. The card said, "Hey little Meglin Kitty, move on down the road. Show 'em what you've got, kid. You're a hoot. Rita."

How did she know? She was so clear the last few weeks. It was like she could see right into Vi's soul.

Adrian had gotten a book on "Special Relationships," but she didn't share Rita's note with the others. Sophie got some fancy lingerie she was embarrassed to show.

Kathy's gift was a professional make-up kit from a Hollywood make-up department, complete with wigs, noses, crepey stuff to make your skin look old—and an autographed picture of Katherine Hepburn. Her card said, "Quit pouting in the wings, detached from life, Kate! Smell the grease paint, take center stage. Your audience is waiting. Break a leg. Rita."

Kathy came in, as if on cue. "Isn't the library sad with all these empty shelves?" she asked.

"Yes, the whole house is forlorn. I'll be glad when we close it up and leave the ghosts for the real estate agent."

Kathy sighed, turned her back on Vi. The only sound in the room was the far-off moan of the vacuum cleaners.

Kathy went up to Rita's bedroom. She wanted to be alone and this was where she and Rita had been the closest. The room was bare, stark, lonely, all traces of Rita gone. She remembered that last visit; how she had realized deep down inside it was the last. Rita. No one quite like her. No one did things the way she did. She was unique and indefinable. How could she be so attractive and yet sometimes grotesque? Classy, but crass? Kathy realized she was envious; that she actually wanted to have little bits and pieces of Rita's characteristics, but didn't know how to sort and assimilate the things she admired. It was easier when they were kids growing up in the valley, but later they both got so extreme in their separate paths.

Memories were oppressing Kathy. *I'll always hear her voice, her laugh, her taunting me to attach back to life.* Why have I ignored my kids just because Jerry turned them against me? I should fight back into their lives. Some day. Not now, when things are so muddled and confusing. *Got to get through this first.* She gazed out the window, collecting her thoughts.

Startled by the sound of laughter which at first she thought was Rita, Kathy took a last look around the bedroom. She rummaged in her pockets and fluffed up her hair with a comb. She looked in the mirror up in the ceiling over where the bed once was. "I'll try, Rita. I really will."

"Hey, Kathy. Come on up to the ballroom." Vi's voice shattered her reverie. Kathy closed the door and climbed the stairs to the third floor.

"There you are. Didn't know where you were." Vi put a protective arm around Kathy and led her to where Sophie and Adrian were sitting on the floor.

Sophie looked up, reached for Kathy's hand and said, "We're all finished. Thought we'd rest a bit and reminisce about Rita's farewell party."

"It was not only a hoot, it was a holler. Definitely a proper send-off. She would have loved it." Vi's eyes sparkled.

"I'm glad the Monday Club members honored the request for the Black and White Masquerade Ball. Real incognito. I sure didn't recognize a lot of them," Adrian said.

"No telling what went on after we left," Sophie laughed.

"It really worried me," Kathy started—interrupted by groans from Vi and Adrian. "Well, it wasn't just that, the pot. What scared me the most was when we told Guido he had to leave. That he wasn't invited." She shuddered, remembering the way he looked at her as she stood firm, hands on hips, and pointed toward his car parked in the driveway. "I think if he'd had a gun I'd be floating around with Rita right now." She decided against telling the others that she was sure someone followed her to and from the bank the day before.

It was late. They were all exhausted. "Let's call it a day," sighed Vi.

Kathy was the last to go out the front door.

"Bye, Rita," she whispered.

_____

18

HOROSCOPE: See beyond the immediate. You are not a prisoner of what people think and say. Break clean in a dramatic way.

SOPHIE WAKENED WITH ONLY ONE THOUGHT IN HER HEAD. SHE WOULD MAKE her bongo brownies for the Feast of Lanterns contest—the Feast of Desserts. This wonderful legendary pageant with entertainment and fireworks extravaganza was sponsoring a new event this year along with the chicken barbeque.

Competition was always a great spur for her. She loved winning and was very lucky. She took first place in jams and jellies at the West Virginia State Fair with her own original creation—a strawberry-rhubarb conserve with nuts and raisins— that won Best of Show. Suppers for Seniors loved the brownies she made from the recipe box she found in Rita's kitchen. Why did Rita have so many recipes when she didn't cook at all? So much about Rita was a puzzle to her.

As she jumped into a sundress and combed her unruly curls, Sophie thought more of poor Rita and breathed a little prayer that she was now in a better place. But heaven would have to be pretty nice to beat Rita's gorgeous home and view in Pebble Beach.

She quietly left the bedroom after one lingering glance at her sweetly sleeping husband. With luck she'd have the bongo brownies made and in the oven before Jack came looking for her and his breakfast.

She hummed their song, "It Had to Be You," as she organized the ingredients for the brownies. When she cooked she liked to get everything out and on the counter before she started, arranged just so in the order of the recipe. Two kinds of sugar, flour, butter, eggs, baking chocolate, and white chocolate for the icing that helped make her brownies special. But the secret ingredient, her new herb, rested cozily in its chunky little blue and white tin. She liked to use an eighth of an ounce. It gave the brownies that extra something that everyone liked. As she turned off the mixer and reached for the tin, Jack walked into the kitchen.

"Morning sweetie, what got you up so early?" he asked.

"I'm making the best brownies in Pacific Grove for the Feast of Desserts contest. I'm about to get them in the oven."

Without thinking, she took the can in her hand and began to measure out a spoonful.

"What is that you're putting in?" he asked.

"Spices," she answered as she measured and stirred it into the batter. "That's my special ingredient," she added proudly.

He looked closer, picked up the can and smelled it. "Ye gods, Sophie, pot! I can't believe you're putting that drug in your brownies. You can't do that!"

"Yes I can," Sophie said. "I already did. Alice B. Toklas did, too."

"But that was Paris," Jack said. "This is Pacific Grove. Please, Sophie, show some common sense. This is America's Last Home Town. No way can you do that. Don't you know this was the last town in California to make alcohol legal? What would they think of marijuana?"

"They'll never know." Sophie was getting angry. "I'm not going to tell them." She did not want anyone interferring with her cooking, not even Jack. Why did he have to come into the kitchen right now, anyhow?

"I don't tell you how to play golf," she said. Her color and her voice were rising. "I don't want you telling me how to cook!"

"But Sophie, you know this is illegal. You lied to me."

"No, I didn't lie to you." She turned so he couldn't see her face.

"You've been lying to me all along."

A car horn sounded outside. Jack's golfing buddy was out there already.

"You think you know best.... Jack, I've let you tell me what to do about everything ever since we married. Most of the time I agree. But I know best about this. I know what makes my brownies have that certain zing. This gives them zest. The seniors love them. And who's going to know?"

The car horn honked again.

Jack tried again. "Sophie, be my good girl." He reached for her. She moved away.

"I'm not your good girl. Sure I love you, but I can't let you run my life. I've got to be my own person. I have to make my own decisions. I did for fifty years before I met you."

She saw Jack take a deep breath. He sighed.

"Sounds like you're getting ideas from those women libbers. I'm disappointed in you."

He slammed the door; left without saying goodbye.

Sophie wiped away a tear from her eye and put the brownies in the oven. "Our first fight," she said to herself.

Later, while she was cleaning her kitchen to be sparkling again, the phone rang.

"Adrian, I'm glad you called. How about meeting me at the Feast of Lanterns? I'm entering my bongo brownies in the contest. Jack's a bit upset with me. I need you there for moral support." With confidence, she added, "I think I'll win."

"He's not even coming? What kind of husband is that? I'll be there."

"Meet me where they exhibit the desserts. I'm glad you're going, Adrian. Bye!"

The day was gorgeous as it can be only in Pacific Grove. Sophie was already standing in place near her brownies and felt a bit self-conscious as if she were being judged instead of her baking.

Adrian strolled up. "Am I in time?"

"Just," Sophie replied. "Take a look at those judges." A trio of two men and one woman looked like they regularly ate more than their share of goodies. "Perfect for the part," Sophie whispered to Adrian, who giggled.

"I wonder if they'll notice anything different about mine." She really was nervous after Jack's tirade and did not want them to identify the mysterious ingredient that made her brownies special. The patients at hospice, in the hospital, and those from the Monday Club loved their new alternative medicine. Everyone who tasted them said, "The best brownies I've ever eaten."

When those who didn't know asked for the recipe, Sophie would say "Sorry, but it has been passed down through the family for generations and the ghosts of my mother and grandmother would haunt me if I gave it away." She crossed her fingers when she said that, knowing it had come from Rita's recipe box. Sophie urged the judges to have another. They became animated and seemed happier after every brownie.

Sophie remembered that other recipes—some from Rita, some from Running Wolf —had worked well, too. The large pinch of it in a tea ball for bongo tea. And the syrup they'd taken to Rita in the hospital that Adrian concocted, marijuana steeped in 150-proof rum for a week, strained into four-ounce brown bottles to look like regular medicine.

The judges were conscientiously taking one small bite after another of all the concoctions throughout the day. Sophie thought they would get sick. "They seem to be enjoying themselves," she said to Adrian.

"You bet," Adrian answered. "I know that fat guy. He loves to eat."

Sophie watched their faces as they sampled her entry. First, the tall, rather glum man who seemed to be Judge #1 broke into a beatific smile. He watched the others as they sampled theirs. They exchanged glances. "Superb," #1 said. "Superb!"

"Superior," the haughty woman said as she smiled in her superior way.

"I say, I think these have it," the short, rotund gentleman said as he quickly polished his off.

"Young lady," he turned to Sophie; "my colleagues and I admire your ingenuity and originality. Whatever secret ingredient you have used certainly makes you the winner. I have been a judge at the Monterey County Fair for twenty years and never have I come close to tasting any brownies so good as yours."

"Fit for the gods," the woman said. "You do have a knack."

Adrian was grinning and elbowing Sophie.

Judge #1 didn't say another word as his mouth was stuffed. All stood smiling vacantly as the cameraman took the photo of the day with Sophie and her charmed judges.

Sophie felt like she was floating. She turned to Adrian, held up the blue ribbon for her admiration. Adrian gave her a hug.

"I'm glad I was here to see your big moment, but I have to run. I've got a date. Too bad Jack wouldn't come. You're super, kiddo."

"But I'm worried what he'll think."

"I don't like to see you worried, Sophie." Adrian said. "What do you actually know about him? You don't know how he'll act."

Sophie stepped back, looked at Adrian indignantly. "I know he loves me. He'll come around."

"How can you be so sure? Think about it. You married a stranger." Adrian turned to leave, shouting over her shoulder, "Call me if you need me."

She thinks he's a stranger? I know him better than anyone. It'll be okay.

After the early serving of the barbeque, Sophie walked home alone and lonely. She carried the blue ribbon in her purse. She hadn't eaten, hoping he might come, but he had not. She gave her barbeque tickets to a small boy.

Victory was bitter. She won, but she was afraid she had really lost. What would happen when she got home? Was Jack a stranger?

That night in bed, Jack seemed indifferent. Sophie cuddled close, scared of losing him. Life wouldn't be worth living without him.

But her bongo brownies did win.

19

HOROSCOPE: Watch out! Durable goods featured, but household items might not please everyone. A surprise comes in a big package. Be on alert; game of hide and seek begins.

THE FUN PART WAS THE MONEY. VI HAD NEVER HAD A LOT OF MONEY BEFORE. She loved the yellow Subaru with the little cellular phone. She liked knowing she could get the roof fixed so her bedroom wouldn't leak this winter, but most of all she enjoyed giving it away. That was Kathy's and Sophie's favorite part of the adventure, too. They got a kick out of tucking twenty dollar bills into their favorite books at Shop and Pray and the library.

Years of making do for Rose and Fred, who had to look successful, had given Vi a few cardinal rules of thrift. Can you repair it? Can you do without it? Can you buy it cheaper? Can you make it last longer? Can you use it less? Can you borrow it?

When Rose was small, Vi organized a sort of lending library for children's clothes. You kept it until it was too small and then turned it in on a bigger coat. Vi liked to think of herself as a shrewd shopper and clever reclaimer, but Kathy had another name for it.

"What a tightwad," Kathy often teased her. "Are you still saving all your old bread wrappers so you won't have to buy baggies, and making Christmas ornaments out of styrofoam trays? Still use each Kleenex three or four times? You're the biggest cheapskate I ever saw. Please give up buying your clothes at the thrift shop."

"Why?" Vi loved recycling her old clothes.

"This is a small town. What if you show up in something someone recognizes as her charity donation?" Vi didn't care.

Now they buzzed around in their new cars, making connections between Running Wolf and the Monday Club, but staying out of the danger zone. They thought. Kathy kept calling Vi on the cell phone whenever she thought "someone suspicious" was following her.

"It's just your imagination, Kathy. You let that prank warning scare you. They just like your jazzy red sports car."

Since Rita's estate sale was so profitable, it was natural that the inspiration to hold more of them evolved and grew. It would bolster the Monday Club's funds so they could provide solace for those who couldn't afford it.

"They've got to be in Pebble Beach at Rita's house. That's the draw," Vi proclaimed.

"Just think of all the money we could make!" Sophie's voice betrayed her excitement. "We could take the remainders down to Shop and Pray. That way we'd be helping even more people."

"Yeah, but who's going to let us old ladies handle estate sales? Where do we get the stuff to sell?" Kathy always worried about the minor details.

It was decided that until Rita's house was sold, they could have them there, and Martha told them they could use her place, too.

It was Adrian who came up with the idea of checking out abandoned storage lockers for merchandise. "Rich people store things and then forget about them," she said. "You bid on them."

The manager came out to announce the rules. He looked bored. *No wonder,* Vi thought. *He's so boring himself.* He was a beige man: beige skin and hair, pale brown eyes and khaki clothes. Forgettable face. His only distinguishing feature was rimless glasses. Even the way he moved was dull. His gestures small and confined. Vi took an instant dislike to him, though telling herself it was unfair. *I'm too old to be fair,* she mused.

"These merchandise lots have been seized by the administration and have been advertised for seven days in the papers. They are now being sold in lieu of rent to compensate the owner."

As he talked, Vi could tell it was memorized, probably required by law. Wasn't even listening to himself.

"You may not examine this material. Each storage unit will be opened for five minutes and you will be allowed to look in before we open the bidding for each space. Successful bidders must provide cash or cashier's check, and within twenty four hours all materials in locker must be cleaned out and carried away. No one can bid without a number. Hold up your card when bidding."

"Sounds easy," Sophie said.

"I don't know about this, Vi. We don't need another business. You just get tired of anything we already have going. You want to try everything new." Kathy sounded scared again.

"This'll be great, Kathy. You know how much money we made on Rita's estate sale. All we do is stuff some of these things into Rita's, and they will sell in a minute."

"Don't worry, Kathy. This is fun." Sophie tried to keep peace between the two.

Vi felt vindicated, although she was nervous looking at the seedy characters standing around the manager's office. They made Pea Soup look good. She eavesdropped on a pair standing near her. An older man in a leather jacket who had white hair tied in a pony tail, and a young—maybe twenty—eager Mexican boy. The old man looked proud showing the boy the ropes.

"It's mostly junk," he said. "Broken appliances, clothes and stuff nobody wants, but you never can tell, know what I mean? Good stuff for swap meets. Or if you're rich you could get enough to open up your own second-hand store. A guy told me he got a whole lot of cash once. It was in a shoebox. Imagine!"

The boy rolled his eyes upward. Smiled. "What does it cost for one locker?"

"Usually can get one for under $500. About the top anybody pays. Good days, maybe $100. Heard about one guy who got some letters from Charles Manson. What a find! Can you guess how much he'd make on a haul like that?"

"What shall I buy?" the boy asked.

"Get yourself a specialty, like tools or stereos or somethin'. When you get to know the guys they'll trade you tools for things they want. It's good to have a specialty."

The boy nodded. He looked impressed with all this wisdom. *Sounds like a bunch of bull to me,* Vi thought.

"Don't stand so close to that man," whispered Kathy. "Something could jump off him."

The four of them looked into the first locker. Five minutes wasn't long to peer around the dark cubicles. It had camping gear, pipes and rafts. Too much junk in the way to see in the corners. The bidding was low and someone got that one for twenty dollars. Sophie was excited.

"I like these prices, Vi. If we can find something we want, I bet we can get it really cheap."

"Yeah." Vi was glad to get emotional support. Even Kathy was thawing. She was a good sport. Just didn't want to catch any cooties from the unwashed men.

Vi was intrigued by the next one—a rowboat and scuba diving equipment—but the others nixed it. Sophie got excited about the third one. Vi saw a TV set, a mattress, some ugly bean-bag chairs, more old furniture. Didn't look like one that would have a shoebox of money. "What's so great about this one, Sophie?"

"Back in the corner by the typewriter and the fur coat. I think that's a big freezer. The good kind that opens from the top. We could get lots of produce, fruit and things for the homeless, for that Project Open Hand where Jack and I volunteer. Farmers give us their excess, but sometimes we get too much on one day and then nothing for a week. With a freezer we could store it. I could try out all those recipes from Rita's box and freeze them. And I could bake lots of brownies ahead of time." Sophie's eyes were dancing with the prospects.

"How much should we bid?" Adrian asked.

"I'd go two hundred," Sophie whispered.

The old man and Mexican boy opened at fifty dollars. Sophie shouted one hundred, waving her auction card in the air. The other bidders glared at them. Vi felt like an intruder. She had the impression the group didn't like newcomers.

The old man bid $110.

"Be cool," Adrian whispered. "One hundred twenty," she spoke slowly and quietly to the auctioneer, like it was all over, and sure enough it was.

Sophie was joyous. "We'll be back this afternoon with a truck," she told the owner as she paid him in cash.

They returned that afternoon with a U-Haul rental truck. Vi was tired of listening to Kathy worry about whether the manager would help them load things up, or whether they dared ask him.

"We have a dolly, Kathy."

"But that freezer is so big. Can we work the dolly?"

Sophie was excited. "I'm thrilled thinking of all the delicacies I'm going to try—things you've never tasted before! And loads of my bongo brownies so we'll always have them on hand. They're in such demand at hospice and the hospital."

As they pulled up in front of the locker, Adrian hopped out, looked around and said, "Nobody seems to be around to help. Guess it's up to us." She started moving boxes. "Come on and help me, you slobs!" Vi thought she was getting pretty bossy, but she and the others pitched in and moved the lighter boxes to clear a path to the back corner.

When they finally reached the freezer, Vi noticed the odor. "It stinks back here. Like something died."

"Oh, my God, I bet it's a rat!" Kathy was panicking again.

After removing the dusty plastic drop-cloth they started peeling away layers of duct tape. "Only a guy would use so much duct tape," Vi mumbled. The smell got worse. Sophie went to get the manager for a crowbar, which he grudgingly provided, but he said it wasn't his job to open it. Vi and Adrian finally pried it open.

"Good Lord in Heaven!" Vi screamed. "It looks like body parts!"

"Well, I certainly hope we're not going to store food in there," Kathy said without thinking. She leaned closer, clapped her hand to her mouth and ran outside to throw up.

The putrid smell was unbearable. The face was unrecognizable on the decapitated head.

After the screaming, there was silence. Adrian bent down to help Sophie, who'd fainted.

Vi put her hand over her racing heart.

All four women had to remain at the locker for what seemed like an eternity. Even sitting outside they could still smell the rancid body. Kathy kept being sick. Sophie was silent, drawing her arms around herself.

Eventually the police came. Kathy had called Chris—the only one she trusted. He was there first. He'd just opened the door of the locker when the lieutenant from Monterey Police Department arrived.

"Connery, sir," Chris said.

"Falcon," he said. "John Falcon." He was short. Vi thought all cops were tall. Looked like his nose had been broken more than once. Mean little eyes roamed the room, looking at everyone like they were guilty. Vi disliked him immediately.

"Who are they?" Falcon motioned toward Vi sitting on the empty trunk, Kathy standing behind, and poor Sophie who was leaning against the wall being comforted by Adrian.

"They found the package." Chris motioned toward the body in the freezer. Vi had thrown a blanket over it.

"Where's Dickson?"

"Retired."

"Too bad. How long you been workin' homicide?"

"This is my first." Chris reddened.

"Whaddaya know so far?"

"Nothing."

Now Falcon looked annoyed. "Get rid of that blanket! Who put that goddamn thing on it? I don't like nothin' changed. When did it happen?"

"By the looks of things, coulda been here a month or more."

"Coulda been? Don't you know? Where the hell's the lab? Get those grannies outa here and find out what they know. Get on the horn and off your ass, Connery. Let's get some action. Move!"

Chris was obviously relieved to be alone with the women in the manager's office.

"I thought you handled yourself very well, Chris." Kathy tried to comfort him. Don't do it, Vi wanted to say. No mothering. Not now.

"I have to ask you some questions here," he said.

"You don't have to, sir. We know them," Sophie said. "We watch NYPD Blue."

He ran through them anyway.

"Is this your storage locker? How did you get this body?" Chris asked. He didn't sound like a police interrogator now. Just a curious kid who couldn't believe it. Incredulous. Like he was asking his mother, "how *could* you!?"

"It's just an accident." Sophie started to cry.

"We really don't know him," Adrian filled in for Sophie.

"It was *not* our locker." Kathy sounded defensive. "It was abandoned. We just bid on it to get the freezer."

"Why?" Chris asked.

Vi began to feel the bind. She wanted to help clear his suspicions but she felt tongue-tied. There were so many things they couldn't tell. Not about putting second-hand stuff in Rita's Pebble Beach home. Not about needing the freezer for storing and distributing Sophie's marijuana brownies. Not about all the extra money they had from Rita's will and payments from the Monday Club. She knew their hesitation made them look guilty. Trouble was, Vi felt guilty. What to say? Questions would arise she couldn't answer.

"For the freezer so we could store food for Project Open Hand?" Vi said softly. It sounded like a question. She felt the sweat around her collar. Couldn't meet his eyes. Felt the heaviness of the silence around her. She was a liar caught in her own trap.

Lt. Falcon came in from interviewing the manager. "Name on the rental agreement is a phony. The guy says you bought contents fair and square, but we're impounding everything for evidence." He glanced at each one in turn. "You can go. For now. Just don't leave town."

(20)

HOROSCOPE: It's not hardening of the arteries you're worried about in someone close. It's hardening of the *categories*. Help your tightly screwed-on friend find ways to improvise more wiggle room—more swagger in her walk, more slack and wander in her talk. Start by helping her change image.

For DAYS ALL THE LADIES WERE STUNNED, HEAVY WITH THE NIGHTMARE. Finally Vi was ready to do anything but sit around and brood. She went back to work at Shop and Pray.

She was off for her lunch hour, and feeling uncomfortable as she opened the door and let herself into Kathy's living room. It was the purple beret she'd purchased this morning at the thrift shop. The moment she saw it, she'd fallen in love with it. Remembering one of her favorite poems, "When I'm An Old Woman I'll Wear Purple," Vi knew she had to have it.

That was this morning. But now going under Kathy's critical scrutiny, she was self-conscious, felt a little silly. Suddenly she imagined what she looked like with the beret pulled down over her short grey bangs. Absurd perhaps. Well, she certainly was not going to show vulnerability to Kathy. Kathy looked up to Vi. She couldn't afford to display a failure of nerve now. They were all so frightened about the scene at the storage locker. Kathy kept talking about a black car following her, or some man in the shadows. The body hung over all their conversations. For several days they hadn't been able to talk about anything else; now they were avoiding the subject.

Vi was right. Kathy kept looking at her new purple hat. "I wish you wouldn't do that!" She shouted, determined to take the offensive.

"What?" Kathy looked startled, apologetic. Vi didn't want to admit it was about her hat so she changed the subject. "Did you go to your poker game last night?"

"No. They cancelled it. I had to do something." Kathy was scowling. "Josephine dragged me to bingo. You know I hate it. She bribed me with buying dinner."

"What was the bingo like?"

"Awful. Had to sit with some ladies from Carmel. Two stiffs and a dull. Honestly, I never thought I'd find anyone more boring than I am, but these three won the prize. Pretty big contrast to you, Adrian and Sophie." Kathy laughed, "and as different as night and day to Rita! I told you about the big argument we had before she died. About the potheads she entertained at the Monday Club?" Vi nodded. "Gawd—if those ladies had heard that discussion . . ." Kathy's voice trailed off.

"Kathy, how long are you going to live your life like that?"

"Like what?"

"Wondering what the neighbors, what those ladies, will think about you. I thought you were over that."

"Well, they've already read *The Herald* about us being connected with the body in the locker, and with the police following us, who knows when they'll read about us again." Kathy sat down on her beige couch. Vi stood towering over her, a position she enjoyed having, being the short one.

"You're making all this up, you know. I don't think anyone's following us." Vi eased herself into the brown leather chair that had been Jerry's. "Have you got anything to eat? My cooking lately is confined to making popcorn in the microwave."

"Sure. I know the only thing you stir up in the kitchen is trouble!" Kathy was beaming now. She liked having someone to fuss over. Preparing food gave her purpose, distracted her for a moment.

Vi moved to the oilcloth-covered table while Kathy stuck her head in the refrigerator to search for snacks.

"What is it you think you could do to stop their talking about you?" Vi knew she was beating the subject to death—or beating it with a dead stick, as Kathy would say—but she couldn't stop.

"I don't want people whispering behind my back."

"They can and will say whatever they want."

"Not if," she hesitated, "I don't give them anything to talk about . . . ."

Vi knew Kathy could tell how lame this sounded.

"OK. Finish it. There's only one way to do that."

"Be perfect. Or dead." Kathy couldn't meet Vi's eyes. Kept her head low.

"Case rests," Superior Court Judge Violet Farnsworth pronounced, throwing her head back and laughing loudly. "You know, I used to do the same thing." Her laughter rose up in the morning air. She roared so long, finally the intimidated Kathy could no longer resist and the two women clutched each other and laughed uncontrollably as only very old friends can laugh. They whooped and hollered and cried out at the silliness of their whole wasted lives lived for "neighbors." Neighbors who didn't even care.

At last, exhaustion created a moment of silence. The seagulls and children on the beach made the only sounds drifting into the room.

Kathy turned back to the counter and put a tuna sandwich in front of Vi. "I don't know where I got that crazy idea. About being perfect. I've had it since childhood."

"Being perfect never helped with Jerry," Vi said.

"Jerry. Biggest damn mistake I ever made." Kathy's face began to flush. She got up and poured herself a glass of wine, not offering any to Vi.

"Being cynical is not the way to deal with the underlying problem." Vi hesitated, cleared her throat. "I know Jerry's an S.O.B. But I don't know why you let him destroy you, your initiative, your . . . sexuality. I think it goes deeper than his leaving you for Susan. It usually takes two to ruin a marriage."

Kathy took a big gulp of chablis. Gazed out the window in silence. The fog was drifting away, leaving the glow of the sunset reflected on the water. Then, "I never thought I'd tell even you." She hesitated. "I knew Jerry played around. I spent years grinning and bearing it, covering up for him. One night I skipped my weekly bingo game and followed him—and there he was picking up some blond bitch. Drove to a motel. I decided 'two can play at this game'." Seeing Vi's shocked expression, her voice cracked as she continued.

"I was active in Little Theater. He surprised me by coming to the theater to pick me up after rehearsal one night. I had stayed late to talk with Tom. Jerry walked in just as Tom put his arms around me, backed me up to the wall and kissed me. I kissed him back. Jerry had me. He yelled and shook his fist, accusing me of having an affair behind his back. Can you imagine the gall? After all the catting around he did?"

"Told you he was an S.O.B.! But what's the big deal? It was just a kiss, wasn't it?"

Kathy's expression changed. A shade spread over her eyes—a glaze. Breaking a long silence, she spoke softly. "It doesn't matter what it was. Jerry was looking for an excuse to split, and he threatened to tell the kids that my 'affair' was why he was leaving me. I betrayed my family."

✳ ✳ ✳

Vi called Kathy later in the afternoon. "I've been thinking about what you said this morning. What if people knew we were all downright disgraceful?"

"I dunno."

"Don't be so underwhelmed by the idea. They'd be excited! In this sleepy little town, something to talk about would be a thrill! Come on, Kathy, rescue the neighbors from boredom. Hannah could have a new topic to gab about."

"It would be kinda fun." Kathy said. "After all, these are our declining years— we can decline to do things we don't want to do; but maybe we can replace them with something else?"

"Right! Let's be outrageous. Defy those stereotypes!"

Another pause. "I don't know. . . ." Vi heard Kathy slipping backwards. "In many ways we *are* stereotypical. Some things about growing old are inevitable. Take for instance —"

Vi interrupted. "Remember that book we liked, *Growing Old Disgracefully* by those old English women who called themselves the Hen Coop?"

"Yeah, I loved it."

"Tomorrow we'll buy outrageous clothes. Maybe color our hair, Dress too young for our ages. Be the emancipated oldsters. The Chicks in the Hen Coop!" Vi was pleased with the idea.

"Who would I look like?"

"Who was your favorite star?"

"Katherine Hepburn."

"There you are. Tomorrow you turn into Kate Hepburn."

"What about Adrian? Sophie?"

"I'll call them. Tell them we'll pick them up."

"Who will you be, Vi?"

"Not sure. I'll think about it and tell you tomorrow."

"I know."

"Don't sound so smug. Just tell me. Who?"

"Scarlet O'Hara!"

"Not bad, Kathy. Not bad at all. Or maybe Tandelejo. Rita loved Tandelejo."

Laughter cheered them again.

(21)

HOROSCOPE: A change of lifestyle may seem attractive right now, but it's important that you take every precaution that you're going in the right direction.

KATHY CAME OVER TO VI'S AND THE TWO OF THEM GOT IN THE YELLOW Subaru. Vi was excited about the changes. She could see by the way Kathy kept jiggling her leg that she was excited, too—or maybe a little nervous. *Treat her very carefully*, she told herself. *Be cool. Don't give her any excuse to back out.* They needed to get with the program of having money. Rita would want that. Besides, what was better than shopping to help you forget the dismembered corpse?

They were on their way to pick up Sophie and go to the mall.

"All right. I'm sure of my decision," Vi announced. "I want to look like Running Wolf."

"Don't be ridiculous, Vi. You want to remake yourself in the image of an almost six-foot-tall drug dealer?" The voice told Vi it wasn't a serious criticism. Just Kathy having fun at her expense. Yeah, she had to laugh at herself.

"I know it's ridiculous, Kathy, but I really don't care. Maybe ridiculous is good. And anyway, I'm not putting my life on hold any longer."

"Maybe you're rushing things," Kathy said.

"No I'm not. I sometimes feel like most of my life has been spent in the waiting room. No more waiting! Wait until you're grown is what my folks were always telling me. When I was sixteen, I'd tell myself just wait until someone loves you and you get married. Later I was waiting for Rose to grow up," Vi said.

"I waited until we got enough money for a new house, and then Jerry ran off and spent it on the bimbo," Kathy said.

"We can't wait. Time isn't something you can save. Rita taught us that," Vi said. "I'm never waiting again for some magical moment when life will start."

Sophie waved goodbye to Jack as the car pulled out of her driveway. She had no idea what she was in for today.

"Sophie, this is quite a day," Kathy said. "We're going to get a whole new image. We've decided to become new women."

Sophie said, "Wow! How are we going to do that?"

"It starts with the clothes. I think I'm ready to give up looking like a prim librarian."

"Kathy! I hope you aren't referring to Nikki," Vi interrupted.

"Hardly. I meant when I was keeper of the books in Modesto. I'm giving up skirts because I hate to wear pantyhose. No truly advanced civilization would include pantyhose. It's time to be comfortable. Classy comfortable."

"That sounds good," Sophie replied.

"Tried to get Adrian to go with us, but I don't know where she is. Kept getting the damn answering machine and left three messages," Vi said.

"Seems strange. She's sure quiet about what's going on in her life," Kathy added.

"Oh, I'm so sorry I didn't tell you," Sophie said. "Poor Adrian. Her mother died. She didn't want to talk about it. Told me the funeral was private. It was yesterday."

Vi gripped the steering wheel in shock. "I can't believe she didn't let us know. I liked her mom the night we had the pot party. I felt quite close to her. Didn't Adrian give you any details, Sophie?"

"She said there was a big argument at dinner last Sunday. Peter and Adrian really got into it. She accused Peter of some terrible things. He yelled back some secrets about her he had promised never to tell. They saw her mother gasping, clutching her chest. She died from a massive heart attack. Adrian feels guilty."

"What does she feel guilty about?"

"I have no idea," Sophie said.

Silence. "Let's stop at Starbucks for coffee before going to Macy's," Vi said. She needed some time to regroup her thoughts.

"What are you going to buy, Kathy? Who do you want to be?" Vi was back on track after the second latte.

Kathy hesitated. "Do I have to *be* someone else? Can't I just be more comfortable?"

"Yesterday you said you wanted to be Kate Hepburn—saucy, outspoken, bright, adventurous—Kate, who doesn't take guff off of anybody."

"You're going to have to change a good bit, aren't you?" Sophie's voice was polite, tactful.

Kathy seemed inspired now. "Long forest green pants, an expensive silk shirt. Maybe a sea-foam green turtleneck. Or a cashmere sweater set—pullover with a classy scarf and the cardigan tied by the sleeves around my shoulders."

"So Sophie, who do you want to be? You're walking towards me and I'm looking at you coming down the street. What do you want me to say about you?"

"Jack always said I could dress more sexy." Sophie was looking down at her lap. She took another sip of coffee. "I could take advantage of what I've got that doesn't show, but I don't know what I could wear to do that."

"How are things between you and Jack now?" Kathy asked.

"It could be better, but we're getting along okay—as long as we don't talk about marijuana."

"Maybe it would perk him up if you wore a shorter skirt," Kathy said.

"Show off a little bust," Vi said, "some cleavage."

"I'd be too self-conscious to wear a low-cut blouse."

"Wear it around the house for a while till you get up the nerve to wear it outside." Vi was feeling enthusiastic. She thought here was a place to exert some leadership.

The three of them rushed up to the designer department at Macy's. "Let's gather some clothes and get a large dressing room," Vi shouted over her shoulder. "Try a bunch of things."

"I'd rather get my own dressing room," Sophie said firmly.

"Okay, but model for us. Let's be really honest with each other," Vi said, "and say how we look in them. We've no time left for being polite. If someone looks like an old scarecrow you have to tell them."

"Well I don't think we have to be rude," Sophie said.

"Girls, here's how it is. My success will no longer be measured by the size of my dress," Vi continued. "We were raised to be too damned good. It was the task of all the 30s mothers to raise good little girls. We were so thoughtful, so polite, we never learned how to shout out a plain old unvarnished 'No'. Too bad. You have to learn how to say no before you can really say yes.... Let's say yes to life. Let's grab it and hug it like Rita did. Today I want you to buy everything—*everything* you want." Kathy and Sophie seemed to be listening.

"I remember when I was young I swore I'd never look like the old ladies I saw. Some of them were so nearsighted they'd slap on make-up that made them look like clowns," Sophie said. "And they dressed like bag ladies," Vi added.

"Yeah, but don't overstate the new you, Vi. I can see you trying colors that would look like a hot air balloon coming down in Albuquerque. It's okay to look eccentric, but not totally crazy," Kathy laughed. "Let's tell each other if we start to look too weird," she added.

"We've got to protect each other," Vi said.

"What are you going to look for, Vi?" Sophie asked.

"Something like Running Wolf wears, but I don't know how it would look on a five foot, one inch frame."

Sophie said, "I saw a woman yesterday who was all in silver. A luxurious leisure-type thing. Even silver tennis shoes."

"Sounds good," Vi said. "Silver's kinda hot."

"But will we have the nerve to wear these things?" Sophie asked.

"Don't worry! Just put your shoulders back, your head up high, and act eccentric. Like the Pebble Beach crowd," Kathy answered.

"What's the difference between crazy and eccentric?"

"A whole lot of money!"

"Gather up some stuff and meet in the dressing rooms," Vi dictated, taking the leadership role again. "And no fair wasting time searching for something to make you look thin!"

They dashed in and out of dressing rooms like schoolgirls. Among other things, Vi insisted on a flowing caftan with a gold moon and silver stars, even though Kathy and Sophie said she was too short for it. Sophie found a silver mylar jumpsuit. Kathy came out carrying a smashing outfit in contrasting shades of green and a bright green, blue and purple jacket. Suddenly Kathy gasped and grabbed Vi's arm. "Vi, look at that man over there!"

"So what? He's probably buying a nightgown for his wife and is embarrassed to be in the ladies' section."

"No! I'm sure I've seen him before. He's one of the guys who's been following me!"

"Nonsense! Get a grip." Vi wasn't as confident as she tried to sound. She dropped her keys. Bent to pick them up. Whispered, "Go back to the dressing rooms."

Now there was no question of privacy. They all huddled in the same dressing room. No one spoke. Memories of the body returned.

"We've got to figure something out," Vi finally whispered, breaking the spell.

"Call the police." Kathy could barely speak. Her eyes were riveted on the door as if the terrible stranger might grab it at any moment and come in.

"I hate to do that because they're already suspicious, and if the —"

Vi's sentence stopped abruptly at the sound. Someone was knocking on the door.

"Oh Lord!" Sophie held her hand over her chest. "He's here."

"Ladies, can I come in?" the modulated voice of the saleslady. "Are you all right? You've been in there so long."

"We'll be out in a minute," Vi replied.

They were embarrassed as they filed out. Didn't want to share their fears. Vi was relieved the stranger was nowhere in sight.

They made it to the car, but just as Vi started to pull out, Kathy started shouting. "There he is again! Just outside the parking lot. He's talking on his cell phone. Floor it, Vi! Move!"

Kathy, still nervous, picked up the phone to call Rita as soon as she got home. It wasn't until she heard the message, "Sorry, the number you've dialed has been disconnected," that she remembered. "My God! Rita's dead. How could I forget?" There were so many things she wanted to tell her, thank her for.

Rita once told her that after her husband died she wrote him a letter telling him things she'd never told him when he was alive. Kathy stood transfixed, looking out the window. Finally, she sat at the old oak desk and began to write.

Dear Rita:

You'll never guess what I did today! And it's all thanks to you that I had the nerve—and the money. You started it with that red muu-muu you got me for Christmas last year, plus all your lectures and pep talks.

Kathy paused, remembering the shopping trip with Rita when she bought a blouse for $250 at Saks, and a whole Jones of New York wardrobe, totaling three thousand. She decided to describe the things she'd bought at Macy's.

. . . Anyway, it looks like I'm entering a new phase. I bought a lot of soft cashmere. Don't you think the materials in the clothes you choose are interwoven with the ages and stages of your life? Remember the starched cotton our mothers made us wear when we were kids? That was fine, as long as she did the ironing. And she always made me wear blue to go with my eyes, or plaid that wouldn't show the dirt.

When I moved into my taffeta phase it was pink—the blush of youth. Remember that eighth grade party dress? The first time Dick kissed me? Swirling fabric that would magically change patterns before your eyes.

I remember longing for velvet. You did, too, because I remember that dress you bought when the song Blue Velvet was popular. And remember my green formal?

Kathy put down the pen and walked to the window, opening it for fresh air. She remembered that first formal she bought. Her mother had a fit when she saw it. Rita loved it. "Maybe that's why I picked out the green outfit today. Going back to rebellion," she muttered as she returned to the desk.

I remember the cotton dress I bought in college which was squiggled with different shades of green (again?) and black. It had ruffles and bows, yet! Jerry took one look and asked me what I'd done with the potatoes.

Then you helped me ease into the chiffon era—fluffy, feminine—a deep aqua cocktail dress with tight belt (remember, I had a waist then!). That dress and I flounced in gay abandon. Maybe someday I'll get back in that mood, right Rita?

Again Kathy paused, then continued.

You often told me you'd buy me clothes as long as you picked them out, but I refused. Now you've made it possible and I can't thank you . . .

She felt the tears coming. Without signing the letter, without re-reading what she had written, she threw it into the fireplace.

Then, remembering the afternoon stalker, she closed the windows, pulled the drapes, and double-checked the alarms. She went to bed, but did not sleep.

(2 2)

HOROSCOPE: Tonight is auspicious for you. You will meet a stranger. Don't discount him. He has valuable information and knows where all the bodies are buried.

SOPHIE WAS SITTING AT HER BLUE AND WHITE KITCHEN TABLE, SERIOUSLY thinking about jam. When she was really depressed she made jellies and jams. Stacking up the clean jars and filling them with steaming fruit restored her sense of control. Jack's temper tantrums seemed to be over. He had left for the golf course.

She needed order right now. Needed to be queen of the tiny kitchen world of berries and Ball jars. The great thing about spending a day at canning was when the day was over, you could point to a stack of jars full of fruit and paraffin and know you had actually done something.

She remembered Rita's recipe box. Maybe she could find a good stew for tonight instead. Here's a different one—Near East Stew, with cut up dried fruit, curry and a little Mary-jane, with shredded spinach added at the end. Well, it's healthy, but a bit strange for the homeless. Better stay with the traditional one.

Sophie worried—what was happening with Jack? He was angry about the bongo brownies and now he's mad about the body. Good heavens, we didn't kill him.

All the while she was railing against Jack, she was cutting carrots. What am I supposed to do about it? I just wanted a freezer for all this food. I didn't know there would be a body in it. It made me faint. What I need is some sympathy.

She attacked the beef. Gave it a vicious chop. *I'm glad I didn't tell Jack someone's following us.*

She turned to the stove to heat the frying pan and oil. The wonderful smell of garlic hitting the olive oil distracted her. The cooking was working its magic. She felt better as she poured the small pieces of chopped up meat into the oil. She forgot about her troubles with Jack and ruled supreme over her kitchen, humming as she peeled the potatoes. She grabbed her special herb in the blue and white cannister and sprinkled it liberally over the vegetables to be added when the meat was browned. There! That will do it.

Tonight should be fun. Kathy and Vi were coming to help for the first time. They all were going to feed the homeless men. Those men were so gentle and grateful, you couldn't help but have a good time.

Sophie didn't like to ask Adrian for a ride, but she needed to get the stew down to the homeless, and she didn't know where Jack was.

Adrian helped her carry the heavy kettle to the soup van. "Don't let Jack get you down," she said, blowing Sophie a kiss as she left.

Sophie had to be driven everywhere. *I should get a license. So I failed years ago when Daddy tried to teach me. I'm not a moron. After all, I was a teacher. Dad lost patience and I lost the will to drive. Could walk everywhere in Moundsville. People always tell me how efficient I am, how marvelous at organizing and executing plans. But I feel inadequate simply because everyone in California drives.*

"I'll think about it tomorrow," she said aloud as she was setting up the tables. I've got to feed these hungry people. *I bet Kathy and Vi will love helping the men,* she thought as she lit the fire under the stew. The few shabby women who come probably used to cook good meals themselves when they had a home. It's a disgrace. *Our government should be ashamed of the poverty in America. I wish I could do something about that.*

I wish the Monday Club business weren't snowballing, but I'm grateful that we can do so much good with the money.

What a rank smell! Vi felt sick. She was at the bait station under the Monterey pier. The wet fog, the smell of dead fish dampened her already soggy spirits. Was it getting dark or was it just heavier fog coming in? She wasn't sure. Dampness ruined her hair, and her shoes were already wet. Vi wanted to be anywhere but here. She'd always said she would do anything for Sophie and Kathy. This was definitely the test of that promise.

Sophie had pleaded and finally prevailed. Vi and Kathy were to help with the Project Open Hand soup van, serving the homeless. Tonight they had stew.

Vi didn't like the look of the large, looming black man leaning on the barnacle-encrusted post. Didn't want to pass out stew to the homeless. What would it be like not to have a home? She remembered how afraid she was that Rose and that social worker would move her out of hers.

She moved over to the soup van. Sophie was covering card tables with newspaper and unpacking the plastic chairs. Vi knew she should help, but felt shy, paralyzed. She was afraid they would see it in her face. The pity. She had to keep that secret from showing. Everyone hated pity.

"Get the pot on the stove and start serving, Vi." Sophie was still setting up tables. Kathy was organizing the line. She looked like Vi felt. Vi was a little less awkward now that she had a big pot to hide behind and a job to do.

"I never have liked to be in just one place. I get restless." A fat old man spoke over his shoulder to an earnest middle-aged guy. "Need to do a job or two and then move on down the road."

Here goes nothing, Vi said to herself. "Would you like some stew?"

"Sure," the middle-aged guy answered. It startled Vi. He had no teeth. "Hi, I'm The Mayor. This lady is Junkyard Doll. She lives here. Most nights we dine on other people's scraps. We look for cans, bottles, anything we can cash in. Stew smells good."

"How do you come to be here, Mr. Mayor?" Oh God, Vi bit her tongue. Maybe I'm not supposed to ask him that.

"Couple years ago I left a bar drunk, crashed my Harley through a storefront, knocked out most of my teeth. At first it was hard losing my home." He shrugged as if to say *who knows why.*

"You get used to things. Now I don't mind much. Just would be nice to be able to chew on a steak."

Later, Vi asked Kathy to take over the serving. She decided to sit down at the newspaper-covered table and have some stew with The Mayor. She liked him. His curly hair and toothless grin were growing on her.

"Tell me something about your life," she said. She could feel Kathy glaring at her. *Guess she thinks I shouldn't be so direct. Well, it's not polite, but I really don't know any other way to talk to him.*

"Worst part of being homeless is like you don't have a face. People don't look at ya. It's a long night of closed doors. It's about waiting. Waiting for morning. Waiting for Sophie to show up with the soup. Stew, tonight."

Vi poured him a steaming mug of coffee from the aluminum pot and one for herself. It was strong. It felt good to wrap her fingers around the comforting warmth of the cup. It shut out a little of this awful cold she felt.

"What I usually need most day-to-day is a place to wash up. They won't let us in gas stations anymore."

He looked at her, embarrassed. "I know I need a bath."

Vi saw a short Puerto Rican coming toward her. She was frightened. His eyes looked awful.

"Hey man, Zedello's selling the peso to Clinton. Raul Salinas sells drugs to the CIA. They feed 'em to black boys in the U S of A. U S goes to sleep with NAFTA. Wakes up with an unscratchable itch between her legs. The U S needs a cold shower."

The Mayor gestured toward the Puerto Rican.

"Don't listen to him. He's pretty much a crackhead."

"I know your kind, lady." The Puerto Rican grabbed at Kathy's hand. She jumped back. "I see you on the street every day. You don't notice us in doorways, in alleys, at the top of church steps under cardboard and rag-tag blankets. Or, if we're lucky, in plastic sacks."

Kathy moved to the space in back of Vi's chair.

"Your dogs ate more today, are curled up at the foot of your beds, can belch, fart, be taken to hospitals."

"Hey, Domi," The Mayor interrupted, "leave these good ladies alone. Don't give them no shit. They supply the Monday Club. They feed your face. These are Sophie's people. Ease up."

"Sorry, folks, I didn't know. I'm strung out, you know. Got any stuff on you now?"

"No," Kathy said stiffly, her disapproval and fear probably apparent to Domi too, Vi thought.

"That's a good thing you're doin'. My kid had leukemia. I woulda done anything for pot before he died."

Domi greeted the next guy carrying two bowls of stew. He was a pimply-faced, freckled nineteen year old, with short cropped bleached blonde hair and spanking new black and white sneakers. Vi couldn't help but wonder where he got the money to bleach his hair and where he got the sneakers.

"I'm trying to put my life back in order," he explained to Vi as he sat down. She passed him the bread. Vi wondered when she saw the tic in his neck and the wandering eyes if it were still possible.

"I'm going to the Academy of Art College," he said. His future looked more likely to be jail. "Hey, you ever see the Grateful Dead in concert?" he asked her.

Domi spoke again. "You know about the bay? They're dumping junk in the bay. Can't fish the steelhead trout anymore. I've seen the otters washed up on the beach. Fuzz cleans it up fast. Wouldn't want to offend the tourists by the sight of death.

"Look into it, lady. They're killing my bay. The fish and the seals are all dying. We'll be next. Sophie, you gotta do something."

He walked over to the stew pot and grabbed her. "Sophie, do something."

Vi rushed around the table and tried to wrap her arms around Sophie. "That guy's just a brain-sprung junky."

"Domi *is* a little brain-sprung, but about the bay? He's got it one hundred percent right. I know." The Mayor was nodding and winking.

Vi could tell it would be a long evening. How does Sophie do this night after night, she thought. She felt good about providing the money, but it was Sophie who supplied the love. Not just here. She spread it all through the Peninsula.

"More stew?" The Mayor pointed at the pot.

"Why not?" Vi's ladle scraped the bottom of the pot. But it was all gone.

(23)

I NEED TO GET ALL THIS CRAZINESS DOWN, **Vi** **THOUGHT TO HERSELF,** **OPENING** her journal. A late summer afternoon, Vi was relaxing on her porch swing. *It's all so amazing, if I don't write it down I'll never believe it all happened. Let's see; I'll start with the police questioning us about the body, then the pot deliveries. I know I want to describe Running Wolf—and especially Sophie. Sophie's a miracle.* She picked up her pen and wrote.

Sophie's taken over the town. She's feeding every bum that hangs out by the wharf.

She got the sewing circle to make quilts for infants with AIDS out of scraps of materials, and they also make scarves for the homeless.

She's organized the Suppers for Seniors ladies auxiliary to deliver all those bongo brownies and Maryjane tea to the shut-ins who can't get to the Monday Club parties.

She had the high school art classes make Valentines for the Veterans.

Her crowning achievement has to be organizing the annual St. Sebastian's rummage sale. I remember some of the nightmare fights before Sophie came. That time when Betty accidentally sold the same headboard twice, and Miriam wasn't speaking to Nellie because she sold her grandmother's hand-crocheted quilt for three dollars; and Martha, in a huff, took her Sara Coventry jewelry set home with her when she saw the price tag was only fifty cents!

The way the rummage sale usually went—they ended up after a week's work with a few hundred dollars, exhaustion and half of the rummage committee not speaking to the other half.

But all that was before Sophie. Sophie has the most uncanny optimism and way of appreciating everyone, even the irritating Hannah. Before long, she gets the ruffled feathers smoothed down and the sale's a wild success. The estate sales run more smoothly because of her. Of course it helps that she has plenty of money from the pot to add a few really good new items, but still the lady really has a knack for organizing almost anything. What will she do next?

As she put her journal down on the swing, she noticed the lights coming on across the street in the Jeffreys' home. *I'm tired*, she thought, and she closed her eyes.

Vi woke to the terrible smell. A smell that brought it all back!

She saw the duct tape again, the white putrified arm, and the head. The head without a face!

Panicked, she jumped forward, banged her leg against the metal table, staggered around it. Her leg hurt as she limped through the living room. Her neck was stiff from the nap.

When she got to the kitchen, she saw it. The stinking mess of a roast covered with burned India spices, scorched garlic, all drying up on the bottom of the pot. And that smell; that awful, evocative smell!

For a moment she thought she would heave, but she righted herself and regained control long enough to dump it all into the sink and turn on the garbage disposal. She ran water in the pot and left it to soak.

Then she opened the kitchen window, sprayed some sickening Pine Sol aerosol and felt nauseous again.

Thank God Rose isn't here to see this mess, she thought. She'd have me put away for sure!

She tried to go back to her journal writing on the porch, but it was too dark to see now and her mood was spoiled. Everything was spoiled. She went back into the living room and turned on the overhead light.

Kathy was due any minute for dinner, but she knew she had to get out of the house.

When Kathy appeared at the door, Vi opened it, already wearing her purple coat-sweater and carrying her black patent purse over her arm. "We're going to eat at Fandango's Restaurant."

"But the curried roast? You were so excited about that new curry recipe of Rita's." Kathy looked confused.

Vi went quickly, graphically, over her terrible flashback and concluded, "I just have to get out of here. I hope I can eat."

"Now that you've shared more than I wanted to know, I'm not too sure I can swallow either," Kathy said.

"Maybe we should go to Tillie Gort's and have vegetarian," Vi said, closing and locking the door.

Out of the corner of her eye, Vi thought she saw something move in the mallow bush by the driveway. Probably just an animal, she reassured herself, but felt that terrible tightness between her shoulder blades. Her body was not convinced.

Kathy walked faster than usual, alternating looking down at the pathway to make sure she didn't trip and glancing over her shoulder to make sure no one was following her. The other night at dinner she detected an unusual nervousness about Vi. She had asked her:

"What's the matter, Vi? You're acting strange. Burning a roast isn't all that bad."

"Nothing's wrong. Absolutely nothing." Vi had smiled but Kathy could tell it was forced. Didn't look like the Boss Lady of the Monterey Mafia. But as the evening wore on, Vi got back in the groove of scoffing at every incident Kathy told her about.

"I kid you not, Vi. Yesterday the same guy was staring at me in the grocery store—the one who was in line behind me at the bookstore counter. I've seen him at least six times in the last week."

"Kathy, you are so paranoid!" Vi sounded more normal. "Ever since we found the body you've been seeing ghosts."

"They are not ghosts! These guys—there's more than one, you know—are real live flesh-and-blood hoodlums determined to watch my every move!"

"Why would they want to, Kathy?"

"Damned if I know. But I don't see why you never believe me."

✲ ✲ ✲

Now, walking along the shoreline, she reflected on Vi's question. Why indeed? But she knew it wasn't her imagination. The fact remained she felt like she was living in a fishbowl. She remembered the days—it wasn't that long ago—when she could walk to town and everyone she saw would smile and say hello. Today they all looked menacing.

As she approached her porch, she looked over at Vi's house to see if she was home. No. Subaru gone.

But why was that black car parked across the street? Two men —didn't look familiar. They seemed intent on watching Vi's house.

"They're not watching me," Kathy murmured to herself as she unlocked her door. *I don't think so, anyway,* she thought as she peeked out the drawn shade.

(24)

HOROSCOPE: Pay attention to your dreams and your nightmares. They may lead you out of the woods.

AFTER HOURS OF SLEEPLESSNESS, VI FELL OFF THE EDGE OF CONSCIOUSNESS. Disappeared into blackness.

Next she was floating in freezing water, terrible bulbous forms bobbing up and down around her. They were white in the moonlight and semi-darkness. She was up to her neck in icy liquid. One of the blobs came toward her. It was an arm with a distorted white hand.

She sat up suddenly in bed. What was that sound? Was there someone in the house? Or had her own scream awakened her?

Then she remembered the duct tape, the body in the freezer. And then, the carcass coming in for a close-up, she had a vision of something she'd forgotten. That decaying piece of arm in the freezer had something on it—a tattoo. Something like a globe with wings attached. And a number. Number 43.

She turned on her bedside lamp, shuffled into the kitchen, yanked open the catch-all drawer and found a pen and pad. Standing in her bare feet she began to sketch what she could remember of the vision.

Late Bloomers, objecting to this change of routine, rubbed against her legs and yowled, complaining loudly. Finally Vi finished; opened the fridge and poured a midnight snack for each of them. Maybe it would steady their nerves.

✸ ✸ ✸

The next morning Vi's eyes searched her yard for some clue: a broken branch, a half-erased footprint in the flowerbed. What haunted her was the uneasy vision of a figure who had stood under the elm in the moonlight last night, staring in her bedroom window after her dream. She half-hoped, half-dreaded there was some evidence to support her night terrors. But she saw only the clarksia dry seedpods. The cosmos revealed nothing except that they were past their prime, the pinks and magentas turning to seed.

She scowled at the stray starlets struggling to bloom too late. Not everything has a chance, she reflected. All would be gone with the first heavy rain.

Maybe she was wrong. Kathy thought someone was following her most of the time now. Vi was afraid it was true. Don't tell her about last night's vision.

Vi sighed. Took one more look at the yard just to make sure. Nothing. Got in the Subaru and headed for the library.

Vi and Nikki were lunching in Nikki's office. "Try harder, Vi. Can't you remember anything else? Nikki asked between bites of her bologna sandwich.

"No. I barely remember the dream, and I've told you all I can." Vi had asked Nikki to research the tattoo.

"Well, no luck. I know you think our Spiders group, Sisters in the Web, can find anything on a computer, but your description's too vague. They're really trying, Vi, but they need more details. It would take weeks to go through all the images of the world, some wings, something over the top and a 43 underneath."

"Maybe I could draw the wings better." Vi wanted to be helpful. She saw Nikki was doubtful. "Don't mention what we're doing to Kathy and Sophie. They're scared enough already. Kathy's mortified because that stupid Sgt. Wyatt Burley insists on having a detective follow us. He's going around town interrogating people, acting like we're the ones who murdered the poor man."

"I'm not surprised." Nikki handed Vi a hard-boiled egg. "That's predictable with police in a small town."

"And what does that flat-footed cretin, Lt. Falcon from Monterey, use for a brain? Do we look like little old ladies who chop people up in pieces?" Vi was immediately sorry she'd brought the subject up. Even now she could see the starting-to-rot dismembered parts laid out in the freezer. She felt dizzy with nausea. "What does he take us for, psychos?"

Nikki shrugged her shoulders, her mouth too full of boiled egg to reply.

"And why would we be dumb enough to stuff the body in a freezer, not pay the rent so the electricity would be cut off, then buy back our own space so we could find the rotting remains?"

"Falcon and Burley make Barney Fife look good. Officer Connery doesn't suspect you. It's my guess the others think you know something you're not telling."

"They're wrong."

"Well, you're not telling them about your little cottage pot business, are you, and maybe you do know something that's important. Think."

"I have. I don't know anything else," Vi answered quietly.

"Go over everything that's happened in the last couple of days."

"Are you nuts? Don't take that moron Sgt. Burley's side." Vi tried to joke but was feeling offended. Was Nikki suspicious of her, too?

"I know you didn't have anything to do with the murder." Nikki must have read the hurt on Vi's face as she tried to sound reassuring. *I should never try to play poker*, Vi told herself.

"I know you don't think you know anything," Nikki continued, "but is it possible someone meant for you to find it?"

"No. Why? What are you talking about?"

"I'm probably wrong. It just seems like too big a coincidence."

"You think someone wanted to get us in trouble?"

"Is that possible?"

"Nobody could set this up. No one knew we were going to buy that particular locker's contents."

"The way the body was chopped up is the way those Mafia hit men or Columbian drug lords do ritual killings that serve as a warning. Maybe they wanted publicity. I don't mean they wanted to get caught, but just wanted other guys to read about it in the paper so they'd mend their ways."

"Oh, brother, Nikki, you have been reading too many of those cheap mysteries you peddle in this place!"

"I know." Nikki couldn't help but laugh. "It doesn't sound much like Pacific Grove. I'm probably off-base, but who would have thought you would find a body? I still think you may know something you don't even know you know."

Something in Nikki's voice caught Vi's attention and she looked at her face carefully. What was this urgency about? "You're worried about me, aren't you?"

"No." She wasn't very convincing. Wouldn't look at Vi. Now that Vi studied her, she could see that Nikki wasn't quite herself—a little off her game.

"Come on, tell the truth."

"Oh, Vi! Last night I got a phone call."

"Tell me!"

"A terrible voice." Nikki was trying not to cry. "A man. He said, 'I know what you're up to. Drop it now or the old dames die'."

✽ ✽ ✽

The next night, Nikki and Vi worked until after midnight in Nikki's private library office.

"What's that?" Vi asked.

Nikki looked away from the computer screen to meet Vi's frightened gaze. "I didn't hear anything."

"Grating sounds. Like someone's trying to open the front door. The janitor?"

"No, he's already been here. Maybe it's an animal on the roof."

"No; listen. It's someone trying to get in."

Now they both heard it. The scraping sound of someone trying to force the door.

"Get down," Nikki whispered.

Vi felt the fear shooting down her back as they crouched on the floor and heard the door begin to splinter. Then a deep voice, glass shattering.

Nikki motioned for Vi to follow and she painfully crawled after her into the ladies' room. Vi heard footsteps coming through the stacks.

Without turning on the light, Nikki whispered, "Stand on the toilet so they can't see your feet. Keep the door closed."

Vi's legs trembled from the pain and her back screamed for mercy, but she didn't dare make a sound.

From Nikki's office she heard shouts, drawers opening and closing, stacks of books hitting the floor.

Something about the voice Vi heard frightened her. It was familiar. She strained to hear the words.

"Shit! This is taking too long. We can't go through all this computer stuff."

"Erase it."

"Don't know how."

"Try, damn it!"

Vi remembered her cell phone in her purse. Felt the buttons in the dark. Nine-one-one. She whispered "Library . . . Central Avenue . . . break-in . . . emergency . . . hurry!" Her legs trembled while cold perspiration ran down her back. She heard footsteps coming to the door. What if they'd heard her?

"What's in here?" Deep voice. Light went on.

"Naw, it's just the can." The light went out. Now Vi couldn't stand it any more. She crawled down and sat on the toilet.

"Crap!" she heard him yell. "Car stopped outside! Wreck the machine!"

Frantic noises of things toppling, crashing. A door slammed. Silence.

The bathroom light went on. Vi's heart froze.

"Nobody's in here."

She recognized the voice. It was Officer Connery. She rushed out of the stall and collapsed in his arms. "Thank God it's you, Chris!"

The next day Vi went back to the library. "I just can't sleep, Nikki."

"I've been pretty jumpy myself."

"I get up at every noise. Sometimes just a branch rubbing against the house. I thought I saw a shadow of a man in my shower window."

"You should get a sedative."

"Last night I even got up and went through the closet to see if someone was hiding there. That's what I did when I was a kid."

"You need sleep, Vi. Better call Doc Spiritos and get something."

"I keep going over and over all the events of the last three days, searching for a clue."

"Me, too. Was the ransacking of the library some kind of warning? What do they know? What are they looking for?"

"That's what I wonder. But a warning about what?"

"It's got to be about the Web somehow. Oh, that reminds me. I called Running Wolf. She's taken over the computer sleuthing since they wrecked mine. She said a Millie Hartman from Michigan logged on. Thinks the tattoo is a symbol used by the armed forces in WW II. Running Wolf needs to see you right away."

By Friday Nikki's computers were back up. She had contacted the Pentagon and about two o'clock, after no lunch and a frantic run of interchanges, Vi and Nikki exchanged hugs. Sisters in the Web had come through. Bless them. They read e-mail from a woman named Sue Kent of Costa Mesa, a history teacher who belonged to the Costa Mesa Historical Society. "Just heard from some old vets at the Army Air Base in Santa Ana. They can definitely identify the insignia from their Army Air Force unit, 1943."

Nikki worked her magic, and by Saturday a full roster of the graduating class arrived. It was alphabetical, starting with Aaron, Boyd. It didn't really bring them any closer to identifying the corpse, but it did contain a nasty surprise. Peter Pellagrino's name was also on the list.

Vi put in a call to Adrian. Would she know anything about her brother's outfit? Was it just an odd coincidence? Could Adrian shed any light on the mysterious corpse?

"Damnation." Adrian wasn't home. Funny. She didn't even have her answering machine on so Vi could leave a message.

(25)

HOROSCOPE: On the surface it may appear that you have to make concessions to demanding family member. Stand firm. It's not what you say that counts, but what is believed. Lie if you have to.

VI WAS IN A SOUR MOOD. THAT OLD SPY HANNAH HAD CALLED ROSE, AND now they were both marching up the driveway. What a vampire Hannah was. Or maybe a dust witch. She could smell trouble a block away. *How did she know about the trashing of my house?*

Vi didn't want to admit, even to herself, how scared she was when she got home and found that someone had broken in—violated her privacy—messed up her belongings.

As Rose and Hannah got closer, Vi was alarmed. *Oh—oh. I know that look on Rose's face. It's her you-have-been-a-naughty-child look.* Just when did Rose become my mother, anyway? That voice she used was familiar. Maybe it's really my voice, the way Rose heard it ringing in her ears when she was a child. Does she really think this is how you express love? *I must have been a bad mother for Rose to turn out so cold and punitive.* Vi felt a lump in her throat and the old panic. She wanted to avoid these thoughts. Years of denial were cracking.

Funny, when she thought of Rose's childhood it always seemed beautiful. She could see her at the beach thrilled with the picnic basket full of chicken. Clapping her baby hands together, full of such spirit. How could that little sprite, that spirit of life, turn into this soggy Christian she saw now? *I must have cheated Rose out of something.*

Vi could feel the burn in back of her eyes. Knew she must not cry. Not here, not now. She put a hand up and covered her face for a moment, trying to erase the picture of the fat, laughing toddler from her memory.

"Mother, who will clean up this mess?" Rose shouted.

This woman, this Rose before her today, was a threat. A threat to her future. This Rose could get a court order. This grim, tofu-consuming fanatic could enlist the aid of Hannah the witch, get a court order and have Vi put away. Would she? Vi couldn't answer, but an inner voice warned: *Be sharp if you are ever going to be again. Lead her off the trail. Lie as you have never lied before. Cover your butt.*

"Rosie, no need for you to worry." *Smile,* she ordered herself. *Look at ease.* "Hannah shouldn't have bothered you. It's nothing important. Probably some teenagers looking for my stereo or the TV set."

Rose saw that the TV was missing. Thank God Vi hadn't mentioned to Hannah that she had taken it down to Bradley's for repairs yesterday.

"What about these men? These dark men Hannah saw?" Rose was like a dog holding one end of a dishtowel once she sunk her teeth in.

"Oh, Hannah. You can't see at night without your glasses on." Vi tried to laugh and look the old witch right in the eye. "I know you're blind as a bat. How do you know what you saw?"

Hannah was nodding now. Vi pushed her advantage. "They were probably a couple of kids."

Oh—oh, Rose spotted the Subaru. *Be cautious.*

"Mother, I hope you are not driving this car."

"No, I'm just taking care of it for the day, Honey," Vi lied.

"You are already a menace on the road. I forbid you to drive a sports car."

Forbid was not a word Vi took kindly. "Don't get your knickers in a knot, Rosie." She could hear her voice was too loud.

"Crude language doesn't become you, Mother."

Vi made a mental note to park the Subaru at Sophie's.

The unusual mixture of noises—cars pulling up with screeching brakes, babble of voices—jolted Kathy from the couch. She looked at her watch. 9 P.M. Must have dozed off. Television still on.

She got up and peeked out the window. Rose's station wagon was in front of Vi's house, as well as a police car with flashing red lights. "What the hell's going on?" She fumbled for the phone, dialed Vi's number.

"Ms. Farnsworth's residence." Kathy recognized the haughty voice of Vi's self-righteous daughter.

"Where's Violet? Is she okay? What's happened?"

"Who is this?"

"Katherine. I'm coming over." She wasn't going to waste time talking to Rose.

Kathy dashed in the door without knocking. The scene was incredible. Vi's house was never very neat, but this was ridiculous. Chairs overturned, lamps tipped over with shattered bulbs; books, magazines and papers tossed all around. All the drawers of the big desk had been yanked out with contents dumped on the floor.

Chris, looking very official in his police uniform, was taking notes while talking to Hannah, who seemed pleased by the attention.

Vi was sitting stone-faced as if in a trance. Rose was standing over her, shouting, "Well this clinches it. You're going to have to move into a safer environment. Now maybe you won't be so stubborn. We'll make arrangements tomorrow."

"No. We won't." Vi looked up and saw Kathy. They rushed to each other for a Mutt and Jeff hug.

"What happened?" Kathy asked.

"Later," Vi whispered.

Turning back to Rose, Vi took a deep breath and said, "Kathy's here now. I'll be fine. The police are doing their job. You can leave."

Rose glowered at her mother. "It *is* getting late, I suppose. Katherine can spend the night?" Kathy nodded.

"Officer, will you please make sure all the doors are locked when you leave?"

"Yes, Ma'am."

"Hannah, thank you for calling me. I appreciate your watching out for my mother."

Hannah beamed. "Happy to help."

Vi looked at Kathy and rolled her eyes.

"As for you, Mother. I'm sure you'd prefer I not take drastic steps."

Kathy was concerned to see the confusion on Vi's face.

"Your mother is a very capable woman, Rose. You'd be surprised at how well she takes care of herself. I'm with her much more than you are, so I know." Kathy was amazed at her boldness. Vi looked as if she were, too.

Rose tilted her chin up and exhaled "Humpf!" as she stomped out the door.

After Chris and Hannah left, Kathy called Sophie and Adrian to come over for awhile. She thought it would help Vi for them to get together. She left a message on Adrian's machine. Sophie hesitated leaving Jack, but when Kathy explained the circumstances, she agreed.

"Okay, let's pitch in and get this mess cleaned up," Sophie said as soon as she came in.

"Nuts to that," Vi replied, taking the bottle of wine Sophie brought. "I've got a cleaning lady coming in the morning. I don't want to face it now."

They settled uncomfortably in one straightened-up corner.

"Rose wants to put me in a home. Thinks I'm stressed. Her idea of reducing stress would be to sit in a rocker like Whistler's Mother with nothing to do or think about."

"That's my idea of death," Kathy said.

"What she doesn't know is that what stresses me is boredom. I remember when I was always right like Rose. Right starts eroding away in your forties. She's not old enough yet to even realize she could be wrong. Everyone else is wrong. She knows it all. Sometimes I think she just wants my house."

"Why would she?" asked Sophie.

"She always wanted to live near the ocean."

Kathy had waited long enough. "Okay. Details. What the hell happened here tonight?"

"I don't know." Kathy didn't trust that answer. She doubted it was just a coincidence—Vi's break-in so soon after the one at the library.

"I saw someone watching your house the other night, Vi. I'm telling you, somebody's been after us ever since we found that body. Maybe since the Monday Club started."

Sophie looked frightened. "Oh, I hope not!"

Vi was silent. Kathy could tell she wasn't even listening. Finally Vi spoke.

"Maybe Rose is right. Maybe I shouldn't live alone. I have been forgetful lately." She poured wine for each of them. "That business of letting the roast burn. In my next life I'm going to have more memory installed."

"Don't worry." Kathy wanted to cheer Vi up. "It's easier to lie about your age when you can't remember it anyway."

"That sort of thing happens to everyone," Sophie said. "I sometimes go into a room and can't remember what I'm there for."

"Talk about senior moments. I tripped while rushing across Lighthouse Avenue at Forest the other day. Sprawled out like a freefalling parachutist."

Vi said, "I lose my keys at least twice a day. I panic. I check my pockets, the table—every logical place. Then I give up logic. Look in the fridge and the medicine cabinet. I want to cry." She paused. "Then the phone rings and I forget I was even looking for the damned keys. An hour later I reach in my pocket and there they are."

Kathy thought of one that might lighten the mood.

"One day last month I dropped a four-liter jug of wine. It shattered. First thing I noticed was the smell. It made a river down the driveway, just as Sgt. Burley and Chris were driving up in their patrol car. They were coming to take my statement on a complaint I'd phoned in about the Wilsons up the street." They all laughed, imagining the reaction. "Chris was so kind. He said, 'Don't worry, Ms. Doolittle. That could happen to anyone.' He helped me clean up the mess while Burley stood there and smirked."

The phone rang. Vi answered, saying "Yes . . . Yes . . . No . . . Okay."

"That sounded like an interesting conversation," Sophie said.

"Just Rose, checking up on me. No point in having any more discussion with her than necessary." Vi shook her head. "Where were we?"

Sophie chuckled. "Last week I saw Jennifer come out of the restroom at the thrift shop with a toilet seat cover hanging out from the waistband of her slacks. We caught her before she went out on the street."

"Yesterday I put my bra on backwards. The depressing thing is, it fit better that way," Vi said.

Kathy frowned. "I'm losing my stamina. After my walk back from town, up that slight incline that seems like a mountain, I plop in the recliner chair with my feet up and my mind in neutral."

Vi said, "I woke up one night lying on my side. I was drooling on my pillow."

The stories seemed less funny. Vi got up and salvaged a can of nuts from the kitchen floor. They munched and drank.

"One time I was baking an apple pie," Kathy said. "I sat down to read while it was in the oven, telling myself I could go downtown to do my shopping at 2 P.M. when the pie was done. Two o'clock came. I put down my book, got in the car, and off I went—not realizing until I returned to a smokey kitchen that I hadn't taken the pie out."

"Oh come on! You never bake pies," Vi said.

"That happened over thirty years ago. I tossed it in to prove a point. We aren't really so different. Think about it. We just believe the propaganda about getting older."

"I don't feel old. I've been rejuvenated," Sophie said. "We should count our blessings."

"We're lucky. We don't get pimples. We don't have to panic if our period's late," Vi said.

"And you, Vi, certainly don't have to worry about Rose putting you in an old folks home. We'll fight her every inch of the way."

Sophie nodded as she got up. "But now it's time to get home. I told Jack to pick me up at ten and I see he's waiting outside." She looked at Vi with concern. "Will you be okay?" she asked.

"Sure. No problem."

"You have to be careful, Vi," Kathy said. She could tell Vi didn't like her echoing Rose's caution.

"I am careful. What could I have done to prevent this?"

"She has a point, Kathy." Sophie turned as she reached the door. "Be sure to call if you need anything," she said as she waved goodbye.

"I'm sure those guys I saw watching your house were responsible for this," Kathy said. "You don't pay any attention to suspicious things. *Pay attention.*"

"Oh Katherine, get off it! It was probably just kids looking for money. Your paranoia is really getting on my nerves."

"You believed me at Macy's. Why are you acting like I'm making it all up? You were scared, too." Kathy was hurt. She forgot about promising Rose she'd spend the night. She left without saying goodbye.

(26)

HOROSCOPE: You find it hard to see anyone's point of view besides your own. Therefore be wary of trusting your judgment or antagonizing someone you need. You may not feel you require support in a current venture, but you do.

"**AT LEAST THEY DIDN'T HURT THE SUBARU.**" VI SAID IT OUT LOUD IN SPITE OF all her resolution not to talk to herself. She was roaring up Sunset on her way to the discount home supply store. "I'd better call Kathy. Haven't talked to her since she walked off last night." It took all day for the cleaning woman to get the house back into some kind of shape after the ransacking.

She dialed her cell phone. "Hi, top buddy. I really need to apologize. I should have believed you before. You've cried 'wolf' a few times without producing a beast, but I should have trusted you."

"Is that supposed to be an apology?"

Vi could hear the formal tone in Kathy's voice. The apology hadn't worked.

"Yes. Of course."

"Well it's not going to suffice, Vi. Sounds like an excuse."

"I am sorry. Really. If I had listened my house might not have been torn apart."

"Don't just dismiss it like that."

"So what should I say?"

"Say you'll respect my opinions in the future. Say you'll listen to my evidence and believe I see what I see."

"Okay, okay. You know you're my dearest friend. I listen to you more than anyone."

"That's the trouble, Vi. You *don't* listen to anyone."

"Oh, come on now!"

"You're a bully. You just run over people. That's what you do." Kathy's voice cracked.

Vi felt hurt. "I know I do. Forgive me. I get carried away."

"Why do you do that?"

"I wish I knew. Enthusiasm, I guess. I love being in charge." Vi moved the cell phone to her other hand so she could turn onto the freeway.

"Well, you can't ignore others and keep friendships. You better learn to listen."

This stung. She remembered all the times she had asked Fred to listen. She remembered the rage she felt because he didn't.

"Forgive me, Kathy. Give me another chance." Pause. "I love you."

She heard a stifled sob. "What's the matter, Kathy?"

"You forget we're old, Vi. Sometimes people ignore us. I see how they snicker at the police department when I report something. Silly old lady, they think."

"No one should ignore you, Kathy."

"They do, though. I feel invisible. And the kids! I've detached myself from them because I can never seem to do or say the right thing. I feel senile around them. Superfluous. Peripheral." Kathy paused. "It really bugs me when they say, 'You're so cute, Mother.'"

"I know. Rose treats me like an ancient crone. You saw how she treated me last night. What else bothers you?"

"When I'm frightened I want someone to care, to look into it. I'm not a joke."

"Of course not! You were right about our being followed. You're a good detective."

"Really? You think so?" Now Vi heard she had said the right thing.

"Absolutely. You're much more observant than I am. You see plenty."

"Oh, thanks Vi. Glad you appreciate me!"

With a sigh of relief, Vi changed phone ears again. Glanced at the speedometer and slowed down. "Now about those crooks. Remember Hannah described them pretty much like you did. I didn't tell the cops. I figured we're in enough trouble with them already."

"I told you the police are watching us, too."

"You're probably right." Vi wasn't sure, but was too politic to say so now that all was well between them. She pulled off the freeway at the Seaside exit.

"The funny thing is they took my journal. I've looked everywhere. Isn't that the strangest robbery?"

"Now you sound like me. Why would they want your journal?"

"Beats me. I've gone over it in my mind for hours. I can't think of anything in there. Anyway, we need to act normal if we're being followed. We need to stall for time while Nikki looks for the tattooed man on the Internet. Still can't reach Adrian to ask her about Peter being on that list."

"You said act normal. What's normal? I'm too scared to act normal."

"I was thinking we could get Sophie and go play bingo. We can talk there. It looks harmless, like what old ladies do."

"I can't do bingo. Reminds me of Jerry."

"It's time for you to get over that."

"Don't be a bully again, Vi."

"I'm sorry. Of course it's your decision. You never have to go to another bingo game in your life."

"Wow, you mean it? You really are trying to change!" Kathy giggled. "You're probably right, though, Vi. I guess it's time to bury the damned past. I don't even miss him anymore. I want to get beyond bingo."

"Thatta girl!"

"I'll call Sophie. This weekend is the Festa Italia. That's normal. We'll do bingo next week."

Good work, Vi told herself as she pressed off the cell phone and pulled into the Sand City shopping center. Locking the car door, she smiled as she looked down at the blue caftan the others said she was too short to wear. Strolling into the hardware store, she started to sing.

(27)

HOROSCOPE: This is the time for breaking free from unsavory situations. Consider your own safety and warn others. Make known your views, emphasize courage, independence, willingness to make fresh start. Love spark ignites.

KATHY HAD SHOWN VI AND SOPHIE ADRIAN'S STRANGE HOROSCOPE. Concerned, they were wandering around the Custom House Plaza looking for Adrian. Kathy was glad Sophie took time off from the homeless shelter to go to the Italian festival.

"It's our best chance of seeing Adrian. She always comes to the Festa Italia. And at least we're doing something fun while we're looking. We need to get our minds off Vi's house being ransacked and . . ." Kathy hesitated, shuddered ". . . and dead bodies."

Sophie and Vi nodded their heads in silent agreement.

Kathy deliberately changed the subject. "So, Sophie, other than that, how do you like living in the Monterey area?"

"It amazes me. There's some sort of festival going on every week! First the Feast of Lanterns, last week the Greeks, now the Italians—I guess the Butterflies next month?" The band was getting ready to play and the tarantella dancers were practicing on the lawn near the bocce ball courts. "Those Italians sure take that game seriously," Sophie said. "They don't even smile."

"Ah, but they take having fun seriously, too," Vi answered, pointing to the Plaza.

"Let's grab some food and sit for awhile," said Kathy. "Adrian will find us; she knows we'll be eating."

They looked at the assortment of pasta, calamari, sausage, pesto spengies, bruschetta, salads and desserts. Sophie asked, "Is this what it's all about? Eating and music?"

"Oh, no! There's the bocce ball tournament and dancing and drinking and buying stuff you don't need." Vi gobbled down a tiramisu, looked up to see Kathy's surprised face and added, "Life's short. Eat dessert first."

"Actually, there's a lot more meaning behind the Festa Italia." Kathy paused to eat a demure bite of pasta. "It's tied in with the Santa Rosalia blessing of the fishing boats, started by the Sicilians years ago. They had the procession earlier this morning."

"According to Adrian, the Pellagrinos are pretty involved," said Sophie.

"Yeah, it's a major family name, well respected. Santa Rosalia made her home on Mt. Pellagrino near Palermo." Vi looked proud of knowing this tidbit.

"Palermo's a hot bed of Mafia types, isn't it?" Kathy glanced around to make sure no one was listening.

"You shouldn't stereotype places or people, Kathy." Sophie sounded motherly.

"It's known that in the old days the fishermen always had a good supply of tax-free liquor. I read the FBI figured there was a multi-million dollar smuggling operation right here!" Kathy was leaning across the table, whispering loudly.

"You may be right," Vi admitted. "I sure don't trust Adrian's brother, Peter." She cringed saying his name.

"By the way, what does Peter look like?" Sophie had been looking around the crowd for Adrian.

"I've only seen him once—never met him," Kathy said. "Looks a lot like Adrian, I think."

"He's slimey! I can't stand him. Can't tell you why. He's so different from Adrian. A scuzzbag." Vi took a big drink of bottled water.

"See over there? That's Adrian under the tree, talking to two guys. The one facing this way looks like her. Is that Peter?"

Kathy and Vi turned to see. Vi nodded. Adrian was arguing with Peter, waving her arms. He was pointing his finger at her in a threatening way. The second man glanced to one side, showing his profile.

"Look!" Kathy was frightened. "It's Guido!"

Peter and Guido left in a hurry, heading out toward the wharf. Sophie jumped up to comfort Adrian.

"Wait!" Vi grabbed Sophie's arm. "Who's that?"

They watched as Adrian ran toward a woman leaning against the wall of the old Custom House. The woman strode confidently toward Adrian. She was tall, dark brown hair cut in a short bob framing her saucer eyes, dressed in tight Levis and a fringed suede vest over a tailored shirt.

Kathy was amazed to see the stranger passionately embrace Adrian, speaking into her ear, and handing her a kerchief to dry her tears. Adrian and the woman walked arm-in-arm across the Plaza, disappearing into the crowd.

The next day, Sophie called Vi. She sounded terrible. Vi and Kathy went right over.

"Did you get hold of Adrian? Did you talk to her? Did she explain about Peter and Guido? Who was that woman?" Kathy didn't pause between the barrage of questions.

"Oh shut up, Kathy, and give her a chance to tell us." Vi took hold of Sophie's arm, led her to the table and eased the trembling Sophie into a chair.

"I tried to phone her last night, but all I got for hours was the answering machine. After Jack and I went to bed, I couldn't sleep, so about one o'clock I tried to phone her again, and the machine didn't even answer. I called at 9:30 this morning and got a recorded message. The number had been disconnected."

"Did you go over to see if she was there?" Kathy asked.

"No. I didn't have to." Sophie got up, went to the hutch near the door, picked up an envelope. "Jack found this under the doormat and brought it in before he left for golf. Would you read it, Vi?"

Vi took the letter out of the envelope, put on her glasses and began to read aloud.

Dear Sophie:

Please, dear old friend, share this with Vi and Kathy. I am writing it to you because I've known you the longest. You have all been important in my life and I owe you an explanation.

I can't live here any more. I just can't. My family is split apart and I can't bear to watch my Mama and Papa's hard work disintegrate. Papa died from overwork, and Peter and I killed Mama.

"Good Lord! What does she mean?" Kathy interrrupted.

Vi glared at her over her glasses, cleared her throat and continued.

The night she died I made some remarks to Peter about some discrepancies in the books. Several weeks ago, when I was working on the books, I came across a strange receipt. I put it aside to ask Peter about it, but after we found the body, I knew what it was. He'd rented the locker under a false name. I was too scared to tell you or confront him, but he must have realized his mistake. He lashed out and said if I opened my mouth, he would tell Mama what he'd found out about me. We thought Mama was out in the yard. I yelled at him about my suspicions, and he yelled back obscenities, calling me a dyke. Said he had pictures to prove it.

Kathy looked puzzled. "God, Peter could have been the killer!"
"Read on, Vi." Sophie got up to open a window.

Mama heard the whole thing. Just stared at us with no expression, and dropped dead.
I can't live here any longer. Becky's going with me. We love each other.

"Whoa! What? Who?" Kathy said. "No wonder she's avoided us the last six months."
"This answers a lot of questions about Adrian," Sophie said. "Even when I was her roommate in college I never dreamed . . ." Her voice trailed off.
Everyone was quiet. Sophie broke the silence.
"I'll miss her. She's the reason we moved here." Silence. "Adrian was alone so long, even with her family. I'm glad she's found love at last."
Kathy nodded. "Why didn't she tell us? Didn't she trust us?"
"There's only a little more of the letter, Vi. Go ahead and finish it," Sophie said.

I'm sorry for running out on you, on the Monday Club, and all that you're doing, but I have to. Without Mama, and betrayed by my brother, I have to start over. Please, please, all of you be careful. There are things going on that I can't tell you or you'd be in worse danger than you are now. I don't know the details and don't want to. Watch out for Peter. He's after you. His friends could kill me for what I know. He's worse than Guido, and that's saying a lot.
Writing this letter is the most difficult thing I've ever done. Please remember me kindly.
Love, Adrian

Vi folded the letter. The three women looked at each other. "I don't believe we'll hear from Adrian again," Kathy said.
"Now we have to get the goods on Peter," Vi said.

(2 8)

HOROSCOPE: Keep your wits about you. Your lucky day is on the horizon. You could win big.

KATHY STROLLED DOWNTOWN TO THE JAVA HOUSE. SHE DIDN'T OFTEN WALK after dark, but she had been upset ever since they left Sophie's. Images flashed— marijuana plants, body parts in a freezer, Guido leering, Peter's face as he talked to Adrian yesterday, Adrian's fear, and the receipt.

Suddenly she heard footsteps running behind her. *Oh, my God! What if . . .* she thought to herself. Her heart went into double-time; she was sure she would wet her pants as she quickened her pace. *Go to a crowded place. Get in a lighted area. Scream.* She thought of all the things people said to do when stalked.

She turned her head, and just as she was about to dash into the corner restaurant, saw it was only a young teenage boy catching his mini-skirted girlfriend by the arm and passionately embracing her in a way that embarrassed Kathy.

I *am* getting paranoid, she thought to herself. She retraced her steps home, didn't want the coffee anymore. Wanted a sleeping pill to pull a shade down on her thoughts.

She glanced at a Jaguar making a U-turn, headlights off, following her slowly down the side street. With chilling panic she walked faster. Then ran, gasping for breath, into her house and locked the door.

As she pulled the drapes closed, she saw two dark heads watching her. The license plate said 'RitaJag'. The car vanished into the darkness.

✳ ✳ ✳

Kathy was quiet on the way to the bingo game the next day. She decided not to mention seeing the Jag.

Vi was chatting. "I think it was a lucky break you caught Jerry cheating. It got you out of a bad marriage."

"Bingo is a great place to pick up bits of gossip," Sophie said as they pulled into the parking lot. "That's true everywhere, even in West Virginia."

"Yeah, I guess so," Kathy said. She tried to remember why she had enjoyed the bingo games back in the valley before Jerry's escapades came to light. Maybe it was because it gave her the chance to be with other people. Bingo and working with the community theater were her only escapes from him.

Vi screeched into the parking lot. Kathy promised herself to enjoy the afternoon, if only to please Vi.

Settling in their seats with their cards, they listened to the babble of voices around them that quieted only when the elderly caller croaked out the letters and numbers.

"I always get the one I wanted the last game," a well-dressed dowager said.

"You have the opposite of precognition. You've got *post*-cognition," her companion said, pleased with his own sense of humor.

"I just want to win back my admittance fee," the woman with dyed red hair said.

"That's what they say in Vegas, Mabel, just before they go broke."

"Look at her. She acts as if she'd won $200 instead of two dollars!" said Kathy. "Not sure I could endure this every week."

During a coffee break they overheard Penelope Pendergast, the town gossip, talking about her Pebble Beach neighbors. Her Mexican maid heard plenty. "Rosa just loves to pass on things from her friend Theresa. I know it's an excuse to take a break from her work, but it is kind of interesting."

Kathy was bored until she heard an electrifying name—Peter Pellagrino.

"He has four fancy cars and a TV screen that fills an entire wall, and more electronic gadgets than Theresa's ever seen . . ."

And then the bingo resumed, cutting off conversation. Kathy had trouble focusing on the game.

On the way back to Pacific Grove, Kathy was still confused. "Did you hear all that? Peter lives in Pebble Beach," she said. "How can he? Adrian always said their business wasn't doing all that great."

"Especially the fishing fleet," Vi commented, whizzing around the curves of Sunset Drive. "Competition from the Japanese. El Niño fouling up weather patterns a few years ago and expected again. Sea lions crowding the harbor and eating the fish."

"So where's he getting all the money? And why the hell did he rent our storage locker? Something else is definitely going on." Kathy was clutching the arm rest, trying not to be nervous about Vi's driving. Sophie was silent in the back seat.

"Let's get Theresa's phone number from Rosa, through Penelope." Vi looked as though she'd just had a brilliant inspiration.

"Why?"

"You'll see!"

The next day when Kathy came over, Vi looked Penelope Pendergast up in the phone book and dialed the number. She had Rosa's phone number within a minute and called it. In another five minutes she'd convinced Rosa that she needed to talk to her friend Theresa for personal reasons, and got that number.

"Vi, what are you doing?" Kathy didn't like it. "What are you going to say?"

Ignoring Kathy's questions, Vi dialed Theresa's number.

"Theresa? This is Mrs. Vanderhoff in Pebble Beach. I have a surprise for you! You've won a one hundred dollar shopping trip to San Francisco next Tuesday." Pause. "Oh, that's the day you work at Señor Pellagrino's? No problem. My maid Carla has the day off. She can substitute for you. We will make the arrangements with your boss so you can go to San Francisco."

"Well, there you are! You have a job to do next Tuesday, Carla!"

"Are you out of your mind? What are you talking about? Can't we just tell the police about the locker receipt?" Kathy asked.

"That's not enough. They'd ask more questions that we couldn't, or wouldn't want to answer. We've got to get more solid information on what Peter's up to. You will resume your career as an actress. Your debut will be as Carla, the housemaid."

"*No!*" Kathy tried to sound firm. "Absolutely not."

(29)

HOROSCOPE: Let go of status quo–don't be prisoner of your inertia. Despite warnings to leave well enough alone, dig deep for explanations, using fantasy to find what's real. Disguise, practice, pretend. Confront and put to rest your past demons.

TWO DAYS LATER, VI AND KATHY WERE STAGING A DRESS REHEARSAL IN Kathy's bedroom.

"How does it look? Do you really think I can get away with it, Vi?"

"*Do you really think I can get away with it?*" Vi mimicked. "You sound like the old Katherine. Of course you can, Kate!" Vi insisted they rummage through the box full of costumes and makeup Rita left for Kathy. "I'm calling you Kate from now on because you're a new woman. You proved it on the Internet web site, showed real leadership talking to the Spiders about community theater and movie nostalgia. No more Katherine. No more Kathy. You're Kate the actress. Kate the investigator who is going to find out what slimey Peter Pellagrino is up to."

"You're right. I'm in show biz." Kathy straightened the dark wig on her head, adjusted the white apron over the black shirtdress, and added more makeup from the cosmetic kit. As she studied her reflection in the mirror, a different person was looking back at her, a mature, dark Mexican woman, with black hair. The contact lenses gave her deep brown eyes which were accented by thick eyebrows. Her figure was well padded to add thirty pounds, and the costume stretched over it was standard professional maid.

"Rita would be proud of you, Kate." Vi was smiling. "You know enough Spanish to get by, and you disguise your voice beautifully with that south-of-the-border accent. Lower your head when you talk to him. No one ever looks directly at a maid anyway."

"Now all I have to figure out is what to say. I've never acted without a script." Kate paused, looking thoughtful. "But you're right. Not sure I'll ever be ready for 'Katie old girl' like Rita called me sometimes, but Kate sounds and feels good."

They put the finishing touches on transforming Kate into a Mexican house-keeper. She was ready for her debut.

"You go to Peter's at ten o'clock. He'll give you a few instructions. You look great, Carla," Vi beamed.

Kate bowed. "Muchas gracias, Señora. I don't think he'll recognize me. He's never really met me, even though he's been following me—he and Guido—so he knows who I am."

"Your own mother wouldn't recognize you, Kate. Now go."

"We do have to get to the bottom of this. The police don't have a clue. We'll give them some." Kate felt more confident.

"Look for anything that will tie Peter to the locker receipt." Vi gave her a quick hug.

Kate parked her car out of sight around the corner from Peter Pellagrino's house. Practicing her part, she strode up and rang the bell. *Hope this works.* She remembered to lower her head as Peter opened the door and she handed him the identifying note from Theresa.

"Okay," Peter said, glancing at the note without looking at her. Pointing at an open closet door, he said, "There are the cleaning supplies. Just dust and vacuum, and be sure to clean the kitchen. Downstairs only. No upstairs. Comprende?"

"Si, señor," she said quickly as she reached for the vacuum cleaner, turning her back on him. She made comments in Spanish and asked questions about his lovely home, speaking more rapidly as she realized he couldn't understand what she was saying. This was fun!

"Su dinero en la mesa si you finish before I get back. Comprende?" He was curt.

"Si, señor. Adios y gracias."

Kate heard the roar of the black Mercedes leaving. Quickly, she raced the vacuum around the carpets in the living room and dining room, whisked the dust mop over the hardwood floor in the massive entry hall, and flicked the feather duster over where it would show an effort was made. After she had given the kitchen a cursory cleaning, she was amazed at how fast she had done so much.

Proud of herself, she pocketed the fifty dollars on the entry table and dashed upstairs to the forbidden territory.

The bedroom looked like what she imagined a male version of a bordello would be like. Red velvet bedspread, oil paintings of voluptuous naked women, a huge mirror over the bed. The open closet doors revealed cashmere sport coats, silk shirts, Armani suits, and more shoes than Imelda Marcos. "Wow!" she exclaimed.

She scurried into the adjoining room—a den or office of some sort. Red mahogany desk and matching file cabinet. A message light was blinking on the answering machine. She decided she'd better not mess with it. Nothing out of the ordinary in the desk drawers. Except . . . there was a stack of newspaper clippings about the body found at Crocker's Lockers in Monterey. She shuddered. Slamming the drawer shut, she noticed a large paper shredder in the corner. *Why does he need that*, she wondered.

Kate was startled when she glanced at her watch. *My God, it's after noon! He could be back any time*, she thought. Her earlier confidence melted in fear.

She eyed the key in the lock of the filing cabinet, and in her hurry to reach it, banged her hip on the corner of the desk. "Damn!" she shouted, by habit looking all around to make sure no one heard her swear.

Turning the key to unlock the drawer, she rushed through typical business folders: employees, taxes, restaurant records, construction, fish orders. Her frustration was mounting as she peeked in a few of the folders. Then she saw one labeled cargo. "That's odd. Cargo?"

Just as she was opening the file she heard a car door slam. "Oh shit!" she whispered loudly, realizing that was exactly what she wanted to do. "Can't let him find me here. Where can I hide?" Heart pounding and legs wobbly, she shoved the file back and pushed the drawer closed. She peeked out the den door just as Peter came into the foyer.

Kate ran over to the open window and saw a ledge which ran along the side of the house. She'd seen a million movies where people successfully hid on ledges. What would Kate Hepburn do?

As she was crawling out the window she remembered she hadn't locked the file cabinet. No time to go back. Maybe he won't notice.

Her feet were too big to stand on the four-inch ledge. Putting them parallel to the scratchy stucco, she inched away from the window, scraping her arms in the process.

Look out, not down, she reminded herself. *Don't lose balance. Got to make it to corner in case he looks out window.* She couldn't breathe. Couldn't move. So she took turns. *Breathe. Move.*

Clutching a window casement, she got a handfull of sea gull poop.

What was that noise? She rubbed her scratched arm and held her breath. She heard a mechanical voice saying, "You have one message. Message one." The voice that followed was familiar. "Peter, we need to meet to discuss the cargo schedule." Good God in Heaven! It was Guido!

Kate could feel her heart pound and a rising tide from her stomach. She froze. Stuck in fear and fatigue, she felt dizzy. Closed her eyes as she listened to Guido's voice.

"I've got a new cover chick down the coast. Lives right on a cove. I can send the flash code from there next Monday night. Meet me at Rocky Point Restaurant." Click.

Kate opened her eyes, tried to breathe quietly. She felt cemented to the stucco as she heard Peter dialing the phone.

"Angelo? Peter here. Gotta meet Guido. Important to keep him happy." Pause. "Yeah, right! You go ahead and meet with Georgio about the Adrian problem." Pause. "You may be right, but I think the bitch will keep her mouth shut about the receipt. She was damn scared. I'll call you when I get back. Ciao."

Kate felt like she was going to vomit. Every muscle of her body was tense. She swallowed three times quickly—a trick Jerry once taught her when she felt sick. *Please, please. Don't let Peter see the file drawer unlocked. Or look out the window.*

Suddenly, the window slammed shut with a bang that Kate felt from the top of her head to the tip of her cramped toes. Thoughts tumbled in her mind.

Can't go back in the window! What if he sees me? Probably got a gun! What if someone drives by and sees me? Then Kate felt a little relief. *Oh, good, the fog's coming in.*

She started inching her way to the next window. Crack! a piece of the ledge broke off—her foot was waving over nothing. She grabbed the top of a rose trellis. Didn't feel the thorn digging into the palm of her hand. She froze until she heard the Mercedes drive away.

Kate noticed the window to the bedroom was open slightly. She didn't want to go back in.

Further along the ledge was the top of a sturdier wooden trellis with crossbars like a ladder. She scrambled down to the ground, ignoring splinters.

She ran to her car, unlocked the door and grabbed the cell phone.

Vi answered before the end of the first ring. "Vi, meet me here, *now!*"

"Be there in five minutes." Vi sounded excited about getting in on the action. Didn't even ask what happened.

✷✷✷

"There, see? The bedroom window is open a little. Come on, Vi. We can climb up the trellis—the way I came down." Kate was leading Vi by the hand as they came up to the back of Peter's house. Role reversal, but she didn't want Vi to know how scared she was.

Vi's eyes had widened in disbelief as Kate told her the details. Kate could see that Vi finally realized the danger they were in, but was still resolute.

"No turning back now. We've got to get some answers," Vi said.

Scaling up the trellis, Kate was frightened—but determined. She figured they had at least an hour before Peter got back from Rocky Point.

Kate hurried Vi through the bedroom into the den. "Wait! I want to look around," Vi protested.

"I told you there's nothing in here. This is his 'Pleasure Palace'. The files are in the den."

Kate went to the cabinet. "Looks like he didn't check the drawer." She pulled out the cargo file and showed it to Vi.

"Here's a document that looks like it's in code," Vi said. "Can't figure it out."

"Don't have time to try," whispered Kate.

"I'll make a copy on his Xerox. Check his computer. Maybe there's a cargo file there, too."

The computer hummed at Kate's touch. "Oh good! I can access it with no password." Her fingers flew over the keys as she searched the menu for "cargo." Finding it had only eighty three K, she said, "I'll make a printout. Easier than trying to read the screen."

Vi shoved the copy of the coded document in her pocket. "Nothing else in this file that helps. Oh wait. I'll copy this time schedule. Doesn't look right for fishing. 'Big Sur Coast. Three miles off shore.' Fishing boats put in at the wharf."

"Sounds more like smuggling!" Kate exclaimed.

Vi copied the schedule. Put it in her other pocket.

"We'll figure it out later. We've got to get out of here!" Vi's voice didn't sound like the fearless leader Kate knew.

"Wait, Vi." Kate was pointing at the computer printout. "Here's a list of some sort. Looks like a roster of a military unit. Eeeeeek!" Kate's scream startled even herself. "Alphabetical, starting with Boyd Aaron—and Peter Pellagrino, too. It's the same list Nikki found on the Internet."

"That's really weird. See if there's a file on any of the names." Vi watched the screen as Kate searched. Both women were perspiring, even in the chill of the darkening room.

"No. But look at this under Guido. Guido the Gopher. That's what he calls him!" Kate scrolled the screen.

"Print it out. We've got to hurry."

What happened next wasn't clear to Kate, but somehow an alarm was set off. A horrid high pitched shriek paralyzed her. It seemed to go on forever. Kathy rushed to close the computer file and turned it and the printer off. At last the alarm stopped and she heard voices from downstairs.

"Vi, get in the closet!" Kate whispered, shoving the papers into her costume.

"What about you?"

"I'm Carla. More reason for me to be here than you."

Vi ran to the closet, closing the door behind her.

Kate reached the top of the stairs just as Peter and Guido were coming up.

This is it, she thought to herself. Everything depends on me. She convinced herself she looked like Carla, she *felt* like Carla. This is what acting is all about. I *am* Carla. "Buenos tardes, señor," she said calmly. "You turn off alarm."

"What the hell are you doing here?" Peter growled.

"Who is she?" Guido snarled.

"Just a housekeeper. She was here this morning. Well, answer me, Carla!" He took a menacing step toward her.

"Left purse this morning. I come back to get it, señor."

"How did you get in?"

"Rang front bell, nobody answered. Heard alarm. Went to back door. It was unlocked," she lied.

"But you were told not to go upstairs."

"Found my purse downstairs." Kate talked rapidly, alternating between English and Spanish, but he insisted she speak English. She maintained her accent. She was Carla. "I hear smoke alarm. I come to check fire. Couldn't find alarm."

It became easier as the excuses and lies rolled off her tongue. Before, she had been trapped in her own ego. Nobody really cared. Now she could be whoever she wanted, do whatever she wanted.

Guido glared at her. "No smoke, no fire. It was obviously the intruder alarm. How long does it take to figure that out, muchacha?" She was grateful Guido hadn't recognized her.

"I just go up stairs when you come in."

"Stupid broad . . . get her the hell out of here, Peter." Guido started walking toward the bedroom. "I need to borrow a sport coat, okay?"

Kate felt the panic return. Vi was in the closet! Her Carla persona was fading as she watched through the open door. Time stood still. The sliding door of the closet opened and closed. At last Guido returned in a beige cashmere jacket.

Thank God. Vi must have gone out the window and down the trellis. At least she hoped so.

"She still here? We've got things to do."

"Shut up, Guido. I'll handle this. You," he said loudly to Carla, pointing his finger in her face like a pistol, "get out and stay out. Don't even think of taking Theresa's place again. If she can't come, the place will stay dirty."

"Sorry, señor. I did nothing *mal*. I clean good. I —"

"Go!"

(30)

HOROSCOPE: Caution! Someone is dangerous to you. Unless you put an end to the problem now it is likely to escalate.

VI WOKE UP WITH AN UNEASY FEELING. SHE WASN'T SICK, BUT IT ALMOST felt like it. She didn't want to see Kate. Not right now. Had to get out of the house before she came popping through the back door. She could come at any minute. Her front door just steps from Vi's kitchen. It was the first time in ten years she was sorry they lived so close.

Kate made some bold changes lately. Wasn't that good? Vi was always telling her to change. "Assert yourself. Get over the guilt. Live a little."

Now that Kate was finally taking her advice, she really didn't like it too well. She might have to behave differently toward her. She had relied on defining herself by the old Katherine. Katherine the timid, Vi the bold; Katherine the guilty, Vi the free. How could she define herself now? Kate was fast becoming her equal. Kate was turning into Rita right before her eyes. It was like their relationship was now unreliable. It was something new. Should be exciting, but it wasn't. Too many surprises. Maybe she didn't like unpredictable as much as she thought she did.

She would quickly feed Late Bloomers and get out to the Subaru so she could escape before Kate got any ideas about coming in to hash over their escapade at Peter's.

She grabbed a can of tuna and the can opener in a frenzy, cutting her finger.

She was nervous. Hadn't even had her morning coffee. *Get out.* That's all she could hear in her head. Get out fast before she catches you. *Hurry.*

She dressed in last night's clothes without showering, ran a quick comb through her hair, sprinted to her car and drove in her usual bat-out-of-hell style down Lighthouse Avenue to the Donut Hole. She needed a sugar rush to calm her down.

The next morning, Sophie was back in her blue and white kitchen searching the recipe box for solace. Another terrible fight with Jack. Now that Adrian was gone, she heard her words even more clearly. "Why did you have to marry him so fast? What do you really know about the guy?"

Could Adrian have been right? Now Jack was carrying on about the library break-in and Vi's house being trashed.

She shuffled the recipe cards looking for something to distract her. Maybe she should consider jams again. No, she would look for something that could be improved by the addition of a little pot.

She hated the idea of people smoking it. Smoking anything couldn't be good for you, she thought. But adding a little to a wholesome casserole of veggies would not only perk up the poor sick people's appetites, but would improve the casserole. Some of the men with AIDS were so thin, they looked like they never had a good meal. She would love to cook for all of them if she could.

She dropped a few of the cards. When she picked them off the floor, wrong side up, Sophie saw the name Boyd Aaron. "Boyd Aaron. Why is that name familiar?" She thought a few seconds, repeated the name.

"Oh, my heart! Boyd Aaron was on the list Vi got from the library." She picked up the morning newspaper and glanced through the headlines. "There it is! 'Locker Body Identified: Boyd Aaron.' The dead man in the freezer!"

She felt sick again, remembering. She had tried hard to put the scene at Crocker's Lockers out of her mind every time it jumped in.

She grabbed her cellular phone and rushed out into the yard for fresh air, dialing Kate as she walked. "Kate, could Rita have known Boyd Aaron?"

"I don't know. Why?"

"I just found that name on the back of one of Rita's recipe cards. I'll call Vi," Sophie said. "Meet me at the Victorian Monarch Cafe in thirty minutes."

The phone call frightened Vi. She hurried out as fast as she could. The sky looked threatening. She dashed back inside for her old tan raincoat and black umbrella. Too bad the weather looked so ugly with the children's Butterfly Bonanza parade scheduled today. All the little cocoons and butterflies could get wet. Just hope it doesn't rain.

Sgt. Burley and the new cop were already putting out sawhorses and blocking off Lighthouse Avenue even though the parade wasn't scheduled until ten. She looked at her watch. Nine-thirty.

"Hi, Alice." She slid into the window table at the cafe so she could keep an eye on the street. Kate came in next, looking over her shoulder as she closed the door. That woman's still paranoid, Vi thought, certain someone's following her.

Sophie rushed in looking like she was also being pursued. Her blouse wasn't tucked in the back and she wasn't wearing makeup. Her hair was sticking out and lumpy. Not like Sophie to be thrown together that way. She rushed to the table and slammed down the recipe box.

"I don't know what we should do." Sophie put her hand over her heart as she caught her breath. "Look, just look! Names and addresses and funny marks on the back of every recipe. What does it mean?" She fingered through them. "Here's the one I told you about—Boyd Aaron." She pulled the card out. "Boyd Aaron is the guy who was killed! Same name that was on Peter Pellagrino's computer print-out." Sophie shook her head. "I'm scared. Why would Rita have this?"

Kate looked at the card. "I know Rita couldn't have had anything to do with whatever's going on." Kate looked terrible. Her voice sounded like someone else's.

Vi sensed fear building. *Okay, Violet, you wanted to be their fearless leader,* she told herself. *This is your chance to act like it. Don't let them know how scared you are. Just create a plan—any old plan—so they won't panic.*

"All right, Sophie, sit down and order a cup of tea," she stalled for time, "and we'll go through the list. Did you bring Peter's print-out, Kate?"

"Yes." Kate rummaged through her purse.

"Sophie," Vi started, "you read the names and, Kate, you check to see if they're on the list. Let's just see if there's more than Mr. Aaron."

Vi had no idea what this would prove, but it would focus them on something to do while she tried to think. Her heart was so loud in her ears she couldn't. Breathe deep, she told herself. Some explanation will come in a minute. Your mind can't remain blank forever.

"Louie de Naye," Sophie read.

Kate scanned down the names. "He's here. But two names don't prove anything."

"Joey Fontaine." The coffee grew cold as they continued through the list.

"Check," Kate replied. That's three of them."

While they checked names off, Vi fought panic. What to do? Or say? She couldn't get a plan; just felt the painful lump in her throat and her blank brain. *Try. You've got to try.*

Suddenly the face of Wyatt Burley, the cop, flashed in front of her. True, he always thought the worst of them, but Chris liked them. They did represent law and order in Pacific Grove. Better confess everything. Ask for protective custody. Let the cops check out all those names. This adventure was getting out of hand. She wanted to sound calm when she told the others. Took a swig of coffee and stood up to gain a little stature.

"Oh, Lord, look—it's Peter Pellagrino and Guido!" Kate's chair hit the floor. She was standing, pointing over Vi's shoulder. "Who are all those guys with them? They see us—They're coming after us!"

"Don't panic, Kate. Go out the back . . . fast." Vi tried to sound calm. In spite of her words, she found herself starting to run. Quickly she felt the other two pushing past her.

When they came out of the alley, the crowds had lined the streets by the old Holman building and filled the center divide. Nowhere to run but straight down the middle of the street.

Vi put one foot in front of the other, her heart pounding so fast she was sure she'd have an attack. As she ran, every breath hurt her chest. Couldn't tell where her feet were going. Was sure she'd fall.

"Vi!" Kate called out. Vi turned to see Kate had tripped. Sophie and Vi grabbed her arms and helped her to her feet. Vi felt a hand grab her and push her back into the crowd.

"Down in front!" a man shouted, so she and the others sat on the curb. They saw the parade coming. Flocks of yellow and brown monarchs fluttered awkwardly down the street carrying a banner, "Mrs. Crain's Kindergarten Butterflies welcome you to the 64th Butterfly Bonanza." Behind was a marching band and a group of green caterpillars.

Out of the corner of her eye, Vi saw a group of men pushing their way through the crowd. Maybe it wasn't Pellagrino and the thugs, but she couldn't take chances.

"Run!" she yelled and bolted out into Mrs. Rankin's third grade caterpillars. A security guard's arm stopped her. Then Kate's voice:

"Bathroom! Urgent! Diarrhea!" The arm relented. They tore through the caterpillars. Up toward the police station. The guard won't let the men cross the parade route, Vi thought. We'll get away.

"Police! Get to the police!" She was panting so hard she didn't know if Kate and Sophie could even hear her.

When she opened the station door, she saw little black spots before her eyes and her knees buckled. She felt Kate's sure arm around her waist and herself melting, sinking onto a bench. It was several seconds before any of them could speak.

"Help! We need help," Sophie gasped.

The man behind the desk was unfamiliar. A fat Italian, dark curly hair. Officer Russ Marotta was the name on his badge.

"I want Chris! Where's Officer Connery?" Kate said. "We're in trouble."

"Or Sgt. Wyatt Burley," Vi said.

"They're busy with the parade." Officer Marotta didn't bother to hide his irritation. "I'll take care of you. What's the problem?" He looked over the top of his glasses at Vi sinking back on the bench. "What's wrong?"

"We're being chased!"

"Someone's trying to kill us!" Kate shouted, leaning over the counter into Officer Marotta's face. "They're right behind us."

"Who?" He backed up to avoid her.

"We don't know," Sophie said. "Peter Pellagrino and a guy named Guido, but there are lots of others."

"They've been following us for months," Kate said.

Officer Marotta seemed openly skeptical.

"Did you report these death threats previously?" His voice was coldly official, as if he already knew the answer.

At that moment the door opened and Sgt. Burley swaggered in.

"Was anyone outside? A couple of men?" Marotta asked.

"No one," Burley said.

"It's all over now," Kate said to Vi. "He'll shatter our credibility."

"What credibility?" Burley said. "You've never made any sense, Mrs. Doolittle. I'm not up for your stupid accusations today. If you want to be credible, show me some evidence."

"Give 'em the recipe box," Vi coached Sophie. "We have evidence about Boyd Aaron."

"Oh Lordy." Sophie looked like she was going to cry. "I left the box at the cafe."

(31)

HOROSCOPE: You need to regain your leadership in a joint endeavor, so call the shots. Since you are too subtle to pull rank, your best bet is to let others think they are part of the decision-making process.

SGT. BURLEY ESCORTED THE TRIO OUT INTO THE RAIN WITH A SNARL. "Enough of your nonsense. We have our hands full with the parade and the Police Brigade this afternoon."

"How will we get the box?" Kate was shivering.

"Can't go back. I'm too scared," Vi answered.

"It's all my fault. I'm so sorry I did that. How could I?" Sophie's voice sounded like a ten-year-old.

"Any of us could have done the same thing," Kate said. "You were scared. We weren't thinking once we saw Guido and Peter. It was a senior moment."

"I'm too young for senior moments." The sob was apparent in Sophie's little-girl voice.

"What can we do?" Vi didn't like the sound of Kate's voice. Thought she heard the old Katherine returning.

Vi felt the cold. Was it the fear inside her, or the sudden winter chill? Soft rain made the street outside the station shine, the vacant lot next door had turned to mud. They stood together in silence.

Sophie reached in her purse. "My cell phone!" She sounded triumphant. "I'll call Jack."

"No! Don't involve him. He could be in danger. If they're watching your house he'd lead them right to us." Vi was shouting over the roaring noise behind her. She turned to see a row of motorcycle cops speed past, spraying drops of mud at their feet.

"What's this?" Kate asked, jumping back.

"The Police Motorcycle Brigades, practicing for the precision competition this afternoon," Sophie said.

"All these police, and no help for us!" Vi was yelling now. "We've got to get outta here."

"Nikki lives right up the hill across the street. Why don't we go there?" Kate said.

"She's down at Running Wolf's working on the Internet. Call her and tell her to come quick. To pick up the recipe box and meet us at her house. Fast as she can. We'll wait on her covered porch." Vi was motioning wildly as she sloshed through the wet muddy vacant lot.

They expected it would take a half hour for Nikki to arrive with the box, but it was longer. From their vantage point on the porch, Vi watched the motorcycle maneuvers form patterns like the old Busby Berkeley chorus lines. She was strangely calm now. No thoughts. Nothing to do but wait. Wait forever for the box to arrive. Wait forever for Peter and Guido to find them—and kill them?

Then she saw Nikki's white car coming up the hill. They all rushed toward her as she opened the car door.

"Thanks, Nikki. You're a life-saver," Vi said. "Maybe they'll listen to us now!"

It was Sophie who grabbed the box and was already sprinting toward the police station, taking a short-cut through the maneuvering motorcycles. Vi, Kate, and Nikki yelled at her to be careful as they followed. It was raining harder now, and the motorcycles, luckily, were cautiously slowing down a little to dodge the ladies hampering their precision.

Sophie took long strides across the wet street, watching for the on-coming motorcycles. When she reached the vacant lot next to the station, she felt the ground ooze beneath her feet and cling to her tennis shoes as she lifted each foot from the mud, slowing her down. Almost to the door of the police station. Almost safe. Now Sgt. Burley would believe . . .

Then she saw them coming from the direction of Nikki's house, behind the other women. Peter Pellagrino and Guido. "Oh Lord, what will I do!? They'll kill us!"

Sophie opened the recipe box and threw the cards into the air. They looked like birds in flight. She didn't know where she was running now. Felt Vi's hand pulling her. Concentrated on breathing and running. *Run. Breathe. Run.* At last, she was climbing the stairs of Nikki's porch.

The women stood silently, panting loudly as they watched the scene below. Peter and Guido, plus some guys in black suits scurrying everywhere, picking up the recipe cards. Motorcycles running over soggy cards, squishing them into the mud.

Nikki had seen it all. She handed Vi the keys to her car parked by the porch.

"Get away, fast! Go to Running Wolf's. Call me when you get there."

(32)

HOROSCOPE: It takes courage to exchange a world of fantasy for one that is real. But here is where the action is. Your future depends on your past. Break through that glass bubble. There will be quick changes and challenges.

SOPHIE WAS SCARED. SHE WAS SAFE IN RUNNING WOLF'S GUEST BEDROOM, but still unsettled. Imagine! Being chased by Mafia-type men! What was she doing here in this strange rich lady's house. Running Wolf—what kind of a name was that? And how could Vi be sure they had escaped? They had made it down to Yankee Point in half the time it would have taken anyone but Vi to drive it.

After awhile, she noticed her surroundings. The pale pink bedroom with the white Louis XIV furniture, the opulence of the bed smothered in satin and a down comforter, and soft frilly pillows. She kicked off her shoes, not wanting to spoil the elegance of this gorgeous bed.

Her hands and knees had stopped trembling. What did she really know about Kate and Vi? Why had she allowed herself to be dragged into this frightening situation? Always in the back of her mind was the horror of that dismembered body. Thinking of it made her shudder. Instead she'd think of Jack, how wonderful he was. Did he still feel that she was wonderful, too?

She glanced out the window at a bluejay perched on the ledge, his tiny eyes looking at her. Was he an omen? If so, he would have to be a good omen: the blue-bird of happiness, after all. Had she thrown her own happiness out the window?

She'd think about something pleasant. Things were not so good with Jack and her right now. Better not think about that. Back to her favorite daydream—the day she met Jack and the sexy night he made her fall in love with him. Sometimes she needed to pinch herself to believe it was true. Fifty five years old, and no one had ever desired her. Not much, anyhow. She recalled a few back seat gropings in her girlhood, but for years men hadn't even noticed her. She was a typical old maid. Nondescript sweater and skirt, hair in a bun, glasses. Just what she had always been—a West Virginia school teacher from a small hill town. She'd given up hope long ago for romance, and she would not settle for less. Then Jack came along and carried her away on his white horse.

Sophie cried so hard she frightened the bird off the ledge. She watched him flying into the trees. Was her good luck flying away?

The next morning, Kate woke up in deceptive serenity with a soft breeze coming through the open window and the sound of waves breaking on rocks. She was glad Running Wolf gave her this room. The rustic furnishings of redwood and pine were in stark contrast to Sophie's feminine guest room. As she stretched and surveyed her surroundings, reality washed over her like the surf below.

What are we going to do now? She jumped into her gray flannel slacks and maroon turtleneck, grabbed her bulky-knit sweater. Out of habit, she grabbed her purse as she went in search of Vi and Sophie.

"How'd you sleep, Kate?" Vi was calmly sipping coffee on the deck overlooking the cove. It sounded like she was enjoying the adventure of being chased by hoodlums.

"Are you kidding? Not a wink!" Kate paused. "Well, actually, that's not true. I was so physically exhausted, the brandy Running Wolf gave us knocked me out cold. I forgot where I was when I first woke up."

Sophie looked awful. Red-eyed and fidgety, her hand shook as she picked up her coffee cup.

Running Wolf came out on the deck carrying a tray loaded with bacon, eggs, rolls and juice. "Got to keep your strength up, girls."

"I don't think I can eat a thing," Sophie said.

Vi patted her back. "It will be okay, Sophie. You can call Jack as soon as we figure out what we're doing."

Kate wished that someone cared for her, would be worried about her. But she shook those thoughts out of her head.

"I'm so delighted you're here this morning." Running Wolf was the gracious hostess. "I have a date with my new man and I'm anxious for you to meet him."

"Well, now. You've been keeping things from us. I didn't know you had a new boy-toy," Vi said.

Kate wondered how they could be so flippant, ignoring their plight. There were important matters to discuss. Even Sophie seemed to perk up a little as she asked, "Is he tall, dark and handsome? Is he romantic?"

Running Wolf laughed. "Oh yes, and sexy eyes, too. Italian—and you know how they are."

"Some of them, maybe," Vi said. "How'd you meet him?"

"You guys left Rita's memorial early. The masked ball was a blast. He was there as the Count of Monte Cristo. So debonair, so suave."

Kate froze, remembering the day of Rita's so-called funeral. Following Rita's instructions, she had told him to leave. He must have gone back after she left. A terrible intuition of what was to come made her afraid to ask. She hesitated.

"What's his name?"

"Guido. Guido Ferrari. Just wait till you meet him. He's making me young again."

Sophie started to say something, but Kate grabbed her arm. Kate glanced at Vi in panic.

"May I have some more coffee, please?" Vi said.

"Sure. Excuse me. I'll go make a fresh pot. Guido will want some, too."

"My God! What will we do?" Kate whispered after Running Wolf went into the house. "Shall we tell her?"

"No. We don't know how involved they are. If they're sleeping together, she won't want to hear anything bad about him," Vi said.

"Can't I just go home?" Sophie said.

"No!" said Vi and Kate in unison.

"We've got to get out of here before he comes. He'll tell Peter and the goons where we are." Kate could not control the panic in her voice. She was glad she brought her purse downstairs with her. Maybe she had some Valium.

"Come on, girls. The car's in the driveway. Let's split," Vi said.

Kate had never seen Vi's short legs move so quickly. She grabbed Sophie's hand and led her to Nikki's car. "Do you have the keys?" Kate asked Vi.

"They're in the ignition. Hurry! Get in."

Sophie crawled into the back seat and looked out the rear window. "Running Wolf is on the deck waving and yelling at us."

"Hate to do this to her, but . . . ."

The tires spun in the gravel as the car peeled out onto the highway, headed south. For once Kate didn't mind how fast Vi drove. "Where are we going?" she asked, wishing she'd gone to the bathroom before they left.

"I met one of the growers. Mr. West. Lives down the road about ten miles. Maybe he'll hide us while we get a plan."

Vi never took her eyes off the winding narrow road. She was driving as fast as she dared. Something between a rain and a mist fogged her vision. She turned on the windshield wipers. Tried to breathe normally but the twisted knot in her stomach didn't let her inhale very deeply. She was afraid to look in the rear-view mirror—afraid she'd see the red Jaguar following them.

The coast was treacherous. She blinked rapidly trying to see better.

In a moment of clarity she remembered the cell phone. Fumbled for it, tossed it to Kate.

"Call Nikki. Tell her what happened and where we're going, in case something happens. Tell her we're taking the Old Coast Road to a ranch called Casa Esperanza. This is her car. She should know where we're going. Tell her to call the cops."

She looked away from the road only a second—long enough to see the terror on Kate's face.

Got to hold it together. Don't show her your fear. Someone has to run this show. She hunched in closer to the steering wheel, heard the squeal of her brakes as she rounded another hairpin turn.

"Lord have mercy," Sophie muttered from the back seat.

(33)

AT LAST, THE TURN-OFF. A DIRT ROAD FULL OF HOLES AND STONES. A MILE or so up, Vi recognized the giant garbage cans, not very well hidden, with marijuana plants five and six feet high. She saw the low Spanish house in the distance. It was starting to rain.

"Jump out and run to the house," she shouted as she turned off the engine.

She could see the pool now. Big and blue. Deck chairs. Orange and white umbrellas.

She could hear Kate panting behind her, feel her own pained breath as they ran up the hill toward the big carved door.

"Let me do the talking. I know him a little bit," she puffed between gulps of breath. She rang the camel bell.

The door opened, but Mr. West was nowhere in sight.

"Buenos dias," said the short, dark lady who stood before them.

"Inglés?"

"No." She dropped her eyes.

Oh lord! Vi struggled to remember her high school Spanish. Maybe Kate could help.

Just then, there was a growing staccato of thump, thump, thump. "Planes!" Sophie yelled. Vi and Kate looked up as the whirring noise of helicopters became deafening. Things around them started to blow like a tornado. Deck chairs and umbrellas were swept into the pool and shingles flew off the roof of a nearby shed. The young, dark woman slammed the door.

"Go for the car!" Vi yelled. "Let's get the hell out of here!"

Kate looked uncomprehending. Just stood there, blank.

"Move," Vi shouted, pushing her forward. "Go! Go!" Kate did not move. Vi wanted to cry, scream. What to do? *Kate's in shock.*

"Kate, come on." She took her hand gently. "Come with me." As she pulled, Kate finally began to move.

Sophie was up ahead. Suddenly parachutes with men dressed in camouflaged fatigues and combat boots were coming out of one helicopter. They were drifting toward the heavily wooded area further up the hill. From another hovering chopper, a pair of men were dangling from a cable, being lowered near the house.

On the ground, cars and trucks everywhere. Men with guns—marines, drug enforcers, sheriff's deputies. Mexicans were screaming, running down the hill, jumping out of bushes all around.

"Sophie!" Vi screamed. "Sophie!" She couldn't hear. "Sophie, don't go to the car—it's out in the open!" But Sophie didn't turn around.

"Run for it," Vi said to Kate as she let go of her hand. "Hide!" Around the corner of the house she saw a shed. A tool shed, she thought. She tripped, fell forward. Kate pulled her up. Vi and Kate pushed through the tiny door, closed it behind them. Plunged into darkness. Only the terrible sounds outside.

"Just be quiet!" Vi whispered as Kate groaned. For a moment Vi felt safe. The door containing the darkness. Then panic. If the door opened they were cornered. *Don't think about it,* she commanded herself. *Don't think at all.*

Sophie ran toward the car. Turning, she saw that Vi and Kate weren't behind her. Furious, she shouted "Vi! Kate! Where are you!?"

Why did they leave me alone? How could they do this to me!? Vi said to go to the car, and they aren't in sight. Sophie's heart was flapping in time with her thoughts. She reached the car and leaned against it, panting to catch her breath. She grabbed the handle. Her rage increased. "Locked! Why in the hell would she lock the damn car?"

She felt her face flush. This looked like a war, and she was in it. Even the marines had landed!

She backtracked to the house. Pounded on the door. Were Vi and Kate inside? No answer.

Down the driveway she saw Rita's Jag—"Oh no! that's Guido and Peter!" She dashed behind a garbage can to hide. She saw a Pacific Grove Police van coming up the hill.

How long were they in the dark while shouts and shooting went on? Vi lost all track of time. Could only pray. Then she heard an alien sound inside the shed.

A phone ringing. Kate must have brought the phone. She crawled toward the sound, and fished it out of Kate's purse. She could see the whites of Kate's unblinking eyes staring as if still in shock.

Vi heard her own voice, low, but almost sounding normal, say "hello."

"It's me—Nikki. Are you all right?"

"No," she whispered now. "Can't talk. Get police."

"I already called them," she said, just as Vi hung up. It seemed like hours crawled by in the dark. Sounds of the helicopters. Screams. Silence.

A sharp slice of white light poured in on her and she saw an outline of a figure in the doorway. Tears of thankfulness filled her eyes, blurring his image, but he was unmistakenly Officer Connery.

"Thank God, Chris!"

"I heard the phone," he said. "Quick, follow me."

She asked no questions. Rushed out, pulling silent Kate behind her.

A few minutes later, Chris was helping Vi and Kate, lifting them gently into the patrol wagon. Vi spotted Sophie inside.

A silence fell over them as the patrol wagon pulled out of the driveway, leaving the sheriff and police cars, marines, helicopters, guns behind. Vi didn't want to look. They were safe. That's all she could think. Safe at last.

Sophie shouted as they made the turn onto Highway 1. "There's Jack! I'm sure it's him. It's our car. Stop! I've got to talk to him."

"Sorry. Can't," Chris replied. "It's important we get out of here. The officers will explain to him and let him know you're okay."

As Sophie was craning her neck to watch Jack's car turn up the dirt road, Vi placed a reassuring hand on her shoulder. "Why are you taking us away?" she asked Chris.

"We're taking you back to Pacific Grove. Sorry, I'll have to arrest you in order to keep you overnight. Peter Pellagrino was arrested by the Feds. Unfortunately, Guido Ferrari escaped."

The three women looked at each other in confused disbelief. Still in danger. So many unanswered questions.

(34)

HOROSCOPE: Get control over your emotions. Get a better idea of what's happening and why. Some puzzle pieces will fall together.

"YOU GOT HERE IN A HURRY. DID NIKKI PHONE YOU?" VI WAS THE FIRST to speak.

"No, we were already on your trail. We picked up the first call from your cell phone."

"What?" Kate was recovering fast now, embarrassed by her earlier inertia. "How could you do that?"

"We didn't want to frighten you, but we've been monitoring your calls."

"More frightened than we were!?" Sophie said.

Chris smiled, then continued. "I realized you were being followed after the break-in at Ms. Farnsworth's. Discovered this Pellagrino character and his cohorts prowling around. Noticed he always had a car phone stuck on his ear and decided to monitor him, too."

Kate was sitting on the edge of the seat, clinging to the safety strap as Sgt. Burley swerved recklessly around the curves. She was glad he was keeping his mouth shut for a change. "I don't understand. How can you hear what people say on their cellular phones?" she asked.

"High tech eavesdropping. Ninety percent of calls can be listened to within a radius of several miles if you have a portable radio scanner."

"Lord, that's how they always knew what we were doing." Vi was irritated.

"Anyway, when I got back to the station yesterday afternoon, Officer Marotta and Sgt. Burley filled me in on your visit. They thought it was a joke. We heard about the chaos during the Motorcycle Drill Team Exhibition, and the men picking up cards off the street. We brought in a few of the cards they missed."

"Oh my! The cards!" Sophie looked like she was going to bounce out of the van. "That was our evidence, and I threw them away!"

"Don't worry," Kate said. "Remember the printouts I got off Peter's computer. They will verify. . . ." Abruptly she shut up, realizing she'd better not say any more about that. Her Carla adventure wasn't exactly legal.

"Even though those recipe cards might have originally been Rita's," she said, "it was Guido who put all those names on the backs."

Chris nodded. "Probably. When we saw the name Boyd Aaron on one of the mud-splattered cards, we figured these goons were connected to the dead body in the freezer. We monitored Guido Ferrari calling Pellagrino to meet him and follow you down to Big Sur. Then we contacted the Feds. They had been scouting that place for some time. They launched the raid."

Sophie breathed a sigh of relief. "Oh good. It wasn't a foreign invasion."

Chris smiled again. "I think there was blackmail going on. These cards must have been what they were after in the library and your house," he nodded toward Vi. "Pellagrino and Ferrari double-crossed the mob, and were secretly blackmailing them."

"Put a lid on the speculation, Chris. Don't tell these dames what you think. We don't really know how much they're involved." Sgt. Burley spat out the words, breaking his stony silence. Chris looked sheepish. Kate wanted to defend him, but kept her mouth shut.

Burley turned on the siren and the three women retreated into their own thoughts. Each reflected on the last few hours, the last few months.

It was out of their hands now.

(35)

HOROSCOPE: Justice must be seen, tested and completed in order to be effective. Within bounds of convention, you'll learn rules, and perhaps break them. Have patience; fame may be on the horizon.

AS THE VAN PULLED UP TO THE POLICE STATION, VI WHISPERED TO KATE AND Sophie. "We'll get one phone call. I'll call Nikki."

"Nikki? No! We've got to call an attorney. We'll hire the best lawyer we can find to get us out of this mess!" Kate was emphatic.

"How? We don't have any money," Sophie said quietly.

"What? That's impossible! We were rolling in dough." Vi wasn't whispering now. Kate shushed her. "Where did it go?" Kate asked Sophie.

"Project Open Hand. Feeding the homeless. Befriend the Bay, trying to research the pollution problem the men down at the wharf told us about. Buying stuff for the estate sales. And remember, Kate, it was your idea to stuff money in books at the library."

"Oh, God. We'll be assigned a lame public defender. That's how it works." Vi said. The van stopped. Vi and Kate were quiet going up the walk.

"Where . . . what do I . . . I'm doomed . . . when will they . . . Ohhhh . . ." Sophie was muttering while eyeing the formidable cement building. It looked like a fortress. She tripped over the doorsill as Chris led her into the police station. She almost fell into a man standing behind the door. She smelled him before she saw him. He must be intoxicated, she thought. The glare of fluorescent lights hurt her eyes. Didn't think they needed to be that bright in daylight. Lots of glass partitions inside between the offices.

Chris herded her to a desk in the corner. Officer Marotta, she thought, looking up at the stern face behind the desk. I know him. The one who wouldn't listen the day of the Butterfly Bonanza . . . when was it? Only yesterday! A metal bar was in front of the desk. "Stop right there, Mrs. Conway," Chris said. His voice sounded kind. Maybe he didn't like this any more than she did. He had played golf with Jack once or twice. What must he think of her?

But Officer Marotta was all business. Name. Address. Telephone number. Next of kin. "You have been arrested on suspicion of conspiracy with Antonio West to grow and distribute illegal drugs. Have the suspects been Mirandized?"

"Yes, they have," Chris said.

"Do you have some identification, Mrs. Conway? A driver's license?"

"No. I don't drive. I have my Macy's card."

"I'll vouch for her. She is who she says she is," Chris said.

Over to the right, a man not much more than a boy, was being fingerprinted. I remember that from *N.Y.P.D. Blue*, Sophie thought. "I believe he's crying," she said half aloud. *Keep a stiff upper lip*, she told herself. *Stand straight. Look the policeman in the eye.*

A lanky woman in a police uniform started to take her purse. "No, Ma'am—I need a Kleenex first, and a comb. May I?" She opened it, took Kleenex, comb and lipstick out, then handed it to the boney police matron.

A door clanged loudly, making Sophie jump. They were taking the boy through the big metal door. He was crying.

"Your jewelry, Miss."

Sophie focused back on Officer Marotta. Looked at him blankly. "I'm not wearing any jewelry."

"Your wedding ring."

"No, I'm sorry. I've never taken that off since my husband put it on at our wedding and kissed it. Noooo," she wailed, feeling herself choking up.

"Your wedding ring, ma'am."

Her hands were trembling so she couldn't get it off. She tugged. She held it in her hand. The wide gold band with three large diamonds. "Take good care of it, please," she said. "It's the most precious thing I own."

The matron was inspecting the purse. "What is this substance?" she asked as she took out a pill box.

"My blood pressure medicine," Sophie replied.

"I'll have to take this for evidence."

Sophie just looked at her, feeling dazed and slightly dizzy. She hadn't eaten for hours. Chris took her arm and led her toward the forbidding steel door. She looked back at the others. Kate was being pushed up to the desk by Sgt. Burley. She looked gray and shriveled. Vi, though, still looked pretty cocky. *I guess wherever Chris is taking me, they'll be there too*, Sophie thought. *My heart! You don't suppose they'll do a strip search like in the movies! I'd be so humiliated.*

They walked down a short corridor. It looked cold with the lower part of the walls gray cement and Plexiglas above. Sophie felt eyes watching her. They stopped at a barred iron door. Entering, she could see into a fairly large room. Seated on one of the cots was a flashy young woman with a blond bouffant hairdo, a short tight leather skirt, and tight red sweater. *Do you suppose she's a fallen woman?* Sophie thought to herself.

"Right over here, Mrs. Conway," Chris indicated a bed next to the floozy.

Sophie looked at him. "I'll never sleep if I can't brush my teeth."

"Sorry, honey. This isn't a hotel. They don't supply toothbrushes," chuckled the blonde.

Sophie's teeth were actually chattering.

"Don't be afraid," Chris comforted her. "Your friends will be along soon."

The door slammed behind him. The woman looked Sophie up and down. "What are you in for? Did you turn a trick, too, and get caught? Is this your first offense?"

Sophie couldn't answer. Put her head down.

Kate was angry after the embarrassment of being strip-searched. She didn't know the female officer. Didn't want to. She tried to gain her composure while waiting alone in the small, brightly-lit interview room for the public defender to show up.

Chris opened the door and ushered in a small bookish-looking man with little beady eyes, made large with coke-bottle glasses. Looked intelligent.

"This is Clarence Dudley, the public defender assigned to represent you at the arraignment tomorrow. Mr. Dudley, this is Katherine Doolittle, one of the three women brought in from the drug raid." Chris sounded very official, yet polite. Kate was grateful he was the one to interview her. She felt comfortable with him. Knew his mother through the thrift shop.

Mr. Dudley nodded in her direction. He moved a chair out from the table, hitting his leg in the process. Dropped his briefcase. His glasses started sliding down his nose as he stooped to pick it up. Kate almost smiled until she realized this was the man who held her fate in his bumbling hands.

"Thought we could have a chat about what led up to this—on an informal basis, mind you—to help your attorney understand your predicament." Chris seemed more self-assured every time she saw him. His mother must be proud.

"Do you understand what an arraignment is?" Mr. Dudley peered at her over his notebook. She wondered if *he* knew. "It's when you enter your plea—guilty or not guilty of the charges," he continued, glancing down at his notes. "And the judge sets bail."

"You'll be taken to the courthouse in Monterey tomorrow for that," Chris added. "Probably be held in jail there if you can't raise the bail the judge sets before the preliminary hearing. That's when the D.A. tries to show probable cause that you were involved in a crime."

"The D.A. is Benjamin Farrell," Mr. Dudley said. "He's a puffed-up grandstander, up for re-election. Probably wants a state office eventually. He'll be tough."

Kate felt panic surfacing. Jail. She couldn't even imagine it. Chris must have seen her face flush, her hands shake. He poured her a glass of water. She accepted it gratefully but found it difficult to swallow.

"What can I do?" she asked.

"Cooperate. Tell us what happened. Everything."

Kate took a deep breath. She knew she had to filter the information. There was more than self-incrimination involved here.

"It all began with trying to help a friend." Kate stood up and paced back and forth as she told them of Rita's illness. About Adrian, Violet and herself plunging innocently into getting a little marijuana to her. She paused frequently, but Chris seemed to understand he shouldn't interrupt. Mr. Dudley took notes. Kate skipped the part about their trying pot themselves.

"Where did you get the marijuana?" Chris asked.

"The Pellagrinos," she replied. No problem admitting that. Adrian had disappeared, Mercedes was dead, and she didn't give a damn about Peter.

"Later on it was Pea Soup and Mr. Big." Chris raised his eyebrows. Dudley shook his head.

"Don't know their real names," Kate added hastily. She really didn't know Pea Soup, and no way was she going to incriminate Running Wolf as Mr. Big.

"What about this Monday Club. What can you tell us about that?"

Kate sat back down. Took a drink of water. Choked on it. "What about it? How did you hear . . . ."

Chris tried to hide a smile. "Word of mouth travels fast. Even my mother heard rumors. We got a call from the guard at the Pebble Beach Gate reporting suspicious groups going in and out on Mondays."

"But we didn't go to the parties," Kate said, looking to make sure Dudley made note of that.

"Gossip filtered through the community about what was going on at Rita Rich's house, but nobody felt like blowing the whistle." Chris paused. "Did you women have anything to do with the plants the goats ate?"

"No! Heard about it, that's all."

"Anyway," Chris continued, "seems too many people knew someone who was being helped and treated it like a popular social service. Word even came down the bureaucratic ladder that there were more important investigations." Chris suddenly stopped talking. Looked sheepish as if he were saying things he shouldn't.

Mr. Dudley broke the silence. "I don't think it will be an issue here. Law enforcement agencies don't mess with rich people. From what I've seen, it's the poor dumb laborers who get busted. Most the time it's only when they're in trouble for something else."

Kate was amazed he could string so many words together at a time, but still say so little.

"Okay," Chris said, "then there's the problem with the body in the freezer."

Kate shuddered. "That was awful! We were upset that the police suspected us. After that, people were following us. We weren't sure if it was the police or the killers, or who. Then there were the break-ins at the library and Vi's house. It all sorta snowballed." She stood up, started pacing again.

Chris cleared his throat. "We didn't think you'd killed anyone. We were keeping tabs on what was going on, through the cell phone conversations and by surveillance. We knew Peter Pellagrino and his friends broke into Mrs. Farnsworth's house. Didn't arrest them because we figured there was something bigger going on."

Kate stopped pacing and grabbed hold of the back of the chair for support. "Chris! Can you get my purse back from the booking desk?" Why hadn't she remembered! She had the printouts from Peter's computer at the cafe before the parade. They must still be in her purse. The list that matched the names on the back of the recipe cards. The fishing boat schedule in Pellagrino's cargo file showing unloading on Big Sur Coast instead of the Monterey wharf. The receipt for the locker where the body was found!

"I doubt it. Is there something you need?"

"Yes! I have evidence. I . . . ." Kate shut up. How could she explain these private papers without admitting she stole them?

Chris and Dudley were both leaning forward, waiting for her to continue.

"It's all right, Mrs. Doolittle. Keep calm. Tell us about it. What evidence?" Chris's voice was quiet.

Kate sat down and told all about Carla the housekeeper who took all this information from Peter Pellagrino's home.

Twenty minutes later, Chris stood up. Mr. Dudley put his notebook in his briefcase. Chris spoke. "This interview falls into client-attorney privilege. For the record, I didn't hear all of it, but was asked by the public defender to get these papers from your purse for thorough examination. Thank you Mrs. Doolittle."

Vi sat on her cot, staring up at the gray ceiling. She couldn't help but think about the humiliations of the day. She tried not to remember the booking, the mannish matron and the body search, but when she let down her guard she saw the scene again, felt sick shame.

Exhaustion. Couldn't think. Couldn't move! The phone call to Nikki they finally let her make didn't help her mood at all, even though Nikki did get to drop off changes of clothes at the front desk for the women.

What a mess. For the first time I can remember, the three of us are silent. What can I say? What can I do? "It really is all my fault. All of it. No one to blame but me," Vi said.

"No, it's my fault," Kate said. "We wouldn't have gotten into this if it weren't for my listening to Rita. Now we're stuck with a dumb lawyer and an ambitious D.A."

"And whose fault is it we don't have a good defense attorney? I could have put aside some of the money," Sophie said.

Vi lay down. Picked up the blanket from her cot, pulled it over her head. Couldn't look at her friends right now. Sleep. That's all she wanted. Sleep, but it wouldn't come. Too many voices, all her own, were screaming in her head.

How could you do this? How could you create this nightmare? How?

It had started as a dream. One afternoon as she walked along the shore kicking stones a vision appeared in her mind. She saw it in full radiance—a new exciting life. Herself a brave leader, an adventuress.

Had any cautions come to her? Wasn't there any warning voice to recommend restraint? She couldn't remember.

There was Kate—Katherine, her great and loyal friend who could never say no to Vi. She should have shown more consideration for her, not charged off without a thought for her welfare. Poor Kate. And Sophie, who never really believed in the whole thing—just wanted to be part of the gang. Now she's in a jail cell.

Why hadn't she thought more about the danger to her friends? Her timing had always been off. "You're some leader," she said aloud to herself. "Like General Custer." She rolled over sadly and tried to ward off her demons with sleep.

No use.

(36)

HOROSCOPE: Heed inner voice. You'll eventually come up with correct answers, but where information came from remains mystery. Friends work on your behalf. Don't ask questions; for a change, just let others do the talking for you.

AT SIX O'CLOCK THE NEXT MORNING WHEN CHRIS PUT THEM INTO THE POLICE car, he apologized for the handcuffs. "It's regulation," he said.

They were taken to Monterey to be arraigned in the Courtroom of Judge Linda Hogan. Clarence Dudley had described her as being something like Judge Judy on television. What would this morning bring? Vi couldn't focus.

Entering the courthouse, Vi was embarrassed but relieved to recognize the sturdy, comforting frame of Agnes Roper. She was the matron assigned to escort them to the jail facility.

Agnes was an avid reader in her late fifties, and an old friend of Nikki's. Vi had seen her many times in the library and they had compared favorite authors a time or two. Agnes was enchanted by Elizabeth Berg, one of Vi's favorites, too. They had hit it off right from the start.

"Hi, Agnes." Vi knew she sounded apologetic.

"Hello, Vi." Agnes smiled, showing her large teeth.

"I'm glad to see you again, but ashamed you're seeing me like this."

"Don't be, Vi. I've seen an amazing array of Pacific Grove's finest citizens in here. It can happen to anyone. Besides, you'll be out in a couple of hours. Have you read the new Elizabeth Berg book?"

What We Keep?

"Yeah."

"No, I bought it, but with all that's been going on lately, I haven't had much time to read." Vi regretted the sentence as soon as it was out of her mouth. Sounded whiney, self-pitying.

"I've got it here. I just finished it. Definitely her greatest yet. I'll bring it in later —to take your mind off things." Again she showed the big teeth.

Waiting in the holding cell for the arraignment, Vi wasn't sure she liked having so much time to think. Maybe Rose was right. Maybe she was getting senile, should give up and go to The Grove. Her mind was far away. She remembered the first time she met Rita. The tap dance, the nickname of Tandelejo. The sorrow when the brightness that was Rita died, leaving a dark hole.

Rita gave her the red shoes so she could tap dance her way back home, but it was Rita—not Vi—who was Dorothy trying to find her way back home to die. It was Rita trying to avoid all the pain of her last weeks.

Well, if Rita was Dorothy, no doubt who the scarecrow was. *Why didn't I use my brain? Why did I always go too fast without looking over my shoulder for what was following me? I was bold, rash, wouldn't listen to warnings from Kate.*

Kate was the cowardly lion, finding all her courage that day at Peter Pellagrino's when the moment called for it. She thought she had lost it all when Jerry left, or maybe that the bimbo had stolen it along with her husband. Not so! Kate had misplaced it along with her glasses and appointment book and everything else you can't find when you're feeling anxious and old. She should be proud now to have found it and used it again.

Who's Sophie? Certainly not the Tin Man. If anything, her heart is too big.

Now the $64,000 question. Who's the Wizard? *Is* there a Wizard out there somewhere? Vi felt like shouting. *Stop wallowing,* she told herself. No Wizard. Anyway, you don't need one. He's just a little old phoney from Kansas. We never needed him. What we needed was the trip. Needed to join arms and skip down the yellow brick road.

Hey, come to think of it, maybe Rita was the Wizard after all. She gave me the ruby slippers and she's the one who had started us on the journey to find what was there all along—friendship.

Rita, I need a little help. What would you say now? I know what you'd say, Rita. "Get it together, Tandelejo. You got them into this mess. Use your brains. Get them out. Stop tap dancing and think. Kick a little butt!"

"Thanks, Rita," Vi whispered aloud. "I'm taking over our case as of now." She hollered for Agnes and asked for paper and pencil. Started outlining instructions for the Sisters in the Web. The clarity and calmness worked wonders. She started to feel like her old self. She smiled, remembering what Kate had told her about Guido's message on the answering machine at Peter's house. "The cover chick down the coast." Of course, it was Running Wolf. She knew where Guido would be tomorrow night.

She banged on the bars the way they did in old prison movies. Feeling like Ida Lupino, she shouted, "Let me out. Get me to the D.A., I'm ready to sing."

At 10:00 A.M. the arraignment finally began. The prisoners were led by Agnes into the courtroom and ushered to seats in the front row. Sophie kept her eyes cast down, afraid to look around. When she did look up she saw Mr. Dudley in a three-piece suit, smiling at them. He didn't make her feel any better.

She felt like she was getting the flu. No wonder, after sleeping in that drafty jail. She supposed, though, it was just nerves. *Occupy your mind with other things,* she told herself, and began to study the judge. To Sophie's surprise the judge was an older woman, capable looking. Somehow she was relieved. An older woman might have more compassion for the three of them, but it was hard to tell.

Next she distracted herself with analyzing Benjamin Farrell, the prosecutor. He was a tall man, dressed in a pin-stripe suit with a gold watch chain draped across his ample frame. He had a neatly-trimmed moustache and hair graying at the temples. Looked like a moral majority politician, Sophie thought.

Finally, she observed the room. It was attractive, in a men's club sort of way. Mahogany wood paneling looked old and the sturdy wood chairs were uncomfortable. There were large tables where the lawyers had papers spread out in apparent disarray. The American flag and the California Golden Bear flag added some color, but the room wasn't very well lit. A bailiff stood in front, looking bored. The court reporter was a slip of a girl.

Sophie smoothed the skirt of her dress. She was grateful that Nikki was able to get them all a change of clothes. The gray, thin wool dress with the white collar made her feel like a teacher again. She used to wear it on special occasions at school. But what was a teacher doing in court? Why wasn't Jack there?

She noticed Vi whispering to Kate, but Sophie didn't say anything. Just waited and hoped it would be over quickly. If only she could be home again.

✴ ✴ ✴

Vi was glad to see that Nikki and Running Wolf were in the back of the court-room. She asked Agnes to give them her notes, in which she explained Guido's involvement and told Running Wolf to cooperate with the arrest by leaving the house before 8 P.M.

Vi was not happy with her outfit. Dudley had insisted she wear a lavendar cash-mere sweater and skirt with a single strand of pearls. Sophie was wearing her prissy gray dress and Kate was told to wear her navy blue suit. Dudley wanted them to look like proper Pacific Grove matrons. What did he know about proper Pacific Grove matrons, anyway? She couldn't think of anyone in town who dressed this way. Playing this part! She hated it. Was sure even the judge would have liked her better in her blue caftan. Oh well, better not offend Dudley. He was dumb, but he was all they had.

Vi was so busy with her ideas for help from Sisters in the Web that she had ignored the reading of the charges.

"How do the defendants plead?"

"Not guilty, Your Honor," Dudley said.

Now alarmed, Vi tuned in to hear the prosecutor arguing the bail.

"These three women sitting here have been highly uncooperative. They have refused to implicate their drug suppliers. If the bail is set below one million, their wealthy drug dealer friends will smuggle them out of the country so fast we'll never see them again."

A million dollars? Dudley was just sitting there making no objections. *Why doesn't he say something? Why doesn't he defend us?* A million dollars! They would rot here, who knows for how long? We told all about Pea Soup. We couldn't help it if he didn't have a name the FBI could find in their computer files. We gave all our evidence against Peter Pellagrino and Guido. They were the real villains. They and their friends. Kate gave them all the papers we'd copied from Peter's house. We'd found the Air Force connection with the dead man. What did he mean "uncooperative"?

She nudged Dudley and made a gesture for him to stand up. "Stand up and defend us," she mouthed, but he just shook his head and put his finger to his lips. She knew what he wanted. He wanted her to sit demurely and look like some-body's grandmother. *If only we could have hired a decent attorney.* Running Wolf volunteered to get one, but Vi was afraid the police would trace the con-nection to her. *I'm not turning her in, no matter what this fat prosecuter says. She's my friend.*

Vi tried sitting calmly, playing her part. Tried not to listen to the lies and accu-sations coming her way, but she couldn't help hearing some of it. Couldn't help but feel her cheeks growing warm, hands fidgeting with pens, paper, anything.

The prosecutor walked past the three of them, stopping for a second at each one, staring each in the eye. Vi glared back at him. He was carrying on like he had been watching too much Perry Mason. Then he turned, walked back to the bench, raised his arm dramatically and pointed at them.

"Don't be fooled by their grandmotherly looks. These three women sitting before us are part of an elaborate drug dealing ring, an operation they themselves set up, an operation involving over one thousand kilos of marijuana distributed to hundreds of adults and countless numbers of unsuspecting and innocent children. They may even have been involved in the murder of Boyd Aaron, and . . ." he paused, "perhaps others we have yet to identify." He turned and walked back toward them.

"Lies! All lies! What does he mean?" Vi said. She felt faint now.

"Objection!" Dudley finally stood up.

"Sustained," said the judge.

"And what did they do with the fortunes accummulated by their immoral and illegal actions? What they didn't spend on setting up elaborate computer systems and cell-phone networks to bring in more loot, they spent on themselves—on fancy clothes, on luxurious new cars. This blood money—make no mistake about it, that's what it was—this blood money led to the corruption and ruin of hundreds in our community, hundreds of decent, law-abiding citizens taken in by these innocent-looking, grandmotherly types. We cannot allow these women to be released back to the community we love, to Pacific Grove, to sow their seeds of destruction. The bail must be set high so there will be no chance for them to poison the mind or body of another single Pacific Grovian."

Vi thought she'd explode. She punched Dudley in the ribs, but he didn't move.

Leaning on a railing, his face just inches from theirs, the prosecutor spoke in a stage whisper. "These women are terrorists, capable of destroying the very fabric of our society. Certainly they are polite—smiling at little children as if there were only love in their hearts. And they're quiet and passive as they casually distribute poison throughout our fair city. But make no mistake about it. They are still terrorists—politely passive terrorists, perhaps, but terrorists nonetheless."

One minute Vi was in control, the next, she was so angry the world looked funny. Not sure what would happen next. Too much energy. Couldn't hold it, scalding her lungs like hot lava, choking up into her throat. Heard her own voice from somewhere out in space. Gutteral, animalistic. Through clenched teeth she shouted, "You don't know what you're talking about!"

"Why is he so angry?" Kate said to Sophie.

Sophie said, "What *is* he talking about?"

The prosecutor ranted on. "Instead of tending their grandchildren and growing old gracefully, these women are like witches on brooms. If children can't look to their generation for moral values, where will our country be? Disreputable pot-smoking elders, trafficking in drugs and Lord knows what else, squandering money on luxuries gained from underworld scum. I suggest that bail be set at one million dollars."

A collective gasp. The man Vi thought was a reporter got up and ran out of the room. Sophie screamed "No!"

Kate looked dazed. "That's ridiculous!"

Vi found herself on her feet.

"Rita gave us that money. Helping her with her pain was a moral thing to do! And I don't have any grandchildren!"

"Mr. Dudley, please control your client." The judge was visably annoyed. "I will not have a shouting match in my court."

At last Dudley rose, glaring daggers at Vi. He took her by the arm and forced her down into her chair.

"I must object, Your Honor. It has not been established that these women received appreciable profit from illegal drug sales."

"Sustained."

Vi wrote Dudley a note, scribbling furiously. "Not true that we made money. Rita gave us her money when she died. Not true she was a big drug dealer. Never made any money on the pot. Gave it out of the goodness of her heart to people from hospice. It was medical marijuana."

Dudley did not respond. Did not repeat any of what she said except the medical marijuana part. Now the prosecutor was tearing him to shreds.

"If it was medical, they should have been screened. Had prescriptions from their doctors. Taken it under physician's supervision."

Vi was on her feet again.

"That might be ideal, but doctors are afraid to be involved. Why would you begrudge dying people their medications?"

"We have reason to believe they weren't all sick, Mrs. Farnsworth."

"Perhaps not. Rita was a generous soul. Maybe she didn't ask enough questions. She was dying. Wanted company. They were friends who didn't desert her. Maybe we were wrong in helping. If we'd thought it out better, maybe we wouldn't have made so many mistakes. But we're not witches. Never did it for the money. Like Rita, we gave it away to sick people who had no money."

"Order in the court! Mrs. Farnsworth, you will not speak again or I will hold you in contempt . . . Court adjourned for lunch until 1:30 P.M." The judge banged her gavel decisively.

Dudley finally turned to Vi, his face pale. "You're getting old, Mrs. Farnsworth. Why don't you grow up?"

After the lunch break, they were escorted back into the courtroom. Dudley leaned over and whispered to Vi, "Be quiet. Don't look at the judge. Write me a note if you hear anything you think we should object to. And behave!"

Vi decided not to take offense at being talked to like a child. She was in too good a mood. This morning she had thought the arraignment might make her nervous. Not so! Her noon hour planning had been productive. She was now on the offensive. This afternoon she knew she was just going to have a helluva good time.

Vi had decided against changing into the caftan, even though Agnes had told her Nikki could bring it. She was sporting her cane with a ribbon tied on it, but she was still wearing the lavendar outfit. She had made Dudley angry enough this morning, and she didn't want him to quit.

Funny, she didn't want to be dismissed as old, but now the stereotype was really working for her. She tried to keep her posture dignified, her manner brave. Now and then, she turned to show her wry smile and twinkling eyes to the crowd that was beginning to form.

Where had all these people come from? And why was a section down front roped off with a lavender ribbon? All sorts of friends were waving. Even Hannah and Rose were there, and Rose waved to her. The courtroom was not exactly noisy, but there was a steady hum of excitement behind her. Good! The word was out!

Kate was confused. The courtroom was nearly empty before. Now nearly all seats were filled. It was Vi. Vi hadn't talked much in the holding cell. She'd taken charge. Kate felt uneasy. She hated the unknown. What was going to happen?

She wasn't even sure of her own identity. Was she Katherine? Kathy? Or Kate? Whoever, she just wanted it to be over.

Vi remembered the movie *Mr. Smith Goes to Washington.* Kate wasn't the only one who could take up acting. Vi felt like Jimmy Stewart battling against the establishment. She was working the room as best she could, playing into becoming a symbol of undefeated aging taking on city hall, and behind that maybe even some larger targets. *We'll just see,* she thought to herself. *Maybe we can parlay this hand into a bigger scenario.*

Nikki had turned out to be the real brains of the outfit, though. Agnes told Vi that since that first phone call, when Vi called her instead of a lawyer, Nikki had been busy. She even had enlisted all the Sisters in the Web—Spiders—so she had plenty of volunteers ready on the Internet or in person to carry out any of her schemes.

Now Nikki made her entrance. Here she came, with five prim, white-haired ladies in lavender sweatshirts and immaculate white duck pants and white tennis shoes. They filed slowly down to the front row and passed out lavender ribbons to visitors on either side of the aisle. What a fabulous entrance! Vi smiled and waved. They created a real hubbub. One woman even crawled over the benches to get her souvenir ribbon. The noise grew like a high school pep rally. Vi fought the impulse to turn around and lead one of her old cheers. Judging from the age of the crowd, most of them would remember the ones she knew:

Give 'em the axe, the axe, the axe,
Right in their backs, their backs, their backs.
Our team is red hot; your team is all shot!

No, not dignified. Wrong image. Dudley was right. Keep quiet.

She asked Dudley for an envelope, put in more of her plans for the Spiders and told him to drop it off to Nikki later at the library.

The judge was banging her gavel now, demanding order. "I'll clear this courtroom if I have to. I'll have the marshals remove those disturbing the peace!"

When the beefy marshals appeared in the aisles, things quieted down a bit. More banging and threats finally restored order.

Vi could read the sweatshirts of the five women in the front row. Emblazoned in gold across their chests: "Politely Passive Terrorists". That's also what it said on the lavender ribbons everyone was trying to snatch.

Nikki smiled and gave Vi a thumbs-up sign. Nikki and Running Wolf strike again. She wanted to disobey Dudley and laugh out loud. But she didn't.

What a great friend Nikki was! She sure knew what would make the six o'clock news.

Vi felt smug. "The plot thickens," she whispered to Kate. "This is definitely headed to the governor's office!"

Kate and Sophie just sat there, looking puzzled.

Vi hugged her arms to her chest so the excitement wouldn't show; had to sit still. Maybe Agnes would smuggle a *Herald* to her in the cell tonight.

The judge's words interrupted Vi's reverie. "Bail is set at one million dollars. The preliminary hearing will begin at 10 A.M. Wednesday morning."

A million dollars! No way could they come up with $100,000 to post bond.

Sophie dreaded another two nights in jail before the hearing. Fearful dark, strange people around. No Jack. The bed didn't look that clean. *What shall I do?*

She took off her shoes and jacket, unhooked her bra. She would sleep in her dress. Use her jacket for a pillow—there might be bugs in the striped one with no pillowcase. She shortened her prayers considerably, but managed a quick Act of Contrition. She was so sorry about the money. Knew she wouldn't sleep a minute.

However, emotionally and physically exhausted, Sophie fell asleep immediately, only to be wakened by a horrible dream. A six-foot tall marijuana plant chasing her down a country road, leaves became hands grabbing at her clothes, catching her hair. She screamed, but the others didn't wake up.

Then the black thoughts came. *Why did I think I could handle all that money? Who put me in charge anyway?* She hated the way Vi and Kate had looked at her when she admitted there was no money left to hire a good lawyer. *I'm the dud more than Dudley.*

Of course all those organizations needed cash. They didn't ask where it came from. There was never enough to help the poor, the homeless, the environment. Sophie thought, *my friends must hate me. I hate me. I hate them, too.*

Whose hare-brained idea was it to get all that pot originally? *Rita, I guess. But we didn't owe her anything. She was just another human being.* But a suffering one, her conscience consoled her.

Another night in jail. *We're in such trouble and everything is so complicated. The things the prosecutor said in court were horrible. They couldn't be true. Not all of it, anyway.* Sophie eventually fell into a troubled sleep.

Once back in their cell, Vi eagerly anticipated Agnes' visit. She didn't have to wait long before Agnes appeared, carrying *The Herald* and a note from Nikki.

"Just look! Your picture's on the front page!" Agnes said, handing the paper to Vi.

The headline read: "D.A. Brands Grannies 'Terrorists'." There was a picture of the three of them. Below that, a photo of five women wearing the "Politely Passive Terrorists" sweatshirts. Looked like it was taken just outside the courtroom.

Running Wolf didn't spend her life as a marketing director for nothing, Vi thought. *I can see her fine hand in this.*

Next, she read the letter from Nikki.

Great minds run in the same rut. We've already organized the Spiders. Running Wolf has supplied the funds for a phone bank at her home. The T-Shirt Shop in Pacific Grove is staying open all night printing more sweatshirts. Tomorrow we'll stage a big TV rally.

You should see all the reporters! Rumors are flying. I heard that Ted

Koppel has a scout checking out whether to take some footage for his
'Nightline' show. I started a rumor that you have been contacted by a
literary agent who has Hollywood contacts. That ought to scare the hell out
of the D.A. He's up for re-election, you know.

We will implement your plans with the governor's office. I will need some
names and addresses. See if Agnes can get you some time on the Internet
so we can talk.

Agnes ushered Vi into her private office and supplied her with a laptop, her
password and e-mail address. "Hurry. This is against all regulations," she said,
showing her teeth in a broad, nervous smile. "Everyone is preoccupied around
here. Seems they're investigating something really important. I've been hearing all
sorts of rumors."

Vi didn't ask what rumors. She was already too involved in the exhilarating conversation she was having with Nikki via e-mail.

Tomorrow morning would dawn on Sophie's Day. Vi was sure she was too
excited to sleep at all.

(37)

HOROSCOPE: Be ready, fight because cause is right. Allies appear out of the blue and circumstances move in your favor. Events transpire that make victory possible.

SOPHIE WOKE UP AND LOOKED AROUND. WHERE WERE THE OTHERS? SHE seemed to be alone. She couldn't believe she had slept in her clothes again. Ugh! She felt dirty and messy. What was she supposed to do? A whole day and another night before the hearing. Where were Vi and Kate? Maybe they sneaked out on her. No, they couldn't sneak out of jail. *This is getting to be too much. I know they blame me because we don't have money for bail.*

"Good morning, Mrs. Conway." It was Agnes, unlocking the cell door. "I've come to take you down to the recreation room. Vi and Mrs. Doolittle are already there, watching the excitement on television."

Sophie was relieved to see Kate and Vi wave and smile at her as she entered the room. They were already seated, and the TV was on Channel 5.

"We interrupt our regular program to bring you a fast-breaking news story. A storm of protest is brewing in Pacific Grove. The case of the marijuana grandmothers has erupted into a major community event.

"I'm Dan Bradford, here on the steps of the Monterey County Courthouse, and I, along with correspondent Dina Rusk, will bring you the latest amazing developments."

Vi was bouncing in her chair. Kate had her mouth open. Sophie said, "I can't believe this is happening! I wonder if Jack is watching."

"Here is Nikki Sullivan, Pacific Grove's head librarian, who has helped organize this fund-raising event. Ms. Sullivan, what can you tell us about what we are seeing here?"

A rumpled-looking woman started up from her chair in the rec room. "They canceled *Days of Our Lives*?"

"Don't touch that dial!" Vi commanded as she moved close to the TV set.

Now Nikki was talking. ". . . and we're calling it Sophie's Day. It's a demonstration of love for the marijuana grannies and particularly for Sophie Conway, who was the administrator and coordinator of all their community charity projects." Nikki faced the camera.

"If you can see us or hear us, Sophie, this is all for you. Our chance to give just a little love back for all you have given the community."

"Why me? I didn't do that much. You two did as much." Sophie was flabbergasted.

"Not even close," Kate said.

"By the way," Dan Bradford said, "I understand that the Chamber of Commerce announced this morning that one of the projects Mrs. Conway has been active in has won the Small Business Award—a church thrift shop, I believe it is."

All three women cheered.

"What will the money you're raising here be used for?" the announcer asked.

"We are trying to raise bail for those three women now in jail so they can at least return to their homes. The bail's been set at a ridiculous one million dollars, so we need a hundred thousand."

Dan Bradford motioned to the crowds behind him. "I see lots of people, must be over a hundred, gathering on the streets and sidewalks. What will they be doing?"

"We'll have a small parade around the park at 9:30, followed by the sale of sweatshirts at ten o'clock." Nikki walked over to a table covered with shirts.

"This is Jack Conway, Sophie's husband, and five volunteers from the Suppers for Seniors organization."

"Jack's there!" Sophie said. "He must have forgiven me."

"A hundred dollars will get you one of these bold, history-making sweatshirts you'll want to pass down to your grandchildren."

Nikki faced the camera again. "If you can't get down here, the folks at Shop and Pray Thrift Shop in Pacific Grove will take your cash, credit cards or pledges. The sweatshirts are available there, too. Their phone number is 408-555-1133."

"Thank you, Ms. Sullivan." The camera moved in on Dan Bradford.

"These sweatshirts created quite a sensation yesterday when a group of women entered the courtroom wearing them to protest the prosecutor's accusation that these harmless looking women were actually terrorists—'politely passive terrorists,' he said, but terrorists nonetheless. This motto seems to have become a rallying cry for the supporters of these women. But let's switch now to Dina, who's at the parade site."

The sound of "The Saints Come Marching In" flooded the rec room as Vi, Kate, and Sophie watched the TV. The reporter was standing on a small knoll in the park as a band marched by.

"This is Dina Rusk, and what you're seeing is the Senior Center Marching Band which was formed in 1922 and, as you can see, is still going strong. Following them are the Drum Majorettes who I understand are from the Pacific Grove Poker Club. I believe one of their members is Mrs. Katherine Doolittle, one of the three ladies who've been arrested."

"Oh, good grief! I don't believe it!" Kate yelled. "Look at Nellie all dressed up in a mini-skirt and white boots."

"What's that banner say?" Vi said. "The Raging Grannies from Carmel Valley. Watch them strutting and chorus-line kicking their way down the street! Sure breaks the stereotype, doesn't it?"

Sophie jumped up from her chair. "There's the Friends of the Sea Otters with their mascot—and look! There's some of the gang from Befriend the Bay!"

Dina Rusk was saying, "Oh look at those Dalmation pups! How adorable! They're wearing firemen's caps inscribed 'Doris Day's Adopt-A-Pet Foundation'."

"What's that next group, Dina?" the announcer at the studio asked.

"It's the choir from The Lord's With It Church in Santa Cruz. They're singing 'How High the Moon'—and what's that on their T-shirts? 'Put a little pot in every chicken.' Well, I'm not sure that's to everyone's taste, but they're sure getting a big hand from the crowd.

"Oh, here's a flock of Pacific Grove's Monarch Butterflies. Some children decked out with large spotted cellophane wings. And who's that with them? It's Madge Kelley. She was the first child to march in Pacific Grove's annual Butterfly Parade. Hi, Madge!" Dina waved; Madge waved back.

"Oh, Madge! I know her from Befriend the Bay," Sophie said.

". . . 'Don't Arrest Our Grannies' is on their T-shirts," Dina was saying. "This community's really backing these women, isn't it? Now back to Dan at the sweatshirt table."

"I'm here with one of the ladies who was part of yesterday's demonstration. She's wearing her Politely Passive Terrorist sweatshirt. Ms. Drummond, what prompts a Pebble Beach matron like you to support this cause?"

"Well, I'm a sponsor of what the district attorney has called 'The Debauched

Monday Club.' That's not what it was at all. It was headed by a fine, generous lady, Rita Rich—rest her soul—and I believed in what she was doing."

"The mike's all yours. I think the TV audience might like to hear what made you such a strong supporter."

"I can't believe they are allowing so much time for this," Sophie said.

"Isn't it wonderful?" Vi said.

Ms. Drummond was telling about her son with leukemia who'd been undergoing chemotherapy for over two years. "If it hadn't been for the marijuana he got through the club, his life would have been much more miserable. I'm not sure he would have wanted to live."

"But didn't you care that marijuana is addictive and anti-motivational?"

"What difference does it make if you're dying?"

"So he goes to the Monday Club for his drug?"

"Oh, that and so much more. They give him support, real support. More than that—respect. He says what he gets there he's never found in any other medical setting. He needed the club not just to ease his nausea and pain, but to remind him why he's putting up with the monstrous treatment in the first place—because life, even with leukemia, can be fun."

"What do you mean? They had wild parties? Sex?"

"No! No! They presented creative possibilities, caring relationships, even fulfilling dreams—with others who were facing death, too. He wasn't just a medical case. It was a chance for him to be useful to someone else. Thank God for Rita's Monday Club!"

"Thank you, Ms. Drummond, and best wishes to you and your son."

Dan Bradford faced the camera. "There you have it. A controversial issue, to say the least. Let's check on the situation downtown. Seth, are you there at the thrift shop?"

"Yes, Dan. I have Margie right here." The TV picture now showed the familiar cashier's desk at Shop and Pray. "Margie, can you give us an up-date?"

"The phone's been ringing off the hook. We're over twenty five thousand dollars, and the pledges are coming in at a phenomenal rate. There's a real chance we'll hit our goal of a hundred thousand by the end of the day! If you want to send in a contribution for Sophie's Day, call me, Margie, at Shop and Pray where all the monies are being tallied.—That's 555-1133."

Margie looked tired, but happy. Suddenly realizing she was on TV, she smiled and waved. "Hi, everybody!"

"Thank you Seth and Margie. We now pause for a station break."

"Wow!" Sophie said.

Kate leaned back in her chair. "This is not really happening. It's too incredible."
Vi just sat there, grinning.

After a few minutes, an announcer was saying, "Here's a human interest story.
Dan Bradford is talking to a man who calls himself 'The Mayor'."

"Mayor of what city?" Dan Bradford asked the bearded toothless man.

"I'm 'The Mayor of the Homeless.' We were gettin' soup under the wharf. Sophie
made it herself, and I mean it was good."

Sophie beamed.

"I remember talking to him," Vi said. "He's the one who was carrying on about
the bay."

"I told Sophie there're bodies in the bay," The Mayor was saying. "Jack and
Sophie looked into it. I gave them plenty of info. Now I'll tell you. Those richy-
bitchy growers in Castroville spray their crops with something that ruins the sex
life of bugs."

"How do you know this?"

"One of the guys at the shelter told me. Domi. He and Baby Louie worked the
strawberry fields last summer. Brazilium it's called. Check with Domi. He can tell
ya more. Anyway, these guys dump the excess in the bay. Monterey Bay. Now this
stuff doesn't kill ya. Just destroys your sex. They've been dumpin' for a couple
years. Pretty soon the seals and sea otters are sterile. I told Sophie."

Sophie nodded. "At first I didn't believe him, but . . ."

" . . . and she got Marilyn of Befriend the Bay on it. They did a biopsy on an
otter. Sure enough. Sterile. Maybe whales, too. Hell, for all I know, the swimmers
down by the pier may have trouble gettin' it up, from swimming in that water. The
fish, the salmon are dying."

The newscaster tried to interrupt, but The Mayor wouldn't stop.

"Then Marilyn, she starts to make a stink. Next thing we know some bulls come
around asking questions about Baby Louie. He had to lay low. I think they were
CIA. This stuff could have come outta Fort Ord. Dunno. Some Cold War weapon.
Anyway, Baby Louie disappeared. I think they bumped him off cuz he knew too
much. I think that right now he's at the bottom —bottom of the bay."

The announcer from the station broke in. "And there you have it. Is this man
who calls himself 'The Mayor' deluded? Demented? Or, perhaps right on the
money about all the shenanigans going on here in Monterey? What connection, if
any, does this story have to do with the drug lords of Big Sur? We'll have more on
this story when further details are known. Stay tuned to Channel 5 for further
developments."

Agnes clicked off the television.

"There you go," said Vi. Can't have better publicity than that! We've got that prosecutor on the run now." She did a high five with Agnes.

"Sophie, I guess you're sitting on top of the world," Agnes said.

"Oh, yes. What a relief to have our concerns out in the open. Such a wonderful community this is!" Sophie actually looked cheerful. "How great to see Jack was there."

"We have a group of Sisters in the Web flooding the governor's office today with telegrams asking for clemency for all of us. I know we're winning. I can feel it," Vi said.

"Well, it looks like all that money you spent did do some good after all," Kate said as she gave Sophie a hug.

"Hate to interrupt, but I'd better get you back to your cell." Agnes sounded apologetic. "Good luck at the prelim tomorrow."

"To hell with Dudley," Vi said. "I'm wearing my blue caftan."

(38)

HOROSCOPE: The time has come to take over the running of your life and quit letting people dictate the terms of your future. Close the door on bad memories of the past.

THROUGH HER MENTAL FOG, KATE CAUGHT VEHEMENT WORDS AND PHRASES spoken by the brusque prosecutor. "Don't let them fool you. They appear to be nice little old ladies, but don't let looks deceive." He paced back and forth in front of the judge, turning to point at Kate. At the arraignment he was different. Was it her imagination, or did Mr. Farrell look a little shaken—not quite as cocky— now that he was arguing at the preliminary hearing.

"Sgt. Wyatt Burley will testify that Katherine Doolittle harassed the Police Department and clogged telephone lines by constantly calling in trivial complaints to divert attention from their illegal drug peddling."

Glancing at his notes, he turned and glared at Sophie. He shook his head and pointed at her. "And this lovely lady disrupted the police motorcycle drill teams by dashing through their demonstration and scattering trash. Not to mention the fact that all three were found in possession of a dead body!"

Kate saw Vi poke Dudley on the arm and whisper in his ear. Dudley hesitantly rose and said, "Your Honor, I object. Irrelevant and no basis established. These accusations have nothing to do with the case at hand."

"Sustained."

"Okay, fine. Let's get to the ladies being caught red-handed at a major drug raid," the prosecutor continued.

Vi started to protest but was shushed by Dudley. "Objection!" he said. "They were fleeing from Mr. Pellagrino and Mr. Ferrari. Fleeing for their very lives. They had no connection with the scene of the raid. These women were only interested in the medicinal . . ."

"Your Honor!" The prosecutor interrupted as he approached the bench. "This propaganda surrounding marijuana as a good medicine being put out by the Proposition 215 advocates is simply a scam and a hoax, using sick people to legalize drugs. The Cannabis Clubs in San Francisco are simply updated opium dens. . . ."

Kate retreated back into her thoughts. Were all those people in the Monday Club really sick? Perhaps not. In fact, she knew they weren't. Rita didn't care; she had just been generous. Farrell was still ranting. ". . . This is not about compassion. It's about dispensing and using dangerous drugs. We will submit evidence that marijuana is detrimental to physical and emotional well-being. It's laced with toxic chemicals having cancer-causing ingredients."

"When you're already dying, who cares?" Vi shouted.

"Counselor, control your client!" Judge Hogan shouted louder. Dudley looked more embarrassed than Vi.

"There are also studies that marijuana can prime the brain for addiction to cocaine and heroin."

Kate heard the voices and wished they'd stop. Why couldn't they just explain their intentions were good? She shook her head and took a deep breath. I should have taken a firmer hand with Rita, she thought. I knew pot was wrong, but it meant so much to her. *She was dying, for God's sake!* I couldn't find it in my heart to say no.

The pounding of the judge's gavel brought Kate's attention back to the courtroom. "Back off, both of you! Your bickering is immaterial to the purpose of this hearing. Get with the program and address the matter before this court with . . ."

The judge was interrupted by the bailiff handing her a note. She read it, peered over the top of her glasses as she again banged the gavel.

"There will be a thirty minute recess. Counselors, meet me in my chambers for a conference. Now."

Vi was talking reassuringly to Sophie as they filed up the aisle. She grabbed for Kate's hand and said, "We need to bolster old Dudley up for his big moment. Coach him a bit."

Kate started to say "How?" but it trailed off into a whisper as she glanced up at the figure standing in the doorway. She froze. If she had been asked for her reaction to seeing her ex-husband Jerry, she would have been unable to describe the cold chill of hatred, the heat of anger, the flush of memories. She felt like she was having an out-of-body experience, unwittingly raising her arm as if to ward off a blow.

"I wouldn't have recognized you, Katherine," Jerry said with the familiar smirk of the superior.

Vi started to pull Kate down the corridor away from Jerry, but Kate shook off her grip. "It's okay, Vi. Go wait for Dudley." Even she didn't recognize her own voice.

"Well, Katherine. Seems you've gotten yourself into quite a mess." Jerry's smile was phony. Kate looked at the rugged face she once thought handsome. It looked leathery and wrinkled. His sexy eyes looked tired, old. Didn't even look threatening any more. Just dull.

"What are you doing here?" she asked coldly.

"The story of your escapade's all over the state. Both sides of the Proposition 215 issue legalizing marijuana are using it as media fodder."

Kate smiled. "Had to travel from the valley to see if it was really inhibited Katherine, eh?"

"Actually, I thought maybe you'd need more than your usual alimony check. To hire the best attorney to get you off. For the kids' sake. I know you're pretty helpless in . . ."

"I can take care of myself!" Kate said angrily.

"I hear you might sign with Hollywood, so you won't need my money then."

Jerry started to reach for her hand, but she jerked it away.

"Katherine, I'm . . . I am sorry for what happened." He stammered. Didn't sound like the old Jerry. "Is it possible you could ever forgive me?"

The shock of his words stunned her, but not as much as the memory of his hands and fists had in the past.

"You've got to be kidding!"

Jerry's face reddened. "I don't understand why you . . ."

Kate didn't want to hear any more.

"Jerry, when you first left, I was full of self-pity and hatred. You made me live in black and white. I wanted technicolor. You wanted me to be perfect. No one is." Her anger allowed her to speak her mind like never before.

"At first I couldn't move. Now, for the first time, I'm letting life take up my time."

Jerry looked skeptical. Kate could see his eyes appraising her change in physical appearance. She could feel his questioning her new identity. She felt strong, attractive, even sophisticated. Confident.

"I have friends who support me. They love me. They understand me," she continued. "I now live with zest." She wanted to tell him about 'Carla' climbing down the rose trellis at Peter's. Better not push it.

For once, Jerry was speechless.

Kate tried to calm herself. Changed the subject.

"How's Susan?" she asked, trying to keep the sarcasm out of her voice.

"I guess she's okay." Jerry was looking down at his feet, hands in the pockets of his immaculate gray flannel trousers. "She left me last month."

"Oh. I'm sorry," Kate said, wanting to giggle.

"Actually, I've been thinking." Jerry hesitated. "Katherine, when this nonsense is cleared up, why don't you . . . the kids would be pleased . . . maybe we could . . . start seeing each other?"

"Screw you!" she shouted, immediately wishing she'd used the "f" word instead.

She turned her back on Jerry, whose mouth was hanging open in shock. She straightened her shoulders and marched away, feeling nothing for this ghost from the past. She would get in touch with her children and regain her place in their lives. Soon.

Back in the courtroom Kate felt a strange calm. She found herself quietly humming. Didn't know what tune—just humming.

In the middle of all this chaos—being accused of heinous crimes, the hearing going badly, seeing Jerry—she'd never felt so good in her life.

(39)

HOROSCOPE: The planets are on your side in legal battle. Facts and circumstances fall into place, even though the more you learn the more you realize there is to know.

KATE BARELY GOT SEATED WHEN THE BAILIFF ANNOUNCED THAT COURT WAS back in session. "All rise," he said as Judge Hogan walked in and took her seat behind the massive desk. She shuffled papers as the bailiff indicated the audience could sit down. Looking over her glasses, the judge cleared her throat.

"Ladies and gentlemen. I have reached a decision. Based on additional evidence procured by the defendants in this case, which the police spent yesterday investigating in cooperation with county and federal law enforcement agencies, we can end this preliminary hearing."

Kate looked at Vi and Sophie.

"What's going on?" Vi mouthed.

"Police successfully apprehended Guido Ferrari, who has confessed his role in this whole affair, and will testify against Peter Pellagrino in the Boyd Aaron murder trial."

Murmuring filled the courtroom. Vi grabbed Kate's arm. "See, I told you it would be okay," she whispered.

"They must have caught Guido at Running Wolf's. What about her?" Kate asked.

"Don't worry. We warned her."

The judge banged her gavel for order. "We will need testimony from the defendants as corroborating evidence. It appears their situation is one of being in the wrong place at the wrong time. No drugs were actually found on them, and they had no control over the premises where the raid was held."

"They've finally seen the light," said Sophie.

"What a relief to not wonder if Guido's following us any more," Kate said.

Vi whispered again. "It's because of your great performance as Carla that we knew about Guido signaling to the smugglers. That's how he got caught."

"Silence in the courtroom." Judge Hogan looked sympathetically but sternly at each defendant. "On the condition that these three ladies are willing to cooperate in all respects with the federal investigation, and testify before the Grand Jury in the upcoming case against Peter Pellagrino . . ."

All three women were nodding their heads in unison.

". . . the matter before this court can be closed in a pretrial diversion."

"What does that mean?" Kate blurted out.

Judge Hogan smiled for the first time. "It means that if the defendants agree to perform certain actions in the form of community service . . ."

Sophie whispered to Kate, "I thought that's what we've been doing all along."

". . . and refrain from all drug-related activity, and do not break the law in any way for a period of six months, the charges will be dismissed."

Kate heard shouts of joy behind her.

"Order! There will be no unruly demonstrations in this courtroom!" The judge seemed intent on restoring her image.

The hot air had been knocked out of Benjamin Farrell. His arrogant posture diminished as he left the courtroom, brushing aside reporters.

Vi, Sophie, and Kate had a group hug. Vi dashed up the aisle to Nikki. Jack came up behind Sophie and they embraced quietly.

Clarence Dudley was smiling. "It helps that the D.A. is seeking re-election and didn't want to go against public opinion," he said to Kate.

Surprising even herself, Kate gave Dudley a hug.

The judge again banged her gavel. "Mr. Dudley, would you bring your clients into chambers for a brief conference."

Kate was relieved that Farrell did not join them in the judge's chambers. She noticed Judge Hogan had pictures of her children on her desk. It was an informal room, littered with law books.

"This is Horst Schuman, the federal officer who took Guido Ferrari's deposition in the Peter Pellagrino matter," said Judge Hogan. "He would like to explain some details of that deposition and then ask you some questions."

Kate looked at the officer and thought his horn-rimmed glasses on his pale